2 -
myst.
fict.

OFF SEASON

OFF SEASON

A Martha's Vineyard Mystery

PHILIP R. CRAIG

CHARLES SCRIBNER'S SONS
NEW YORK

Maxwell Macmillan Canada
Toronto

Maxwell Macmillan International
New York   Oxford   Singapore   Sydney

Copyright © 1994 by Philip R. Craig

Charles Scribner's Sons
Macmillan Publishing Company
866 Third Avenue
New York, NY 10022

Maxwell Macmillan Canada, Inc.
1200 Eglinton Avenue East
Suite 200
Don Mills, Ontario M3C 3N1

Macmillan Publishing Company is part of the Maxwell Communication Group of Companies.

Library of Congress Cataloging-in-Publication Data
Craig, Philip R., 1933–
Off season: a Martha's Vineyard mystery/Philip R. Craig.
    p.   cm.
ISBN 0-684-19617-4
1. Jackson, Jeff (Fictitious character)—Fiction.
2. Private investigators—Massachusetts—Martha's Vineyard—Fiction.
3. Martha's Vineyard (Mass.)—Fiction. I. Title.
PS3553.R23038   1994

813'.54—dc20   93–47100
                CIP

10 9 8 7 6 5 4 3 2

Printed in the United States of America

*To my sister, Martha Walker, and my brothers, Kenneth
and Howard Craig, who stayed in the mountains
when I went to live by the sea.*

"Perverseness is one of the primitive impulses
of the human heart."

—Edgar Allan Poe

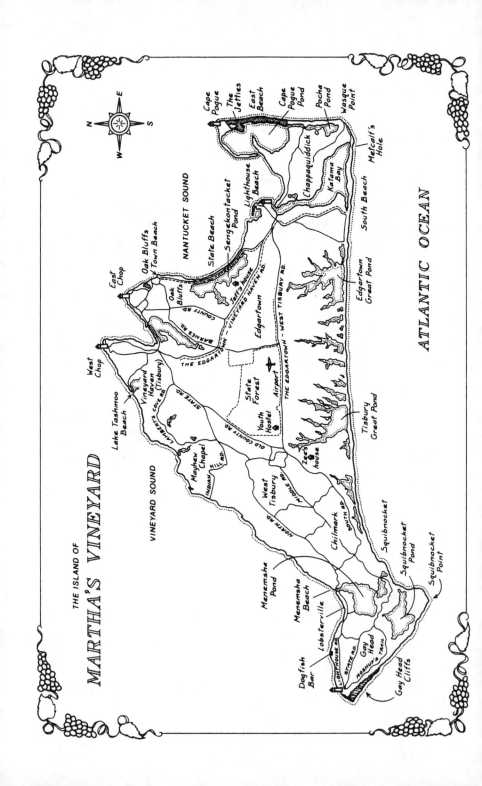

THE ISLAND OF
MARTHA'S VINEYARD

N E S W

VINEYARD SOUND

NANTUCKET SOUND

ATLANTIC OCEAN

West Chop
East Chop
Oak Bluffs
Oak Bluffs Town Beach
Lake Tashmoo Beach
Vineyard Haven (Tisbury)
Lambert's Cove Rd.
State Rd.

Cape Pogue
The Jetties
East Beach
Cape Pogue Pond
Pocha Pond
Wasque Point
Metcalf's Hole
Chappaquiddick
Kalama Bay
South Beach
Lighthouse Beach
State Beach
Sengekontacket Pond
Zeb's House
Edgartown
County Rd.
Barnes Rd.
The Edgartown – Vineyard Haven Rd.

Edgartown Great Pond
Tisbury Great Pond
State Forest
Airport
Youth Hostel
Zeb's House
The Edgartown – West Tisbury Rd.

Mayhew Chapel
Indian Hill
West Tisbury
Chilmark
North Rd.
Middle Rd.
South Rd.
Old County Rd.

Squibnocket
Squibnocket Pond
Squibnocket Point
Menemsha Pond
Menemsha Beach
Lobsterville
Dogfish Bar
Gay Head
Gay Head Cliffs
Lighthouse Rd.
State Rd.
Moshup's Trail

OFF SEASON

— 1 —

The evening that Mimi Bettencourt shot Ignacio Cortez started out as just another chilly but peaceful fall day on Martha's Vineyard. I happened to be at the scene because Manny Fonseca, who, like Nash Cortez, was a shootist and a hunter of both birds and deer, had come by that morning and asked me to go to the meeting. I did a bit of hunting myself, because I like to eat goose and duck and venison, and Manny wanted hunters to be at the hearing because he was sure that Mimi and Phyllis Manwaring and a bunch of their pals would be there causing trouble.

When pressed by people like Mimi, who considered hunters akin to murderers, I justified my shooting on the basis of the anthropological\theological argument that people have always eaten meat and fish and that you are allowed to kill animals as long as you eat them, because it's all part of God's master plan.

Mimi, of course, was not persuaded by this reasoning, being a vegetarian for both ethical and medical reasons, and often warned me of the dire consequences of my barbarism. She was a vital, attractive woman, who lived alone in a large old farmhouse out by the state forest, surrounded by gardens of herbs, flowers and vegetables. She had grapevines and fruit trees, and milked goats from which she made excellent cheese. Her hair was long and beginning to gray, and she liked to wear long homespun skirts, loose sweaters, wraps of exotic design and heavy earrings. In mud time she exchanged her skirts and sandals for rubber boots and oversized jeans. She was nearsighted, walked with a slight stoop and looked, I thought, like a bohemian mother superior. She was a widow who had one daughter living on the island and another with children of her own living on the mainland. Mimi was both bright and emotional, and had always treated me well even though she disapproved of my shooting.

I didn't mind needling her. "I kill fish, too, Mimi," I would tell her. "Lots of fish. I do it for a living."

"That's just as bad," she'd say, but you could tell that a dead fish didn't arouse the passion that a dead bird or mammal did.

"Maybe plants have feelings, too," I'd say. "Who says it's worse to kill an animal than a plant?"

"I eat grains and fruits, mostly," she'd say. "Nuts and flowers. I don't kill things."

"How about mosquitoes?"

"All right, all right, so I swat mosquitoes. I'm not a pacifist. If something attacks you, you can defend yourself. Get out of here, J.W.!"

She put up with a lot from me, and had ever since I'd dated her youngest daughter, Angie, back in the days before I met Zee. "I only go out with your kid because I'm trying to get in good with you," I'd tell her. We'd stayed friends even though Zee had long since gotten my mind off Angie and the other women I'd been with in the B.Z. days.

A few days before Mimi shot Ignacio Cortez, I had finished replacing the floorboards of the rottenest part of her screen porch, and had gotten, in exchange, the Norwegian wood stove that Gus, her deceased husband, had used to warm his studio behind the house. Mimi didn't use the studio anymore and therefore didn't need the stove. I had had my eye on it for a long time.

Gus Bettencourt's family had enough money so that Gus hadn't actually needed to work at his art or anything else, so I had admired him for not becoming another dilettante, but a good and a productive painter. I felt the same way about Mimi, who had never ceased to labor just because she had married a wealthy young man. While she and Gus raised their family, she had planted and harvested her gardens and orchard, and sold their produce to the island grocery stores and, later, at the farmers' market.

Gus had not been an avid hunter, but I had seen him a few times in duck blinds, clutching his ancient 12 gauge, and sometimes encountered him on the beach trying for bluefish. Vegetarian Mimi and omnivorous Gus had struck some sort of compromise on the issue of food while he lived, but after his death she had increasingly protested the right of hunters, and to a lesser extent fishermen, to take animals' lives. She wrote letters to the *Vineyard Gazette*, she spoke at meetings, she marched in the Fourth of July parade carrying signs opposing hunting, trapping and fishing, and she appeared at hearings.

"She is a pain in the you-know-where," said Manny. "Her and that Phyllis Manwaring and those other weirdos. They'll be there tonight, you can bet on it, raising a stink about how awful us hunters are, and how dangerous it is to shoot on that land, and all the usual stuff they say. We need some of our guys there, J.W. Otherwise the goddamned Commission may stop us from using a hunk of land we've always hunted on! Here, lemme help you with that."

I was setting up the Norwegian stove on one side of my living room fireplace, and running the stovepipe up beside the fireplace chimney. The stove was heavy, so Manny's help was welcome. We got it where I wanted it.

"This thing will use less wood and throw out a lot more heat than the fireplace," I said. "The price of oil these days, I hate to use the furnace if I don't have to."

My house had some leaks that let the wind in, as had been the case ever since the house had been only an old hunting camp. Although I had sought the leaks, I could never find them all. I was looking forward to stoking up my new stove and sitting in front of it in the evening while I read a book. I wasn't enthusiastic about going downtown to a Commission hearing.

"You don't need me down there," I said to Manny. "There are plenty of guys on the island who'll be there. I don't like to get mixed up in these arguments."

"Look," said Manny. "This island is getting smaller every day. People are buying up land and building houses where there never were houses before. Sometimes they just buy the land and close it off to the public. Pretty soon there won't be any hunting land left at all. We've got to make sure that when the Commission buys a piece of property like this one we'll still be able to use it like we always have. You're a fisherman. You know how it is. A while back you could drive down to the beach somewhere, and now you can't. Some goddamned developer or house owner from off island has closed off the road!"

A point well taken. Still, I didn't want to go. I had not moved to Martha's Vineyard to get involved in the teapot tempests that occupied the islanders in the off season. During the summer, the local people were so busy making money that they didn't have time to get their teeth into each other, but in the winter, when there was time on their hands, they scrapped with enthusiasm.

"There are more of you than there are of them," I said. "Besides, you're the ones with the guns. You should be able to hold your own."

"Don't give me that," said Manny. "Nobody's going to go that far. Jeez." Then he had a thought and raised a brow. "Unless Nash Cortez tries to be funny, of course. He's just liable to show up carrying a mounted deer head or some such fool thing. He loves to stick it to Mimi Bettencourt and her gang. 'Vegetarian terrorists,' he calls them. Sometimes I wish that guy would just stay home."

"Why, Nash is your main man," I said. "He's out there shooting off his mouth when the rest of you are home with your wives watching TV. Nash loves to natter at Mimi. Every time she writes a letter to the editor, he writes one back. He's an actor, and this meeting is like a stage. Nash isn't going to stay home."

"No, he won't. And that's just the point. We don't want the commissioners to think we're all as crazy as Nash Cortez. We need some normal types, like you, to help us make our case. Hell, I doubt if Mimi Bettencourt could bring herself to cuss you out in public. She'd have to treat you nice."

"Mimi may be nice most of the time, but not when it comes to hunters. She's a fanatic when it comes to them, and that includes me."

Manny shook his head. "Nah, she likes you. Come tonight. You'll be a restraining influence."

I didn't want to be an influence at all, but Manny seemed to be willing to argue all day if he had to, so I said, "Okay, okay, I'll be there. For a little while at least."

Manny was happy. "Good." He patted my new stove. "Fixing up the place for Zee, eh? I heard that you two decided to get hitched. Be the best thing that ever happened to you! Prettiest girl on the island. Congratulations!"

"Thanks."

He wandered around and found the pile of old padlocks that I'd brought in from the shed out back. He also found the fruit of a summer yard sale.

"What are these things?" He picked up the pack and looked at it.

"It's clear you're no burglar. Those are lock picks. I got a little book to go with them and some skeleton keys from the widow of a locksmith up in West Tisbury. I've been saving those padlocks for years just in case I happened to find a key to fit one of them, and now I'm trying to open them with the picks."

Manny was pleased. "Never saw these things before. Always wanted to be able to open locks myself."

Every English teacher I ever knew wants to own a pub, with a dart board and maybe a skittles table. The rest of us all want to be able to open locks. So far, I'd gotten one of mine open. My career as locksmith did not seem bright. On the other hand, I had my locks and my picks, so future entertainment was free.

Manny went away, and I started putting up the stovepipe. I could do that and think about Zee at the same time. I saw her in her white uniform at the hospital, then in her waders at Wasque Point hauling in bluefish, then in my yard, lying beside me in the summer sun, getting an all-over tan. I saw her dark hair spread like a black halo on my white pillow while she smiled and reached for me.

At noon, I warmed up the rest of the kale soup I'd had for supper the night before, and ate it with the last thick slices of Monday's bread, washing everything down with some jug burgundy. Homemade bread and soup do not last long at my house, so I decided to make more of each tomorrow. Security is having a container of kale soup in the freezer and a loaf of new bread in the fridge.

By late afternoon, I had the stove installed, so I fired it up and watched to see what it would do. It did just fine. It was an airtight stove with a glass front so you could see the fire. Once it was going, you could adjust the flue so it would throw out just about as much heat as you wanted. I diddled with the control for a while until it seemed about right, then got a beer and sat down with the *Gazette* to find out what the Commission hearing was about.

It was about fifty acres of land up near the state forest that the Commission was thinking of buying. The Commission was a well-funded private organization that had been around for years. It used its money to buy land for conservation purposes before developers could get their hands on it. The Commission held meetings to get public input about what lands it should buy and how the land should be used afterward. Some people who had always used the land in a certain way wanted to continue to use it that way. Other people didn't want it used that way anymore.

There seemed to be no limit on the restrictions some people wanted imposed upon those new land purchases. They wanted no trespassing signs, no walks, no bird-watching, no fishing, no picnicking, no anything. Those were the No People people. They wanted land to revert to its wilderness state, and they were very firm in their views.

Other people wanted the land to be made available to human beings and their activities. The most extreme wanted no rules at all. Others wanted limited access: paths and walkways, benches installed at scenic spots, access for picnickers and bird-watchers, and such. Fishermen wanted to be able to get to customary angling spots; hunters wanted to keep using their traditional hunting grounds. These were the People people, and there were more of them than No People people. Alas, they, unlike the highly unified No People people, were often at odds about just which human beings should be allowed use of the land. A classic case was the hunter\non-hunter conflict, with Mimi Bettencourt and Ignacio Cortez as representative zealots for their causes.

Sometimes the No People people didn't even argue their case, apparently believing that the People people had gone at each other so fiercely that the commissioners would have to decide to keep everybody off the land just so the fight would stop.

I didn't hunt deer much anymore, although I didn't mind eating the venison if I could get hold of some. The last time I had killed a deer I hadn't enjoyed the experience as much as I planned, so I hadn't done it again. As fate would have it, my last deer had been killed along a game trail in the fifty acres the Commission was planning to buy.

It was land owned by Carl Norton, a frugal New Englander and one of the numerous Martha's Vineyard Nortons, whose families have been on the island for centuries. As a young man, Carl had done his own hunting. Later, suffering with failing vision, he made a deal with hunters using his land. They could hunt, but he got some venison. He had gotten a hunk of my last deer, in fact. Eventually, continued ill health had led him to leave the island to stay with his daughter on the Cape.

His fifty acres had long been of interest to developers, but Carl had, instead, made it available to the Commission. For the right price, of course.

I had never liked Carl Norton. He had a quick, lacerating tongue, which would have been all right had it been accompanied by any sense of humor. But it was not. It was a knife without a sheath, and, combined with a parsimony of both purse and spirit, made him a man I did not care for. His sole act of generosity was his willingness to let deer hunters walk his land, and even that, it was said, was because his father, a hunter, had forced him to swear that he would do it. Even for Carl Norton, an oath was an oath, and he had stuck to it.

The oath his wife had taken when she married him was not, on the other hand, enough to keep her with him. A few years into the marriage, she had taken their boy and girl and fled across the Sound to America, where she had gotten a divorce. Thereafter, Carl had lived alone, his tightfisted lifestyle apparently sufficiently unattractive to prevent any other woman from permanently entering his household, although there were rumors of certain women coming and going from the farm. As the local sages observed, men cannot resist beauty and women cannot resist money.

I had not been able to figure why Carl hadn't just sold out to a developer. Developers had more money than the Commission, and Carl, being a man who loved a penny, could probably have made more money from one of them. But he had not. He had offered to sell to the Commission for admittedly a lot of money, but for a lot less than he could otherwise have gotten. Why?

I could not imagine. But then I live in an old hunting camp and my checkbook has never been balanced in my life, so I obviously am not a guy who can hope to understand money or the people who actually believe it's important enough to think about very much.

I wondered if, now that I was going to get married, I should make a real effort to live a fiscally sound life. That would be a real challenge. Maybe I should let Zee take care of the money, if we ever got any.

Zee would not be visiting me tonight, but would be going right home from the hospital to her house on the West Tisbury/Chilmark line to do some womanly things that could not be done at my place, so I ate supper alone, after a Tanqueray vodka martini: Tanqueray vodka (kept, of course, in the freezer) and nothing else, in a frosted glass.

Supper was Oysters Rockefeller made from oysters from the Edgartown Great Pond and spinach from my own garden. I had considered making a rolled fillet of sole, but the idea of Oysters Rockefeller was so appealing that I made a whole meal of just that, and washed it down with a chilled St. Emelion. It was clear that life was good, and there was a God.

By the time I finished washing the dishes and stacking them beside the sink, I was already late for the Commission hearing. I am never distressed at being late for meetings, however, so I did not speed to this one. The meeting was in the Edgartown town hall, but this being late October I had no trouble finding a parking place right on Main Street.

As I walked in the front door I was met with a cacophony of human sound coming from the meeting room down the hall. Strident voices were raised in anger and dispute. I thought I recognized Mimi Bettencourt's voice among other feminine shouts and cries. These were mixed with masculine bellows and yells. Unimaginative curses were pronounced, and voices shouted in vain for order. Someone identified himself as a policeman and called for quiet which he did not get. I walked down the hall and into the room just in time to see Ignacio Cortez, tall and lean, and wearing a moth-eaten coonskin hat and coat, bend toward Mimi Bettencourt, shake a bony fist in her face and call her the worst name he could think of.

"Off islander! That's what you are! A damned off islander! Trying to come down here and tell us how to live! Go back to where you came from, and take all of your kind with you! Get out!"

"That does it!" shouted Mimi. "Here! This is what you and your sort deserve!" She reached into her huge purse and her hand came out with a pistol. A gasp of fear and astonishment rose from the throats of those citizens who saw the gun.

Before Nash Cortez could react, she shot him in the head. He staggered back and slapped a hand to his forehead. The hand came away red. Someone in the crowd saw the red hand and screamed. One of the people at the table in front of the room was banging with a gavel. I was moving, but before I could get to the pistol and wrest it away, Mimi had shot Nash again, right in the heart.

— 2 —

Nash Cortez stared at his hand. Then he stared down at the red fluid trickling down his raccoon coat. The room was in turmoil. Someone fainted. Those nearest Nash and Mimi seemed bewildered. I looked at the gun in my hand. Plastic. I looked at Mimi Bettencourt. She was pale-faced and furious. I saw Tony D'Agostine, one of Edgartown's finest, come pushing through the crowd from the table in front of the room. He looked serious, and I wondered how much he'd seen.

Nash Cortez put one hand on his dripping head

and the other on his dripping chest. Mimi stuck her face up at him.

"Now you know what it feels like to have somebody shoot at you, you ape man!"

Nash looked at his hands again, then sniffed one.

"Cherry soda. Cherry soda! Cherry goddamned soda!" His eyes dropped to Mimi's. "You got me covered all over with cherry soda! Why you . . . !"

I stepped between them, but Mimi stood on her tiptoes and stuck her head over my arm. "Just be glad it isn't red paint, you lummox! That's what you and your raccoon coat deserve! And who do you think you are calling me an off islander? There've been Bettencourts on this island for a hundred years!"

Tony D'Agostine finally got through the crowd. He was red-faced. "All right," he said in a controlled voice, "I want you two out of here right now. You can come quietly or I'll arrest you both. One way or another, you're going." Then he noticed the soda all over Ignacio. "Jesus, Nash, what happened to you? Is that blood?"

"Cherry soda," I said, handing him the water pistol. "Here's the murder weapon."

"Cherry soda and some red vegetable dye, and I'm your killer. I confess!" Mimi looked at Tony over my arm. "It'll do Mr. Nimrod good to know how some poor deer or duck feels when it gets shot at. And I'm not sorry!"

"Assault!" yelled Nash, over his initial shock and back into his theatrical mode. "Assault with a dangerous weapon! Arrest her, officer. She's dangerous!"

Tony got Mimi by the arm. "All right, Mrs. Bettencourt, you're coming with me."

"That's it, that's it!" cried Nash. "Take her away! Anybody from the press here? Anybody got a camera? This should be on the front page!"

Tony pushed the water pistol under his belt and grabbed Nash with his other hand. "You too, Mr. Cortez. You're coming, too."

"Me?" exclaimed Nash. "Me? I'm the victim. I haven't done anything."

"You've been disturbing the peace for the last half hour," said Tony firmly. "And I imagine I can come up with some other charges, if I have to. Now come along, both of you."

He led them away. I became aware of the gavel still being pounded on the table at the front of the room. Everyone was talking. The woman who had fainted seemed to have been revived. She was slumped in a chair while a friend fanned her pale, moist face with a white handkerchief.

"Order! Order!" cried the gavel thumper, but it was a while before things quieted down. I found a chair beside Phyllis Manwaring.

"Exciting times," I said. "Did you know Mimi was packing iron?"

Phyllis was, as always, impeccably dressed. I had never seen her otherwise. She was one of those well-to-do women who summered on the island and shared weekends there with a husband who flew off island on Monday morning and flew back again on Friday evening. He was a Connecticut commuter, and whatever he did over there in America brought in the big bucks. Phyllis, like many women in her circle, was involved in causes. She was on committees and was interested in various charities. She was a neighbor of Mimi's and shared her sentiments about killing animals, having even gone so far as to give her furs to her daughters when she herself had converted and joined the animal rights crusade. A long, lovely fall had kept her on the island later than usual this year, so she was here for this meeting instead of wherever she would normally have been on the mainland.

"Heavens, no!" said Phyllis. Then she allowed herself a tiny conspiratorial smile. "Actually, yes. Some people throw paint on people who wear furs, you know. One of my friends actually had that happen to her cousin! Can you imagine? Well, naturally we didn't want to do anything like *that*, but cherry soda and vegetable dye will wash out, so that seemed all right. We just knew that Ignacio Cortez would make some kind of a scene, so we decided that we'd give him tit for tat. Do you think that Mimi's really going to be arrested? Not that she'd mind. She'd be glad to go to jail for the cause!"

"Gee," I said, "they might get you, too. Accessory before the fact."

Phyllis's smile went away. "Me? Why, I didn't do anything. I couldn't. . . . I mean, I wouldn't think of ruining someone's clothes. Do you really think that the police might . . . Oh, dear."

"It's something to think about," I said, as the gavel at the table finally pounded the audience into silence.

Actually I imagined that once Tony got Nash and Mimi outside, he would try to talk both of them into going home and staying out of trouble. If a cop can do that, he usually will. On the other hand, if they gave him any grief, he might decide that a night in the county jail might not hurt either of them. He could PC them and let them go in the morning.

I saw Manny Fonseca on the other side of the room with some other guys who hunt. They looked determined, but it was clear that their man Nash had seriously undercut their hopes of presenting a calm, rational argument for their right to shoot on the fifty acres the Commission was in the process of buying. On the other hand, Mimi hadn't done a lot for the animal rights cause, either. In the audience only the No People people looked happy.

Happiest of all was Chug Lovell, who owned an acre beside Carl Norton's place, and had gone back to nature several years earlier. His once pleasant little shack was now surrounded by high grass, overgrown bushes, thriving scrub oak and encroaching ever-greens. Chug was about forty. He was round and bearded and was said to live on berries, nuts and bread. He was deliberately uncivilized and apparently believed everyone else should be, too. His critics ar-gued that Chug was a perfect illustration of the max-im that a developer is a guy without a house and a conservationist is one who already has his. They also pointed out that Chug could afford to live as he did because he didn't actually have to work for a living, being, reputedly, the heir of some tobacco king in South Carolina. Chug and I occasionally met, and he had always treated me okay, so I had no opinion of him one way or another. At the moment, along with a few other identifiable No People people, he had a wide, beatific smile on his face.

At the front table, a member of the Commission ad-visory board leaned forward and gave a final rap of his gavel.

"Ladies and gentlemen, please! This must be a ra-tional process. Everyone who so wishes will have an opportunity to speak, but we must have order. Please keep in mind that the Commission has not yet com-pleted the purchase of the Norton land, and that, as is often the case in these matters, the purchasing process is a delicate one. Until that process is final-ized, our discussions about possible use of the land should be constrained. So, please, if you have some-thing to say, and we hope you all do, say it calmly. Thank you."

I sat and listened to the familiar arguments. I some-times think that people are born with certain predis-positions that incline them to points of view which are foreordained and not, in any way, the result of the logic and study that they think they bring to issues. Some people seem doomed to be liberal and others conservative and others indifferent. They seem to have little control over their beliefs or their philo-sophic and emotional inclinations. Thus, while I lis-tened to the hunters and anti-hunters argue their positions, I had the sense that it was the doom of each individual to hold the views he or she held. Reason had less to do with their conclusions than did their ge-netic strains. What would keep them from each oth-er's throats, if tensions rose? Would a shooter one day shoot the protester carrying an animal rights sign? Would a paint thrower one day throw acid or poison at the lady wearing mink?

I was slightly depressed when I left the meeting, and so, remembering the adage that a case of beer is good for a case of nerves, went home and had a Sam Adams. While I drank, I phoned the jail. Neither Nash nor Mimi had been offered board and room. Tony D'Agostine had prevailed over their passions and sent them home. All was as well as it could be. I sat in front of my new stove and enjoyed the heat still emanating from it. When the Sam Adams was dead, I stuck a couple more sticks of wood in the stove and went to bed. There was a whiff of Zee's perfume lin-gering on her pillow. That wasn't as good as having Zee herself there, but it was better than nothing.

The next morning, early, I drove down to Wasque Point to try for the champion bluefish that I had not caught during the bass and bluefish derby which had ended just the week before. The nineteen-pound, seven-ounce bluefish which had won the prize was a good two pounds bigger than my best effort had been. It had been caught on the next to the last day of the derby, giving credence once again to the ancient maxim that the big blues come in just as the derby is ending, and it had been caught "on the south shore," according to its captor. The south shore of Martha's Vineyard is twenty miles long, so even if the fisherman had been telling the truth, which no one particularly believed, he was giving away no valuable information. I knew he hadn't caught it at Wasque, because I had been there since before dawn on the morning he caught his winner, and I had not seen him.

Wasque Point is on the southeast corner of the sometimes island of Chappaquiddick, and is therefore on the south shore of Martha's Vineyard. It is one of the best spots in the world for surfcasting for bluefish, since the Wasque rip tosses up a lot of bait that appeals to the blues. This morning, since the derby fishing frenzy had passed, I was not surprised to see no fresh tracks in front of my lights when I turned off the pavement at Katama, put my rusty Toyota Land Cruiser into four-wheel drive and started east along the beach toward Wasque. All of the other people who had been fishing night and day for the last month were probably home in bed, recovering. I was the last lone fisherman. I wondered if I should scratch "lone" and replace it with "dumb."

Chappaquiddick is hooked to the rest of the Vineyard by a narrow sandy beach which runs for a couple of miles between Katama Bay on its north side and the Atlantic Ocean on its south side. Sometimes a storm will knock a hole through the beach, and for a while Chappy will be an island. Usually, though, it's just a peninsula reachable by boat, four-wheel-drive truck over the sand, or via the tiny, four-car On Time Ferry, which runs back and forth between Chappy and Edgartown, the Vineyard's prettiest village.

In the chill, late October morning, I had South Beach to myself. Elsewhere on the island, duck and goose hunters were hunkered in their blinds waiting for sunrise. But the weather was too good for duck and goose hunting. The worse the weather, the better the shooting, they say. Today was too nice. No howling wind, no driving rain, no sleet. Instead, a clear sky with a few stars still in view, a nippy wind out of the south and the promise of a sunny morning. Fishing weather.

I fetched the Wasque reservation, and drove along the road through the dunes. There was a brightening of the sky in the east, where the fall sun was rising over toward Nantucket, that other island on the horizon that I had yet to visit. I had been to Vietnam, but I had never been to Nantucket. So things go in these modern times.

I parked where I could see the light buoy out by Muskeget channel, and climbed into my waders. I put my topsider over my sweater, got my graphite rod down from the roof-rack and tried to guess whether I should use metal or a popper for a lure. What the hell. I snapped a Hopkins on the end of my forty-five-pound leader, walked down to the small surf and made my cast.

Nothing.

I fished for half an hour, changing lures now and then, then went up to the Land Cruiser, put the rod in the spike on the front of the truck and had some coffee while I listened to the C and W station in Rhode Island. Tanya sang a song about a good woman loving a not so good man. The sun hesitated beneath the horizon and I watched for the green flash. Suddenly, the orange ball peeked at me and began to climb. No green flash once again. You can't have everything. It was another incredibly lovely morning, like the beginning of time.

A half an hour later, something very big hit my Ballistic Missile. An incredible hit! Thank you, God, for making me use a twenty-pound test line! The fish ran off almost all of that nice strong line before I got it turned and could jack it in a little way. It ran again and this time I thought it was gone, but again it slowed and I was able to turn it. It walked me down the beach, and I was able to get a few more cranks on the reel. Then it pulled me down the beach farther. A hundred yards west of the Toyota I got the fish stopped enough to reel it in a bit more. Then I went down the beach some more.

It was a fine fight, and I was a long way from the Toyota when I finally got the fish onto the sand. I hooked my hand in its gills and dragged it up away from the water.

A monster bluefish! I carried it back to the Land Cruiser, and hung it on my scale. Wouldn't you know it? Twenty-two pounds! The biggest bluefish I'd ever caught, but a week too late to win the derby. More proof that not even Martha's Vineyard is perfect.

I looked at my watch. If I hurried, I could show this beauty to Zee before she went to work. She would be wild with jealousy. I put the fish in the fish box and headed for West Tisbury.

— 3 —

When I was a small boy and first came to the Vineyard with my father, the islanders made most of their tourist money between the Fourth of July and Labor Day. Since then, the season has stretched out quite a bit. People come down earlier and stay later. The fishing derby brings in a crowd between mid-September and mid-October, and a lot of people make it down for Columbus Day weekend, Thanksgiving and Christmas. On balance, though, once Labor Day comes and school begins, the island empties out. A hundred thousand tourists and summer people go away and ten thousand year-rounders once again have the place mostly to themselves.

You can find parking places on the town's main streets. Except for Vineyard Haven, which has a flotilla of sailboats all year round, the graceful yachts disappear from the harbors and are replaced by rough and ready scallop boats. Most of the restaurants, hotels and shops close up for the winter. Lovely Edgartown, whose stores once catered to the everyday needs of its citizens, but now are almost totally oriented toward summer tourist trade, becomes silent and empty, save at the end of Main Street where the locals collect at the Dock Street Coffee Shop and, for a month, the fishermen weigh in their fish at derby headquarters across the parking lot.

There is a nice emptiness about the whole island. You can feel space around you. The beaches are almost abandoned. You can walk the long beach between Edgartown and Oak Bluffs and not see anyone else. No more towels, umbrellas or kites. No more lines of parked cars. Only the water lapping at the sand. On South Beach, only a few cars still park at Katama while their owners walk the lonely, lovely, windy shore, hand in hand, looking at the cooling sea.

Summer greens fade and are replaced by tans and browns. After the leaves have fallen, you can drive along the roads and see deep into the forests. Houses that you never knew were there come into view. Vistas hidden by verdant summer trees and bushes are now revealed. There is a sense of cozy roominess about the whole island.

When you meet people in the streets or along the highways, you now often know who they are. Out-of-state plates are more rarely seen, mopeds disappear, the summer-long traffic jam in front of the Edgartown A & P is gone and it becomes easy to make left-hand turns all over the island.

In September and October, the waters are still warm enough for swimming, the air often comfortable enough for shirt sleeves, the gardens are full of fall veggies, the bluefish are back and the scallop and hunting seasons have begun. Later, when winter arrives, it rarely brings the cold or snows that hit the mainland, because the same surrounding water that cools the island in the summer warms it in the winter. By January the seed catalogues are being studied, and by March the question "Got your peas in yet?" can be heard among the gardeners.

When you live on the Vineyard all year round, it's easy to understand why the tourists like it so much, but it's also nice to know that they mostly come only in the summer. The rest of the time the island belongs to you.

And the year-rounders make both the worst and best of the off season. For some, it's a time for malevolence. Old antagonisms, put on a back burner during the busy money-making season, reappear. Meannesses, both petty and grand, manifest themselves in and out of court. Tire slashers make their presence known. Anonymous telephone callers and letter writers harass their victims. Drink and drugs continue to mix with driving and the abuse of relatives and associates. Arguments break out over fences or in committee meetings, threats are exchanged, angry letters appear in the papers.

For other islanders, the winter season is a time of special blessing when, no longer obliged to structure their lives around the activities of a hundred thousand visitors, they can pursue their private intellectual and aesthetic interests. Their enthusiasms for culture and the arts flourish, with concerts, benefits, dances and lectures being attended on a nightly basis. People go to theater, listen to speakers, plan charitable events, gossip and otherwise use the off season to good advantage.

The islanders also exchange buildings and businesses in a sort of giant, real life Monopoly game, and, in like fashion, also exchange spouses and lovers rather actively. A popular joke is that of the small boy who, when challenged by a rival about whose dad could win a fight, replied, "Your dad can't either lick my dad. Your dad *is* my dad!"

In these ways, the island is a microcosm of the world, with all the good and evil, mediocrity and extremism you can find anywhere else, and in about the same proportion.

As I drove to Zee's house, I considered my options for the day. Zee herself, unfortunately, was not one of them, since she was working the day shift at the hospital. That being the case, I had other choices, all appealing. After showing the fish to Zee and establishing bragging rights for the biggest blue of the year, and after filleting the wonderful fish and sticking all or part of it into my freezer for future reference, I could go shell fishing or duck or goose hunting, although it was a little late in the day for hunting, or I could do some ahead-of-time cooking which would also go in the freezer. Some seviche made from part of my fresh bluefish and to be eaten tomorrow would also be nice. Or I could sit in front of my new stove and read another one of the books I'd gotten at the summer book fair in West Tisbury. Or maybe I would do nothing at all. By noon the sun would warm things up enough to allow me a midday snooze out in my yard. Maybe I would do that. The joys of the bachelor life on Martha's Vineyard were many.

Soon, of course, those joys would end for me, and would be replaced by the delights of marriage. After saying no to my proposals for more times than I could remember, Zee had shocked and delighted me by saying yes. Now we were officially an item. A couple. Engaged.

Engaged. Soon to be married.

Married. I had been married once, long before. Zee, too, had once been wed. Now we had agreed to try it again. The triumph of hope over experience.

As a married man, could I ever again decide to do nothing at all, just because I felt like it? Now I owed nothing to anybody, but when I married, Zee would be part of every decision.

Or would she? Were there, even in marriage, areas of privacy which needed to be maintained? Both Zee and I were used to living alone and making decisions for ourselves. Neither of us was the dependent type, neither inclined to ask permission for how we lived.

Hmmmm.

But the thought of her in my house forever filled

me with joy and amazement. I shed not a tear at the thought of giving up my bachelorhood. It couldn't happen too soon.

I got back to the pavement at Katama, shifted into two-wheel drive, and decided to take the Meeting-house Way shortcut to the West Tisbury road. Mistake. Meetinghouse Road is Edgartown's worst public road. It is corduroy from end to end and will shake your car to pieces in short order if you drive it often. I take it every now and then just to see if it's been improved, but it never has been. It doesn't get any worse, because it can't, but it never gets any better, either.

By the time I got to the West Tisbury road, my teeth were loose in my gums. I lived in a house con-verted from a hunting camp, I drove an ancient, rust-ed-out Land Cruiser, I was always short of money and I had other problems, but at least, by God, I didn't live on Meetinghouse Way, so things could have been a lot worse.

I drove up past the contested fifty acres belonging to Carl Norton, past Mimi Bettencourt's place and the acre of jungle that surrounded Chug Lovell's sagging house, then past Phyllis Manwaring's huge house. No one seemed to be up and around. I went on to West Tisbury, passed the mill pond and took a left. I drove by Alley's general store on the right (long since owned by people other than Alley) and the field of dancing statues on the left, and on to Zee's driveway.

Perfect timing. Zee, in her white nurse's uniform, was coming out of her house just as I pulled in. I sat and ogled her. Her raven hair was pinned up, her tan was still smooth and dark, her great dark eyes were bright and her teeth flashed when she saw me. I got out and put a modest expression on my face. She was immediately suspicious.

"All right, Jefferson, what's going on? I've got to get to work, so don't take too long."

"You wound me," I said. "Have I ever done anything that was not in your best interest? Have I ever been self-serving in my actions?"

"This sounds worse by the minute."

"I brought you a surprise. I know you'll love it. Come and see."

She walked to the Land Cruiser. I bent and offered pursed lips. She kissed them.

"You smell like fish. Fish. You've been fishing!"

"I only got one little one. I'd give it to you, but it would embarrass me."

I opened the rear door of the Land Cruiser and took the lid off the fish box. Zee looked in.

"Oh, my God! You devil! Where did you get that fish?"

"Shall I describe the scene? Me, all alone at Wasque. The sun coming up. A green flash . . ."

"A green flash?! Don't tell me you saw a green flash, too?!"

"Well, all right, there was no green flash, but the rest is true. I had some coffee and listened to some C and W music, you know . . ."

"Get on with it, Jefferson! I have to go to work. Besides, it's bad enough just knowing you got this fish while I wasn't there. I don't think I should have to listen to this drawn-out tale. Why didn't you get me up so I could go with you? Why is it that I'm always home when the big ones come in? Why me?"

But I knew how long it would take her to drive to the hospital, so I stretched the story out until the very last second, giving her details both real and imagined, until she absolutely had to leave.

"I hate you," she said, giving me a goodbye kiss.

"You'd better not try this sort of thing after we get married!" She got into her little Jeep and started out of the driveway. Then she stopped and stuck her head out the window. "A dynamite fish, Jeff, if I do say so myself!"

"Come for supper," I said.

"I will." She grinned and was gone.

A most successful visit. I drove home and dressed out the fish, throwing the bones into the woods behind my house so the worms and maggots would have something to eat. In a couple of days the flesh would be gone, and there would be no bad smells even if the wind came around to the northeast. I skinned and cut the huge fillets into meal-sized portions and put all but one in the freezer. It is comforting to have a freezer full of fish.

It was too late for hunting, too early for sunbathing, and the tide was a bit too high for scalloping. I got keys from the drawer in the kitchen, climbed back into the truck and went to check out the houses I look after in the winter. If you're going to live on the Vineyard in the wintertime, you pick up a few bucks wherever you can. I make some fishing and some more being a caretaker and handyman.

I had a dozen houses, and I went to them all. Everything was fine. No broken windows, no broken shed doors, no sign of vandals. Pipes were drained and the power was turned off. The houses and barns were cold and dead-looking, the way empty buildings are in the winter. I checked everything, then went down to Collins Beach, got my dinghy and rowed out to the *Mattie* and the *Shirley J*. Both were catboats and both swung at stakes between the yacht club and the Reading Room. The *Mattie* belonged to Professor John Skye, and the *Shirley J*. belonged to me. Both of them stayed in the water all winter, and I watched over them.

All was well with the boats. I sat in the cockpit of the *Shirley J.* and looked out at the harbor. It was almost empty, with only a couple of sailboats still out there on moorings. Across the water was Chappaquiddick, most of its houses now vacant and tranquil. The sky was pale blue and the water was darker blue and rippled by a cool, gentle breeze. It was a peaceful scene.

After a while I rowed back to shore and pulled the dinghy up away from the tides. The beach was lined with scallop boats with their culling boards, drags and winches. In a week or two, when the commercial scalloping season began, they would be out at work every day. I would be out with Dave Mello, since he had a work boat and I didn't. There is a lot of money to be made scalloping, especially in the first few weeks when the scallops are still plentiful and the weather is good enough to make dragging for them fairly comfortable. In early November, therefore, a lot of guys are out in their boats; later, when the pickings get slim and winter arrives, the scalloping crowd thins out considerably. Dave and I were two of the guys who dragged all winter, and on the really bad days we earned our bucks.

But the commercial season hadn't arrived yet. Instead, the people with family permits were out on the flats getting their bushel a week. Even though I had my commercial license, I was also a family of one, so I could get my bushel, too. I checked things out. The sun was high, the air was warming, there wasn't much wind and the tide was now halfway down. Perfect. I put the dinghy in the back of the Land Cruiser and went home to get my gear.

Before the beginning of the commercial season, I, like most family scallopers, use a dip net, a bushel basket floating in an inner tube and a glass-bottomed peep-sight known locally as a Buck Rogers (this because it had reminded some past scalloper of the noted 25th-century adventurer's space helmet). I collected all of my equipment, got my waders and headed for Katama.

I put the boat in from the beach beside the launching ramp that was wrecked by Hurricane Bob back in '91 and was always too sanded in to use before that (another example of man proposing and nature disposing), piled everything aboard, started the little Seagull and putted out to the flats in the middle of the pond. I had so much gear that the dinghy looked top-heavy. When I got where I wanted, I anchored and climbed overboard into the knee-deep water. I could see several other boats anchored here and there on the pond, and other scallopers who were busily dipping up their prey.

Scallops lie right on the surface of the bottom of the ponds. You spot them through your Buck Rogers, snag them with your dip net and dump them in the basket you have floating beside you. Nothing to it, on a day as fine as this. No wind to build up waves, plenty of light, warm weather. Mighty fine. Next to eating them, netting them is the most scallop fun you can have. You can see the results of your work, the company is good and you can sing or meditate or otherwise enjoy yourself while you're filling your basket.

The scallops were numerous if not thick, and I was back on the beach in an hour with what I thought of as a nicely rounded bushel, which meant one that was more than level, but not so much more that the fish warden would make me throw some back, if he happened to see me. Next would come two hours of extracting the little rascals from their shells. Unlike any other island shellfish—quahogs, steamers, mussels or oysters—all of whose innards are eaten, only the scallop's large muscle is deemed eatable. Because you have to separate the muscle from the rest of what's inside the shell, it takes a bit longer to open scallops than to open other shellfish. I reached my top opening speed several years ago, and have not improved with time. I'm not bad, but there are a lot of people who can cut scallops faster than I can.

Although opening them is the worst part of scalloping, even that isn't too bad if you have a good place to do it and remember that once you've opened them you can eat them. I opened mine in the shed behind my house, and planned to feed some of them to Zee for supper, so I was well motivated. With luck, I might persuade Zee to spend the night. I would ply her with fine food and liquor. It seemed like an excellent plan.

When I wasn't thinking about Zee, I wondered what was going to happen between the hunters and the anti-hunters. I didn't think any of them were going to change their minds. Was there going to be trouble right here in River City? Or was peaceful coexistence possible? Maybe we should put all of the combatants on a boat and send them to the mainland. After all, Adam and Eve had been tossed out of Eden because they couldn't leave well enough alone, so there was precedent.

If I were God, what would I do with Nash and Mimi and their crowds? I put the question aside. I had no interest in being God. Just being a human being kept me busy.

— 4 —

"You know, of course, that Heather Manwaring is supposedly sneaking off for lurid romance with the man of her dreams," said Zee, sipping her martini in front of my new stove between bites of bluefish pâté and crackers.

"Who's the man of her dreams, and how do you learn all this stuff?" I asked.

"Hospitals are rumor mills," smiled Zee. "Sooner or later everybody goes to see his or her doctor, and people speculate and talk. You know. I don't know who the man is. I just know there's supposed to be one. I approve, by the way."

"I'm trying to imagine Heather's type."

"Everybody's somebody's type. You, for instance, are my type in spite of your inclination to go fishing without inviting me. I deserve better."

"You're about to get it. Dinner is served."

Dinner was scallops, simmered first with wine, salt and pepper, a bay leaf and a celery stalk, then combined in a baking dish with sautéed sliced mushrooms and chopped onion and green pepper, covered with a roux flavored with thyme and pimento, topped with some bread crumbs and grated Parmesan, and baked until bubbly.

This I served with some whipped potatoes, a salad and a bottle of sauvignon blanc that I'd been saving.

Zee, who has the body of a nymph, also has the appetite of an elephant. She and I had little to say for several minutes, while we concentrated on eating. Finally she touched her napkin to her lips. "A notable meal, my dear chef, even by chez Jackson standards. I take back all the nasty stuff I said about you earlier."

"Madam is too kind."

"I like your new stove."

"It's not as pretty as the fireplace, but it does a better job of heating. Why, I'll bet that if you took off all of your clothes, you'd still be warm as toast."

"I dare say, but I plan on finishing this meal before testing the rest of your domestic offerings."

"We could take turns eating the remains of this repast off various parts of each other's body."

"I don't believe I've ever heard you mention this particular urge before."

"I've been waiting for just the right moment to tell you."

She gestured with her fork. "Eat, Jefferson. You're the guy who doesn't even like to go on beach picnics because you're afraid you'll get sand in your food. You shouldn't be thinking about eating off a body that's been in an emergency ward all day."

"Romance is dead, just like people say."

Afterward we sat in front of the new stove and had Brie, French bread recently from my oven, coffee and cognac.

"So Phyllis Manwaring's little girl is swinging with somebody, eh? I always imagined Phyllis had some Yale lawyer and a big formal marriage in mind for Heather. I wonder if Heather's guy meets the standards."

Zee gave me a wry smile. "I don't know, but it doesn't make any difference because as far as I know, Phyllis doesn't know anything about it. Heather is trying to make it on her own. She doesn't confide in Mom and Dad."

"I thought you girls told your mothers everything."

"Sure you did. I wonder what Vincent will think of the beau, if he ever meets him. I mean, Vince Manwaring's so straitlaced that he's still got his tie on when he comes down to the island for the weekend. And ever since he's decided that Connecticut needs him as a senator, he's even worse than before. Having a daughter sleeping with who-knows-who can't be a political asset."

"Maybe Heather is picking out the man of her parents' dreams."

"Who knows? Maybe she's slumming."

"Maybe he's a caveman."

"Some women like the caveman type."

"Now, now, let's not talk about your feelings for me. Let's just gossip about other people. What else is hanging on the hospital grapevine?"

"Well, Cotton Williams seems to have a new woman."

"Where's the news in that?"

Cotton Williams, better known as Shrink, was a psychiatrist who had landed on the island several years before. He was then newly shed of a wife and needed a change of scene from New York. He had settled into the Vineyard lifestyle quite nicely and now had a good practice, since islanders are just as prone to psychological malaise as anyone else. He had not remarried, for the very good reason that a long string of attractive women had found him irresistible for varying lengths of time.

"If my rumors bore you, you can give me yours."

I looked at my nails. "Sorry, I never gossip."

"In that case, I'm going home."

I hooked an arm around her shoulders and slid her closer to me. "Wait a minute, wait a minute, I'm thinking, I'm thinking! Let's see. Did you hear that Jeanette Norton wants Carl to sell his land to a developer instead of to the Commission?"

She snuggled against me. "Who's Jeanette Norton? I've heard of Helene Norton. She's the daughter Carl is staying with on the Cape, isn't she? Who's Jeanette?"

"Jeanette is Carl's ex. Helene's mom. When she left, she didn't get much from old Carl. Now that he's getting old and sick, she wants him to leave as big an estate as possible. Ergo, a developer should get the land."

"If she's his ex, what difference does it make to her what his estate is?"

"Because she and Helene are close, and she figures Helene will inherit and then share with Mama!"

"I see, said the blind woman."

"And since Carl is staying with Helene, Jeanette figures that Helene can maybe get the old man to change his mind."

"And Jeanette has some developer in the wings, eh?"

"Eh, indeed. You're a smart cookie, for a nurse. In fact, Mom's developer is now dating Mom's daughter. Is that some kind of incest?"

"Where did you get this bit of gossip?"

I had a sudden foreboding of danger. "My sources are confidential, I'm afraid."

"Well, I've got to go now." She wiggled within my arm, and pretended to try to sit up. I didn't want to let her go, and made a quick, wrong decision.

"Okay, okay. Angie Bettencourt told me all about it the other day. She and Helene go way back, and I guess they still talk a lot."

I could feel Zee get a little stiff. "I didn't know you and Angie were still seeing each other."

I was suddenly irritated. "We met at the A & P, down by the fruit and vegetables where we always have our passionate encounters. Nobody pays any attention to us there, and we can put our pants on the potatoes while we cuddle on the floor. You know how Angie is. She can't restrain herself, but she hates to have her clothes get dirty."

Zee was not amused. "Don't be funny with me. Have you been seeing her?"

I tried to push my temper away. "Look, I see Angie about once in a blue moon. We bump into each other at the store or on the street now and then. We don't date and we haven't for years."

"I'll bet she'd like to!"

"I don't know about that." I was at once angry and worried. "Are you okay?"

"Let me go." I did, and she got up and stood, rubbing one arm with her hand in a nervous way. "I don't know . . . All right, I'm sorry I said that about you and Angie. I don't know what's the matter with me lately. I guess I'm just nervous about . . . "

"About what? About getting married?" I stood up, too.

"Yes, I guess so. Look, I'm sorry . . . I think I'd better go on home."

"Wait," I said. I put my arms around her and she let me pull her to me. I held her taut body against mine for a moment, then kissed the top of her head and stepped back. I put my hands on her shoulders, and looked down into her great, dark eyes. When my voice seemed ready for words, I said, "I love you. I want to marry you. I know you must wonder how much your life will change if we get married, and I understand that the idea must be nerve-racking sometimes. I want you, but I don't want to push you, and I don't want you to do anything you're not sure you want to do. Do you understand?"

"Yes." Her voice seemed small.

"When we marry, I plan on having it last as long as we both live, so I want you to be sure."

She shook her head, and the lamplight glittered on her long, dark hair. "Oh, I am sure. It's just that I get so touchy sometimes that I don't like myself."

"I want you to be happy. I'd rather have that than to be married to you."

She put her arms around my waist, and laid her head against my chest. Her voice seemed lost in my shirt. "I love you, but I'm going home. I don't feel like very good company tonight."

I tried a joke. "Excellent. I'm not very good company."

She tightened her arms around me. "Yes, you are." She lifted her lips and gave me a kiss, then stepped away. "I'll see you later. Thanks for supper. It was super. A super supper." She gave a wan smile and went out.

I felt empty as a new tomb. What had happened? A wonderful day had turned into mud in the blink of an eye. I walked around like a robot, picking up dishes, washing them, and stacking them in the rack beside the sink. I straightened up the living room, tried to read, then tried to sleep, then listened to the radio beside my bed far into the night. I put out my hand to touch Zee, but of course she was not there. I was awake a long time.

— 5 —

"It's just nerves," said Manny Fonseca, pouring coffee from his thermos into a cup. "When I got married, I almost wet my pants, I was so nervous. It's normal to be jumpy. Don't worry about her."

To the east, the sky was brightening over the Edgartown Great Pond. Our blind was west of the pond, and there were ducks out there in the middle of it, talking to each other in that way ducks have of quacking when they know they're beyond shotgun range. The brightening water and sky showed a flight of a dozen or so birds coming in from the south, but too far out to give us a shot.

It wasn't miserable enough to be a really good day for duck hunting, but there was a cold wind off the ocean, and some promising storm clouds upwind, so Manny and I were not without hope.

Manny had been married a long time, and considered himself an expert on the subject of matrimony. Maybe he was.

"I changed my mind a dozen times after Helen and me got engaged, and she did too," said Manny, sipping his coffee while eyeing the sky in hopes of seeing a shootable duck. "I was having fun being single, you know, and I didn't want to give it up. But I didn't want to give Helen up either. You know what I mean?"

"I think so."

"Anyway, I almost called it off, then she almost called it off, then we tied the knot."

"Wet pants and all."

"Yeah!" He laughed. "Fifteen years, now." He paused and frowned. "Or is it sixteen? Geez . . ."

Small flights of ducks flew in from the west and north, and landed out toward the middle of the pond. All out of range, of course. Most of duck hunting consists of sitting in a blind being cold and uncomfortable and not getting to shoot at ducks. They, like Canada geese, will let you come right up to them until the day hunting season starts, then they start hanging around out in the middle of ponds where you can barely see them. All of which once more raised the question: who were the real birdbrains out here, anyway?

I poured some more coffee to ward off the chill of sunrise. A single duck came over us from the west. Too high. Manny raised his gun, but didn't shoot.

"Anytime now," he said, lowering the gun.

"Any news on the Norton land?"

"Nope. Saw Nash Cortez, though. A couple of days ago. He said he was thinking of suing Mimi Bettencourt for assault."

"With a water pistol?"

"Hey, don't ask me. I'm no lawyer. You know Nash. He likes to give Mimi and her crowd a hard time." He gave me a thoughtful look. "Tell me, did you ever get the impression that Nash is just putting on a show?"

In fact, I had. There was something contrived about Nash's ranting and raving about Mimi and her animal rights friends.

"What do you mean?" I asked.

"Well, you know, it's like he's showing off, or something. Like a kid who'll burn rubber driving his car out of a lot, or who'll risk his neck swinging from a tree, or some fool thing like that. You know what I mean?"

"Maybe."

"On the other hand, maybe he really is going to sue Mimi."

"Good grief, what next?"

"Well, archery season for deer is coming up in a couple of weeks. I think Nash is going to get himself a license, even though I don't think he ever shot an arrow in his life. He'll probably get himself a black powder license, too, just so he can give those animal rights people more to stew about in December."

"Does Nash have a cap and ball rifle?"

"He came by my place and looked at my Hawken, and had me show him how to measure powder and like that, so maybe he's planning to get himself a black powder gun. Look there! Here they come!"

He pointed and I turned. Four ducks were coming past, flying low.

"I'll take the two high ones on the right," I said, and swung my gun up. I led the first duck and popped my cap. The duck folded and fell, arching down toward the water. Beside me, Manny's gun barked, then barked again. I led the second of my ducks, but it swerved away as I shot, and was quickly out of range. Manny's two ducks curved into the water. Since Manny was about twice as good a shot as I was, I wasn't surprised that he'd gotten twice as many ducks.

We reloaded. Manny had a little six-foot dinghy that we'd brought out in the back of the Land Cruiser, and I got into that and rowed out to retrieve the three ducks. The wind was cold across the water, but I decided it was going to be a nice day after all, in spite of the storm clouds down off South Beach. It wasn't going to be a nice day for these three ducks, of course. Their nice days were over.

Between mid-October and mid-December, and then in late January and early February, there is a lot of hunting on Martha's Vineyard. Goose and duck seasons usually start in mid-October, and pheasant season starts a week later. Normally, the archery season for deer starts in early November and runs for two or three weeks, then the regular deer hunting season replaces it toward the end of the month. In December you can hunt ducks and geese again, and in the middle of the month you can hunt deer with black powder rifles for a couple of days. Finally, you can try for geese again for a week or so in late January and early February. The more you like miserable weather, the more you like hunting. My appetite for being cold and wet was not as great as it once had been, so I only got out now and then.

"I had a bow and arrow once," I said. "I made the bow out of a piece of yew, and made arrows out of willows. I used any feathers I could find. I was inspired by Errol Flynn as Robin Hood. I knew a guy who kept horses and who had baled hay in his barn. I used to sneak in there and shoot my arrows into the baled hay. It was a lot of fun. You're a noble redskin, so you should know all about that sort of thing."

Manny Fonseca was a firearms enthusiast who for years had thought of himself as just another islander whose ancestors had come over from the Azores. However, he had recently discovered that he had just enough Wampanoag blood in him to qualify as an official member of the tribe, and he had made a rapid social adjustment. Now he tapped his Remington automatic.

"No more of that bow and arrow crap for us original Americans. Look what that got us. Lost the whole damned country to a bunch of paleface outcasts from over the big sea water just because they had fire sticks and we didn't. Bad mistake. Next time the white eyes get the bows and arrows and we get the gunpowder. Were you any good?"

"No. Crooked arrows don't go where they're supposed to. If Crazy Horse, or whoever it was, had equipment as bad as mine, he'd never have whupped Custer."

"Hey, you got it. Out there on the Little Big Horn, the U.S. Cavalry wasn't the only ones with rifles, and see what happened. Maybe if they'd had all this new-fangled archery gear back then, compound bows and all, my relatives would have massacred yours just as easy as they did with guns. Modern archery equipment is really something."

"Anglo technology," I said. "We'll get you guys out of the Stone Age, yet. Pretty soon you'll be wearing regular clothes just like us, and you won't have to live in skin tents anymore, either. You'll like it."

"Here comes one," said Manny.

"It's yours."

Manny lifted his gun, but the duck swung away and went off to the north. We heard a shot from another blind up that way, but the duck kept flying until it was only a dot in the sky.

Manny sat down again. "Mimi Bettencourt and her pals used to belong to an archery club or something, did you know that?"

"No. Must have been a long time ago."

"They wore white uniforms and they shot at targets. I saw some pictures of them once. Maybe it was back when they were in college."

"Where'd you ever see pictures like that?"

"At Mimi's house. Several years back. I was up there doing some cabinet work for her and Gus, and there was this album. Angie and Heather were looking at it. They thought their moms looked pretty funny in those uniforms. I didn't think they looked so bad, myself. Nice-looking young girls back then. I was married when I saw those pictures, but that didn't mean I was blind." He cocked an eye at me. "You don't get blind when you get married, you know."

"I know. So you have a Hawken, eh?"

All I knew about a Hawken was that it was a muzzle-loading rifle that had been popular in the nineteenth century during the early hunting days out west. But for the time being, I had had enough advice about being married, and I knew that all I had to do was mention a gun to Manny, and he would forget everything else and entertain me forever with talk about firearms. He loved guns and all the equipment that went with them, and he did not disappoint me. He told me more than I wanted to know about powder, flint, caps, balls and other subjects of small arms conversation. By the time he was done, it was time for us to collect our decoys and go home. Manny had to go to work.

I dropped him off at his house, and went home and dressed out my duck and put it in the freezer. Then, because my house felt lonesome, I decided to go down to the Dock Street Coffee Shop for breakfast. I liked having an occasional meal there both because the food was good and reasonable, and because the cook was a master of his work whose every move was a model of efficiency, grace and beauty, although he no doubt would have been surprised to hear about it.

I was finishing up a second cup of coffee when someone slipped onto the stool beside me. I glanced up and found myself looking into the dark green eyes of, wouldn't you know?, Angie Bettencourt.

Angie was about five four, weighed about one ten, had yellow-brown hair and looked quite smashing in her neat skirt and blouse. Once I had seen a great deal of all of Angie, and though that had been some time ago, I had not forgotten.

"Hi," she said in her throaty voice.

"Angela. Aren't you supposed to be working? How

can this great nation of ours be expected to prosper if its ace entrepreneurs hang around in coffee joints instead of keeping at the old cash registers?"

Angie owned Angie's Place, a snappy clothing store in Vineyard Haven which catered to youthful, wealthy and wild-dressing women, some of whom were year-rounders, but most of whom came to the island in the summer.

"It's Sunday," said Angie. "The store is closed. I'm going to church when I leave here. You should come, too. Do you good. You're a lost soul."

Sunday. When you live the way I do, it doesn't make much difference which day it is, so you don't keep track. I like it that way. I wondered if that would have to change when I got married. Probably, since Zee had a regular job. Then I wondered if I was still going to get married.

"You've got enough soul for both of us," I said. "You can represent my spiritual interests and make my donation for me."

"What's the matter? Something's eating you." Angie was, as usual, sharp. "Coffee, black," she said to the waitress. Then, to me, "Woman trouble. I can tell. What's happened?"

I quoted Manny Fonseca, the oracle of matrimony. "It's just nerves."

"You mean somebody's nervous about getting married? I wouldn't blame Zee for being nervous. The idea of marrying you would make anybody nervous. But if you're the one who's nervous about marrying her, you're just a nut."

"Thanks a lot."

"Well, if she throws you over, which I wouldn't blame her for doing one bit, let me know. I have worse taste than Zee Madieras, and I could probably put up with you."

"You had your chance, and you let me slip away. Now it's too late. I think our tragedy would probably make a nice two-hankie movie. We could film it right here in Edgartown. Lonely man, lonely woman, growing old, always seeing one another, but doomed to live tormented, loveless lives with other mates. If Olivier and Leigh were still alive, he could be me, and she could be you. Sort of a 'Wuthering with the Wind' combination. What do you think?"

"Sounds good." She drank her coffee. "Is this going to be an old-fashioned, black-and-white movie where the man and the woman flash their eyes at each other on-screen, but all the really good stuff happens off-stage, or is it going to be in living color and include the modern obligatory nude sex scenes?"

"Why do you ask?"

"I thought maybe we could write, direct, produce and star. I mean, it is our film, after all. I think the modern version would be best."

"We'd have to rehearse, I suppose, just to get it right."

"You and I could play the roles in the flashback scenes, when we were still young and juicy. We could get Olivier and Leigh to do the parts where we're old, if only they were still alive."

"At last, a way to earn a living on Martha's Vineyard. I've been trying to figure out how to do that for years."

She glanced at her watch. "Oops, time to go, or they'll start without me." She got up and let her eyes range up and down me, from toe to pate. "Get to work on that script, J.W."

She arched an eyebrow and went off. I watched her go. Nice hips.

— 6 —

I went out and walked to the edge of the harbor. A couple of sailboats still hung at their moorings out beyond the yacht club. Between the yacht club and the Reading Room, several fishing boats and the *Shirley J.* and the *Mattie* swung at their stakes. There were dinghies pulled up on the dock at my feet, and some scallop boats tied alongside, but the only person there besides me was the chief of police, who was leaning on a patrol car drinking coffee. I deduced that he had come into the coffee shop and gotten a cup while I had not been paying attention. I advanced this theory to him.

"You are as keen a thinker as ever," he said. "When I went in, you were being distracted by Angie Bettencourt. And you an engaged man, too."

"I notice that you noticed her. And you're a married man."

"I am a minion of the law. I'm supposed to notice things." He put his cup on the hood of the car and got out his pipe. He stared into its bowl, poked at it with a finger, then stuck it in his mouth and pulled out his Zippo.

I inhaled the fragrance and decided again that maybe I'd start smoking my own pipes again. I still had my rack of them at home, even though I hadn't smoked for years, and I still got the urge whenever a pipe passed me on the street.

"You just stoke that thing up to make me edgy," I said.

He looked around. "Quiet, isn't it? I like it. Maybe when I retire, I'll live here winters and go to Nova Scotia summers. They say Nova Scotia's like the Vineyard was thirty years ago. You know, slow and easy.

Like the island is right now, only up there, it's like this in the summertime." He gestured up Main Street. "Look at that. Parking places everywhere. Nobody walking in the streets. Quiet."

"Not always. Not as long as Mimi Bettencourt has a supply of water pistols, for example."

"Wasn't that something?" He shook his head. "Those two! I can remember when Nash Cortez and Gus Bettencourt were pals. Used to go goose hunting together. Fishing. Now look at him and Mimi. It makes you wonder."

"I hear that Nash is threatening to sue."

"Talk to the lawyers about that, not to me."

A large car came down Main Street and parked beside the patrol car. A large man got out of it. I recognized Vincent Manwaring, Phyllis's husband, would-be member of the U.S. Senate, rumored cuckold. I looked for horns, but didn't see any. He was a tall, florid man who appeared to be in good shape. One of those people who worked out at the gym when he wasn't working out at the bank or the office or the stock exchange or wherever it was that Vince Manwaring made his money. He had a good set of teeth and a studied air of frankness, but his eyes had no warmth in them.

I had attended a couple of island cocktail parties which had included him, and I thought I knew the secret of his social success and his strength as a political candidate. He would keep his mouth shut and look a speaker in the eye when he was being addressed, and then would nod thoughtfully and arch a brow. He might say, "Ah," or he might say nothing, then move slowly away, as though to ponder the speaker's thoughts. He thus created the impressions that he was actually listening, when indeed he might not be, and that he considered the speaker to be an insightful and possibly subtle thinker. The speaker, flattered, felt Manwaring to be a splendid, intelligent fellow, and became a convert. As someone said, if you can become the friend of fools, you can get elected to anything.

Manwaring looked at me, smiled and nodded, trying but failing to remember if he'd seen me somewhere, then faced the chief. "I'd like to talk to you, Chief." His eyes flicked toward me. "Privately, if I may, if you don't mind, sir."

I didn't mind and moved toward my old Land Cruiser. Behind me, I heard Manwaring's voice say, "It's about this Cortez fellow. He worries me. My wife is very disturbed . . ."

Phyllis Manwaring wasn't the only one who was disturbed. I was disturbed about Zee. But to whom could I go for solace? No one. Except, possibly, Angie Bettencourt, and that didn't seem like a good idea.

It was still cool and partly cloudy, but the threat of rain seemed to have diminished, so I decided to go after some oysters while I planned what to do with this morning's duck. Maybe I would make a meal with both oysters *and* duck. I could invite Zee, and I would be damned careful about not mentioning Angie Bettencourt. Or any of the other women I used to see before I knew Zee. It irked me to think that I should have to be careful about mentioning women who really didn't mean anything to me anymore, but if that was what it took for Zee to be happy, I would give it a shot.

I drove up Main Street to the four corners, turned left on South Water Street and drove past the huge pagoda tree that some nineteenth-century sea captain had brought over from the Orient in a flowerpot, then took another left down to Collins Beach, where I got my dinghy and put it in the back of the truck.

I drove up Cooke Street, seeing only a few late season walkers here and there, as they admired the white houses and the cedar-shingled houses and the silent, narrow streets of Edgartown. I passed the A & P without even having to slow down for any left turners, and went on out to my place.

From the shed behind my house I got my waders, my Buck Rogers, my innertubed basket and my oyster tongs, and headed for the town landing on the Edgartown Great Pond. This necessitated a drive down Meetinghouse Way, but I crept along that wretched road at a turtle's pace and managed to save my shock absorbers from an untimely demise. At the landing, I put the dinghy overboard, climbed into my waders, loaded the rest of my gear aboard and pushed off.

My little Seagull pushed me smartly across the pond toward the fingers of land that reached down into the pond from the north. Just around the end of the proper one of those points, there were some excellent oysters. As I rounded that point, I was surprised to discover visitors ahead of me. Most unusual. A canoe with a person in it, and another person in the shallows, tonging for oysters.

I got closer and saw that the tonger was none other than Chug Lovell and that the canoeist was Phyllis Manwaring's youngest, Heather, attorney-at-law. They waved as I killed my engine and let the dinghy slide up and nudge the shore. I pulled the boat up a bit, got my gear and walked out toward them. Heather had a wineglass in her hand, an old-fashioned lunch basket at her feet and a large, rather summerish hat over her long yellow hair.

"A popular spot on a Sunday morning," I said. "I hope I'm not intruding."

Heather waved her glass and shrugged and smiled.

"There is no privacy on Martha's Vineyard. If you want to be alone, go to Boston."

Curly, chubby, slightly grubby Chug sloshed up and shook hands. "There are some good ones here, J.W. Nice size. Plenty for one and all."

Chug's disintegrating house was about a mile straight north, and there were narrow roads winding down through the woods to the pond.

"How come you came down in your canoe?" I asked. "Why didn't you just drive?"

"Canoes are more romantic," said Heather, lifting a bottle from the floor of the canoe and emptying it into her glass. "Don't you think so?"

"Actually, it's because somebody bought this point and built a house right on the other side of these trees." Chug pointed and I saw through the trees that there was, indeed, a new house there. "And they're here this weekend, and they've got No Trespassing signs up . . ."

"And a big dog . . .," interrupted Heather.

"And a big dog that barks and growls," agreed Chug amiably. "So we came by sea. One, if by land, two, if by sea . . ."

"And there are two of us, so we came by sea." Heather smiled.

She had her shingle hanging in Oak Bluffs, and, instead of leeching off rich Dad, was making a living, if not thriving, on island business. It seemed that the hospital gossip line had been right. Shiny clean Heather had a beau, and unkempt Chug was it. Not the oddest couple on the island, perhaps, but contenders.

"They'll be gone on Monday, probably," said Chug. "Then we'll have the point to ourselves again." He rolled his banjo eyes at Heather and snickered. "Won't have to paddle down here, then. Hee, hee!"

"Oh, Chug! You're such a card! Isn't he a card, J.W.?" Heather laughed and spilled some wine and pawed at round Chug, who allowed himself to be patted.

Young love. I felt a flicker of jealousy.

"Maybe I'd better find myself another spot," I said. "You two act like you want to be alone."

"Oh, J.W., you're a card! Isn't he a card, Chug?"

"An ace," said Chug. "But we don't want to try anything in a canoe, sweets! That'd, hee, hee, be dangerous. A feller could upset and get drowned, hee, hee!" He peered into his basket. "I think we got enough of these little rascals, sweets. I figure we can let old J.W. have the rest. What do you say?"

"Anything you say, Chug. You're the one who opens them. I just eat them." Heather winked at me. "Oysters are aphrodisiacs, you know, J.W. We may get home just in time!"

I felt a smile on my face. "You'd better get started right now," I said. "And make sure you don't eat any of those guys on the way, or you may explode before you get to the house."

"You got that right, old buddy!" said Chug, after Heather had reaffirmed that I certainly was a card. He climbed into the canoe and found a paddle. "Come on by the place one of these days, J.W. Got some venison you might like. You ready, sweets? Okay, then, stroke, and stroke, and stroke."

The canoe moved off around the point and disappeared.

South of the point, across the pond, I could see the inner edge of South Beach, the world-class beach that runs the whole twenty miles of the Vineyard's south shore, from Wasque Point to Gay Head. Beyond that the gray Atlantic swept uninterrupted all the way to the West Indies. Around the pond there were woods and meadows, and, here and there, houses that were almost completely out of sight during the summer, and only a bit more visible in the winter. There is a whole subculture of people who live around the edge of the pond. If you aren't one of them, you'd never know they were there. There are lots of such subcultures on the Vineyard, known only to themselves and their friends.

Far out in the center of the pond floated the large flock of ducks that had been there earlier that morning, when I had been gunning. The ducks knew where to be during hunting season.

It was a lonesome, lovely, cool place, and I was glad that Chug and Heather were gone so I could have it to myself.

The water where Chug and I had been standing was murky from the movement of our feet, so I moved off where the visibility was better, and began my oyster hunt.

Oysters live inside laminated shells that are often stuck together or are attached to rocks on the pond bottom. Inhabited oyster shells are usually clustered together with empty or broken ones, and the whole mess can be pretty ragged or muddy. When you tong up oysters, you have to knock off all the waste material before you drop the oysters in your basket, or else your basket will end up being full of useless crud. I use my oyster tongs to do the knocking.

As I picked my way over the oyster bed, I thought about Zee, and about my possibilities as a husband and potential father. I thought about Chug Lovell and Heather Manwaring, the recluse and the lawyer, having a thing together. Why not? I wondered what her very proper father would think. And I thought about Chug's offer of venison before the deer season even opened. Could it be that nature boy Chug was jacking deer? If so, I did not intend to call in the law, since a dead deer doesn't know whether it was killed in season or out. Hunting seasons, like fame and money and other things we take very seriously, have no reality outside of men's minds.

By noon I had a nice basketful of fair-to-middling-sized oysters. I shellfish professionally for quahogs and scallops, but I am only an amateur oysterer. My oysters are solely for me and my guests. I could eat oysters eight days a week. Fried, Rockefellered, stewed, on the half shell, any way at all.

Oysters, oysters, rah, rah, rah!

I put my basket of oysters in the boat and climbed in and sat there for a while in the quiet of the cove, feeling myself ebb comfortably—too comfortably, perhaps, for a man set upon marriage—into solitude. Then I motored out into the pond. The noon sun was in the south, giving much light but little heat. The wind was out of the southwest. I swung around to the point where once I had seen otters playing on a mud bank. No otters today.

I was putting an oyster sauce together in my mind, and trying to taste it with duck. Not much luck. Too many flavors for my imagination to handle. But it had real possibilities, that was for sure. I headed for shore.

Somewhere off to the west a distant shotgun fired, then fired again. At this time of day? High noon? With the sun high and bright? Who was fooling whom?

Out of the west two ducks came flying fast and low. They zipped across the water and then rose over the trees and disappeared.

Had there been four ducks before? Three? Had the gunner missed both times?

Life was full of mysteries.

— 7 —

I called the hospital and invited Zee for supper. She said she had a headache. Hmmmm. Tomorrow night, then? Okay, she said. She really did have a headache today and would see me tomorrow. Great.

I believed her about the headache. I had had one myself before I went oystering.

I spent some time working my way through my cookbooks, trying and failing to put oysters and duck together in one dish. I couldn't get the tastes right in my mind, and my cookbooks seemed to agree. So things sometimes go, in the cooking game.

But there are always other possibilities. I took some of yesterday's scallops, put them in a layer in a baking dish, covered them with fresh dill, a quarter cup of sugar and a bit of salt, and squished them down hard with a little plate topped by an old flatiron held in place by big rubber bands. I put the dish in the fridge to meld. A sort of scallop gravlax. Would that be gravollops? I only had a little over twenty-four hours to blend the flavors, instead of the seventy-two I would have preferred, but it would still be good when Zee arrived.

Maybe I should have a supper of seafood tapas. Lots of little plates of lots of good things: oysters on the half shell with caviar, gravollops, smoked bluefish with cream cheese and thin-sliced red onion, seviche and like that. All served with fresh, homemade French bread.

My mouth watered. On the other hand, I had that new hunk of bluefish fillet in the fridge and my fall veggie garden. Plenty of stuff for a major meal.

I had a Molson and thought about menus.

The phone rang.

It was Mimi Bettencourt. "My back steps just collapsed. Can you come over and fix them?"

"Anybody killed?"

"No, but almost. I was bringing in the laundry, and my foot went right through. I should have had you do them while you were doing the porch, but . . . "

"There's some wood left out in the studio. Maybe there's enough. I'll be right out."

I got my woodworking tools together and drove out. There was still some laundry hanging on Mimi's line. Like me, she preferred to use the solar dryer whenever possible. It not only saved on electricity, but the laundry always smelled sweet and good when it was dry. You could put your nose in it and inhale it and you felt clean and happy.

I carried my toolbox around back of the house and examined the steps. There were three of them leading down from the little porch in back of her kitchen, and they were not only sick, but dead.

Mimi came out on the porch, crossed her arms over her flat stomach and looked first at me and then at the broken steps. "Well, doctor?"

"*C'est mort*, all right. I'll see what there is in the studio."

Mimi used Gus's old studio as a barn. It was full of useful and not so useful stuff. Part of the useful stuff was a stack of boards of different sizes. I'd used most of them for the porch, but there were some left. I spotted a ten-foot two by twelve and got that out, then found some shorter hunks of two by ten and pulled out three of them. I carried the boards back to the porch, ran my heavy extension cord into the house and got to work.

I was half done when I heard a car pull into

the yard. Then I heard voices at the front of the house, and then Mimi and Nash Cortez came walking around the corner of the house, headed for the garden. Nash was carrying an empty basket. He had seen my truck out front, so he was not as surprised at seeing me as I was at seeing him.

"You have your bulletproof vest on today, Nash?"

"Now, J.W., you know me. Never one to hold a grudge. I just came by to get some of Mimi's good, green vegetables."

Mimi gave him a sharp look, but nodded. "I can use his money to pay you, J.W."

Nash gave me a large wink, and followed her. I stood up and stomped around to get the blood circulating in my legs, and wondered why Nash hadn't just gone to the A & P for his veggies.

The answer was not long in coming. I heard a shout of rage from Mimi, and looked up to see Nash, laughing, come running from the garden, his basket shedding brussels sprouts and greens. As he ran, his long legs striding high, he was tossing money over his shoulder, dollar bills that swirled in his wake like fall leaves behind a speeding car.

I looked at Mimi. She had her skirts bunched up with one hand and a garden rake in the other, and she was running after Nash, red-faced and furious. But her short legs were no match for his long ones, and she was losing ground with every stride.

"Yah hoo!" shouted Nash, and then he was gone around the corner of the house. Before Mimi even got to me, I heard his truck's engine roar into life, followed by the squeal of tires as he floorboarded it out of the yard.

Mimi steamed to a halt beside me.

"That son of a bitch!" she cried, panting. "Did you hear what he said?"

"No. Calm down, now. He's gone."

"After he got his basket full, he told me—oh, the nerve!—that he wanted my vegetables because they were the very best on the island . . . "

"What's wrong with that?"

"Because he's gonna use 'em to fatten up his rabbits, that's what! He wanted me to know that I was really helping him out and that from now on every time he kills a rabbit for supper, he'll include me in the blessing! That low-life creep! Can you imagine the nerve?" She threw the rake down so hard it bounced.

I looked down at the rake, and didn't say anything.

"And don't look like that! Don't you dare laugh! Don't you dare!" She kicked at the rake and ran around the corner of the house. She seemed to be crying.

I walked back toward the garden and picked up the dollar bills that lay scattered beside the path. There were quite a few of them. Nash had paid well for his joke, I thought.

I took the money to the front of the house, but Mimi wasn't in sight. Inside, probably. I put the money in my shirt pocket and went back to work on the steps.

I am not the finish carpenter that Manny Fonseca is, but I do all right as long as things don't get more subtle than two by fours, so when the steps were finished, they were fine. I walked up and down them a few times, just to be sure, then put my tools back into the truck, cleaned up the site and knocked on the back door.

Mimi, still a little red in the eyes, answered it, and I gave her the money. She thrust it back at me.

"I don't want to touch it. It's yours. Oh, that man! I am going to get him! You just wait and see!"

"Now, Mimi . . . "

"Don't you 'now, Mimi' me, you cannibal! You're as bad as he is."

"Now, Mimi . . . "

"You want a cup of tea before you go?"

"You bet."

We went inside. Mimi already had a pot of tea going. Something made out of the leaves of the herbs in her garden. It was good. Not too bland, not too zingy. She pushed some cookies at me. I touched my shirt pocket. "This is really too much money for the work I did."

"Keep it! I won't touch it! I saw Angie in church. She said she saw you this morning. She said you had woman problems. Do you?"

"Well, thanks for the tea," I said.

"Sit. Well?"

"Nothing compared to your troubles with Nash Cortez."

"Someday he's going to do the wrong thing to the wrong person. I just hope I'm there when it happens!" Then she sighed. "Just what is that man up to? Why does he do these foolish things?"

"Maybe old Nash is just bored. Maybe being a bachelor is catching up with him."

"Maybe it's catching up with you."

"I want it to end with me."

She leaned back, not displeased. Like most women, even the deliberately single ones, she basically thought that all decent men, and most of the others, should be married. There were only a few men so rotten that they didn't deserve to be married. I figured that maybe Nash Cortez was one of those, in her book.

"So you're ready to tie the knot. Good. Zee Madieras is a real catch. Smart, good-looking, sexy . . . "

"Of course that's a perfect description of me, too. Zee and I have those attributes in common, along with character, terrific personalities and the other qualities that make our nation great. That's why we're such a fabled match."

She rolled her eyes. "You don't deserve that girl. Poor thing. Imagine having to live with such crap for the rest of her life!"

"She's got a steady job, too. Don't forget that. A beautiful, sexy woman with a dependable income doesn't come along every day, you know. A man can't let a chance like that go by when he encounters it. It wouldn't be fair to their children."

"You've explained all that to Zee, of course."

"Of course. She holds my reasoning in high esteem. As, naturally, she should. I imagine Just Ted has explained things to Angie in much the same way. Women appreciate candor."

Ted Just was an accountant and Angie Bettencourt's current beau. He had once been asked his name, and having just completed a bunch of those forms where you put your last name first, had answered, "Just, Ted." Thereafter, island humor being such as it is, he had become Just Ted.

"Just Ted would never try anything like that with Angie," said Mimi.

"Maybe he should, so you can get started on some more grandchildren."

"Oh, dear, I don't know if I'm ever going to have any more grandchildren. You know, none of Angie's gang, the girls she grew up with, have gotten married. Heather Manwaring, Helene Norton and Angie. Three bright, attractive young women, and not one of them married. It wasn't like that in my day. I suppose I'm just not in step with modern times, but, here they are, all pushing thirty, all with good educations and good jobs, and not one of them married."

"Maybe they're trying to decide whether they should become nuns."

She laughed. "It sure isn't that. They've got men in their lives, they're just not married to them! Maybe that's smart! They can shake the dust from their shoes when it gets too thick."

"If dust comes with the marriage, I want it to pile up," I said.

Mimi approved. "That's the way to think. But there won't be much dust in a house with you and Zee. One time, you know, I thought that you and Angie might make it together, but I guess that was not to be."

"Just Ted is a nice guy, although I imagine he eats meat."

"Can't leave it alone, can you? You're as bad as Nash Cortez. Well, Angie eats meat too, just like her dad did. I'm the only one who doesn't."

"I hear Helene Norton has a guy on the string. I haven't seen her since she moved over to the Cape to get closer to her mom and farther from her father."

"Not that her plan worked. Carl's over there living with her, you know."

"So they say."

"I understand that Helene's going with a real estate developer. Some guy with big ideas, deep pockets and her mom's blessing."

"They don't always go together."

"Rumor has it, by which I mean that Angie tells me, that Helene is beginning to think that her greatest charm, as far as her mom and beau are concerned, is the fact that she may be able to talk Carl into selling his land to the boyfriend instead of to the Commission."

"Aha. Skullduggery instead of true love, eh? Well, now that Carl is over there with Helene, the boyfriend can sweet-talk them both at the same time."

Mimi arched a brow and smiled a wee smile. "My sources tell me that Helene might be switching beaus before that can happen. Chug Lovell has been catching the *Island Queen* over to Falmouth several times a week, it seems."

Chug Lovell? Chug Lovell, who this very morning I'd seen sharing his canoe and his oysters with Heather Manwaring?

"Chug Lovell? I thought that Chug Lovell was . . . " I shut my mouth.

". . . Wasn't the type to attract a woman like Helene? Well, apparently he is." Mimi did not seem displeased.

I was mystified. "You're a woman, so maybe you can tell me. What is it about Chug Lovell? He lives in a shack that he's letting fall down around him, he never shaves, he's got that crazy giggle and he looks like a pumpkin. I mean, I get along with Chug just fine, but he doesn't fit the Romeo mold. So what is it about him?"

"You men!" said Mimi, shaking her head. "He's lovable. He's roly-poly, and childish and lovable. He's also got enough money so he doesn't have to work, he's got an education, and he likes women and they know it. You and a lot of other men could learn a thing or two from Chug Lovell, Mr. Jackson."

"You mean that if I was more like Chug, I might have had a chance with you, Mimi?"

"More tea?"

So I had some more tea, and then I went home and made myself a supper of refrigerator soup, bread and white wine. Afterward I sat in front of my new stove and read until I was ready for bed. I stepped out onto the porch first, for some night air. The fall wind sighed through the trees, and the night sky was bright and clear. I wished that Zee was with me, and wondered if she wished that she was. I also wondered if Mimi Bettencourt knew that Nash Cortez didn't have any rabbits.

—— 8 ——

"I thought you didn't use electricity," I said. "I thought you were living the uncivilized life."

Chug had just handed me three cold packages of venison. He grinned. "I got electricity and I got my truck, too. Some things you just can't do without. Hee, hee!"

"I knew a guy once who tried to go all the way back to the old days. Built himself a wooden boat, using only old tools. Had a wood stove and oil lamps and a wooden bucket instead of a water closet. Sailed the boat off to Mexico, then came back and sold the boat and gave the old days up. Said he'd found out he couldn't live without paper towels. Everything else he could handle, but he had to have paper towels, so he resigned himself to living in the twentieth century."

Chug giggled and nodded. "I know whatcha mean, I know whatcha mean. Now, you enjoy that meat, J.W. It's fresh and it's good. Don't let the game warden catch you with it, though. You know what I mean? Hee, hee!"

"I'll be careful."

Chug tapped one of the packages. "These are steaks. That one's a roast and this one you'd better grind up and make into venison burger. It's a sort of tough hunk."

"Just like you and me, Chug."

"Hee, hee!"

Through the sagging door leading to a back room, I could see a compound bow leaning against the far wall. Chug's idea of primitivism apparently led him to eschew firearms, even the muzzle-loading kinds, but not modern bows. I let my eyes drift by and come back to Chug. I put a finger against his chest.

"You be careful, Chug. There are a lot of people on this little island, and you never know when one of them might be walking through the woods bird-watching or something just about the same time you might be lining up the next deer. They'd have the warden on you like ugly on an ape."

He looked up at me with his big frog eyes and grinned his innocent grin. "I don't have any idea what you're talking about, hee, hee!"

"Besides, there's Mimi and her gang, and they'd have you in jail quick as a wink if they caught you. And Vince Manwaring was complaining to the chief just yesterday . . . "

"Now, don't you go worrying about me, J.W. You want to worry about somebody, worry about Nash Cortez. Now, there's a man who's made some real enemies."

True. And he seemed to be working on making them madder every day.

"I think you're right, Chug. I'm going to stop worrying about everybody, especially you and Nash."

"That's smart, J.W. People got enough to worry about if they just worry about themselves. No need to worry about other people, too."

"I owe you," I said, hefting the packages. "How about some scallops? Come by and pick some up."

"I've got all the scallops I can handle, J.W., but thanks. Hee, hee."

I went out of Chug's falling-down house and drove home, the three packages of meat beside me on the seat. If some zealous policeman happened to stop me and see them, would the U.S. Constitution protect me from search and seizure? I didn't know.

Driving down my long, sandy driveway, I decided that I would get rid of some of the evidence of the crime by eating it. Dinner for Zee and me would be a nice venison roast, with brussels sprouts and little boiled potatoes with a butter and parsley sauce. First, though, oysters on the half shell, with a bit of caviar, maybe, to go with cocktails.

There is a lot of good food and drink in the world, and I intend to enjoy as much of it as I can grow or catch or buy.

The table was set with my best almost matching china and silverware, and the food was coming along when I heard Zee's little Jeep come down the driveway. I mixed her perfect martini as she shut down the engine: a chilled glass, a bit of dry vermouth poured into it and then tossed out, two olives (Zee had developed a taste for black ones) and Tanqueray vodka straight out of the freezer. No ice. As she came through the door, I met her with this in one hand and the bedroom slippers she kept in my closet in the other.

"Ah!" she said. "The old ply the maiden with booze and slippers trick, eh?"

"I'm a desperate man."

She kissed me and took the glass and sipped. "Works like a charm. God, I'm such a traditionalist." She kicked off her shoes, and put on the slippers.

"You go up on the balcony, and I will join you with goodies. You might take that blanket with you, because it may be a bit chilly."

"If we freeze out, we can come down here and sit in front of your new stove. It's cozy here."

"Cozy is my middle name, but let's go up first."

She went and I loaded a tray with oysters, crackers and brie, and the Tanqueray bottle, and followed her.

From the balcony over my porch, on a clear, dry day, you can see Cape Cod on the other side of Nantucket Sound. Farther to the south you can see the Cape Pogue lighthouse on the northeasternmost point of Chappaquiddick.

Between the balcony and those far-off places are, first, my garden, second, Sengekontacket Pond, known as Anthier's Pond to those who don't speak Wampanoag, third, the spit of sand that carries the road and the State Beach between Oak Bluffs and Edgartown, and fourth, Nantucket Sound. In the summertime, the road is lined with parked cars belonging to people who are spread out all over State Beach with bright umbrellas, sailboards and kites. On the other side of them, motorboats and sailboats move over the blue waters of the Sound.

In October, the summer people are gone, and the sailboats are gone, and save for an occasional fisherman heading in or out, there is nothing to see but the sea, and scallopers dip-netting in the pond.

I put the tray on the table between Zee's chair and mine. The sun was almost gone, and the air was cooling. The wind hushed through the trees, and a bunny, surely one of the fearless Bad Bunny Bunch who are a constant threat to my garden, had come out of the oak brush and was looking through my chicken wire fence at my fall veggies.

"Get out of there!" I yelled, and threw the shell of the oyster I had just slurped up. Yum! But the oyster shell fluttered off to one side and was ignored by the bad bunny, who also ignored my yell.

"I thought you were going to be nice to your bunnies," said Zee, laying down an empty oyster shell and taking up a full one.

"They're not my bunnies," I said. "And I am nice to them. I could be up here shooting at them, you know. It's not illegal to shoot rabbits, you know."

"Sure," said Zee. "I can just see you up here with your twelve-gauge blasting little bunnies into smithereens. Ha!"

"All right, so I probably wouldn't do that. That proves I'm not mean to them. So I throw an oyster shell now and then, but so what? You ever try to hit anything with an oyster shell? You see how that thing went flip-flopping off toward my shed? Looked like a scud missile. That bunny knew he wasn't in any danger. Look at him!" I threw another wobbly shell which the bunny ignored.

We sat there and ate oysters and crackers and brie. Now and then I ducked down to the kitchen to make sure things were on schedule. The sun went down, and the air grew cooler, and Zee wrapped the blanket around her. Lights began to flicker on Cape Cod, and the Cape Pogue lighthouse began to flash. I reached for an oyster, but they were gone, and I found Zee's hand instead. I got a good hold on it and felt her get a grip of her own. Suddenly I felt better than I had in quite a while.

Then it was time to eat, so we went down.

The secret of preparing good venison is to cook it rare and slice it thin. I served the roast and fixings with a bottle of Australian merlot that I'd come across sometime or other. I hold that there is no bad merlot or cabernet sauvignon, so I buy whatever brand is cheap, when I happen to have the money. The Aussie stuff was quite up to my exacting standards.

"Yum," said Zee, after sopping up a last bit of juice with her last piece of bread, popping it into her mouth and touching her lips with her napkin. "But isn't it a little early in the year to be eating fresh venison?"

"For a goddess such as yourself, hunting seasons do not apply." I told her where I'd gotten the meat.

She arched a lovely eyebrow. "So Chug has been jacking deer, you think? I thought he lived on nuts and berries, or some such stuff."

"I guess he's in his hunter-gatherer stage, or maybe even his early planting period. He's got a sort of garden back of the house, too."

"He's a funny little guy. There are a lot of characters on this island." She paused and looked happily at her empty plate. "Including you and me, probably."

"No question about it." I told her about Nash Cortez's visit to Mimi Bettencourt, and about Mimi's tales of Chug and his new girlfriend, and about the snatch of conversation I'd heard between Vincent Manwaring and the chief. And then I told her about finding Chug and Heather together. "So your rumor mill was right," I said. "Heather seems to have a beau. Of course if Mimi is right about Chug and Helene Norton, Heather may not have him long."

"Gossip," she said. "I love it. You're getting better at it, I'm glad to say. When we get married, I can tell you the hospital gossip and you can tell me the Edgartown gossip. We'll never be bored."

When we get married. A golden phrase.

I put her in front of the new stove with a glass of cognac while I cleaned and stacked the dishes. Then I went in and sat beside her, and we watched the fire through the glass door of the stove. She leaned against me and put her head on my shoulder, and I told her about Edgartown nicknames old and new: the guy who became Two Tailed Rat because he swore he'd seen one; the man who became Littleneck because he got caught selling, then stealing back, the same limit of quahogs, over and over; the two guys called Pete Vincent, neither of whom was actually named Pete Vincent; the guy called Big Octy because he favored Octagon soap, and his namesake son, Little Octy.

"Like Chug Lovell and Shrink Williams, eh?"

"And Just Ted. Some things don't change. The island will always be the island."

"I hope so. I worry about guys like Nash Cortez, though. He seems to want to start a fight."

"With Mimi Bettencourt. He's been pretty obnoxious, all right."

"You know what he reminds me of ? A braid puller."

"A what?"

"A braid puller. One of those boys who pulls a girl's braids because he doesn't know how else to get her attention. Anyway, he's always been polite to me."

"That's because you're the most beautiful woman on the island and you have a healthy effect on everyone you meet, even Nash Cortez."

"Nash is a widower, isn't he? Does he have any children?"

"All grown up and off island, I think."

"No wonder he's being obnoxious. No family."

It was an explanation I should have anticipated since Zee was, in Mimi Bettencourt's words, getting broody. The idea of family was one of the reasons we were getting married. I might not be prime husband material, but Zee, not quite thirty, claimed to hear her biological clock ticking, and professed to liking the

idea of me as the father of her children. I heard no
such clock, but liked the idea of being no more than
sixty when my children, our children, would be
grown. Maybe Zee was right. Maybe if I was a widower and my children were gone, I would be as much of
a troublemaker as Nash Cortez. I didn't like to think
about being a widower, so I cut that thought off
abruptly.

"The thing is," said Zee, "that Nash may make
somebody so mad that they'll do something. Or
maybe he'll get so mad that he'll do something. He
needs a woman in his life."

"Maybe we can get him and Mimi together. She
needs a man in her life."

Zee looked up at me. "Remind me to remind you
not to take up matchmaking as a profession."

"Well, in a couple of weeks the archery season for
deer starts. Manny Fonseca thinks that Nash may get
a license just to annoy the vegetarians and the animal
rights people. Then later on Manny says Nash may
get a black powder license, too. Again, just to rub it in
Mimi's and her friends' faces."

"And naturally, he'll hunt during shotgun season,
too."

"Naturally." In Massachusetts, it's illegal to hunt
deer with rifles. It's shotgun country. A lot of hunters
have rifles, though, and use them to hunt in Maine
and other states. My father did that. His 30.06 and
shotguns, now mine, are in my gun cabinet with the
.38 revolver I used when I was a Boston cop.

"What'll he do with all that venison? Good grief, he
could kill a lot of deer!"

"Leave it on Mimi's porch?"

"Yech! Disgusting!"

"Most hunters don't kill anything. They just hunt,
then come home and talk about it and drink and play

cards, then go out again the next day. More money is spent on booze than on bullets, and more deer are killed by cars than by guns. Most deer are still walking around when the season's over. And that's even truer of archery season and black powder season than of regular season. Nash might not get a shot, let alone hit anything."

"Are you going to hunt?"

"No. I think my deer hunting days are over for the time being. I'll just eat what other people shoot."

"I'm glad."

"Me, too."

"Do you think it's time to bank the fire and slip off to bed?"

"I'm sure it is."

So we did that.

— 9 —

In August, islanders begin to take an interest in tropical storms, since that is the beginning of hurricane season and coastal New Englanders still remember the devastation caused by historic storms in the past. This year, in August, September and October, all of the hurricanes went into the Gulf of Mexico. However, in early November, a bit late for hurricanes, another one brewed up west of the Sahara and moved across the Atlantic in an arc that brought it up toward Bermuda.

Until Bob blew in, in '91, we hadn't had much in the way of hurricanes on the Vineyard for several

years, so there was considerable discussion about this
one between those who figured that since we'd only
had Bob lately, we probably wouldn't get this one either, and those who figured that since we'd only had
Bob lately, the law of averages said that we should be
getting one and that maybe this was it.

Mimi Bettencourt was with the first group and
Nash Cortez, as soon as he learned this, was loudly a
member of the second.

"What's a damn off-island woman know about it,
anyway?" he liked to ask anyone who was nearby.

I happened to be nearby one day. It was one of
those sharp, clear, late fall days when the water is dark
blue and Cape Cod looms at you across the Sound,
dancing on a layer of air between it and the water. We
were on the beach at the end of Fuller Street wading
on the flats outside of the lighthouse. Nash was dip-
netting for his family bushel and I was just strolling
around with my Buck Rogers, checking out the size
and number of the scallops there, in case Dave Mello
and I ran short of them in Cape Pogue Pond, where
we'd been dragging since the commercial season had
opened. You can't know too much about where the
scallops are, after all.

"Doesn't look much like hurricane weather to me,
Nash," I said, waving an arm in a gesture that took in
the bright sky and water and everything else in sight.

"You're a damned off islander yourself," said Nash.
"What do you know about it?"

It was true that I was an off islander. To be an islander, you had to be born there. Some said that your
parents had to have been born there, too. I had been
born in America, over on the mainland, and thus
would never really be an islander, no matter how long
I lived on the Vineyard. I figured that Nash's people

must have been islanders for at least a couple of hundred years.

I said, "I know that when a hurricane tracks up toward Bermuda, it goes out to sea and never gets close to New England."

"Doesn't mean a damn thing. Hurricanes do what they want to do. Remember that one back in—when was it, fifty-four?—that looped out to sea, then came back in again and tore things up? They're like women. You never know. That's why they used to name them after women before these women's rights people raised a stink about it."

I wasn't even alive in 1954, so I didn't remember the looping hurricane. "You're just hoping it'll bring some bad weather with it up the coast so you won't have to go bow hunting this week."

"No sir, we're gonna get a real blow. You mark my words. A real blow." He emptied his net into his heaping basket, then shook the load down. He was one of those guys who stacked his basket as full as he could get away with.

I was about through with my explorations when he had his basket piled to his satisfaction, so I waded ashore with him, got hold of one handle of the basket and helped him carry it across the little bridge and up to his pickup, which was parked beside my old Toyota Land Cruiser at the end of the street.

"Come on by for coffee," he said. "Damned house is empty since the cat ran off and never came back."

That sounded good, so I followed him to his house and helped him put the scallops out back in his garage, where he could open them later. It was sunny and comfortable, a good day for opening scallops.

Nash's house was neat and still showed his late wife's hand in its decor. Her curtains were still in the

windows, her lace still decorated the arms of the overstuffed chairs in the sunny living room, her collection
of china knickknacks still lay in their glass-fronted
cabinet across from the fireplace.

Nash had a coffee maker, and pretty soon we had
cups of strong brew in front of us on the kitchen table.
Nash found some day-old doughnuts to go with them.
Not a bad meal.

"Lot of guys out with commercial licenses," he observed, sitting down across from me. "Must be good
dragging."

"There are always a lot of guys out there while the
picking's easy. When you have to actually work for
your limit, there are a lot fewer boats."

"True enough," he nodded. "If I was a young guy
trying to make a living down here, that's the way I'd
do it. I'd scallop as long as I could get my limit quick
and get back ashore to do my normal work. Big jump
in my income. When scalloping began to cut too deep
into my other work, I'd give it up."

I nodded.

"Depends on the price of scallops, of course," he
went on. "The higher the price, the longer I'd stay out
there. Common sense. How'd you know I was going
bow hunting?"

"I figured you'd do it just to be ornery."

The corner of his mouth flicked up and then down
again. "Can't stand those animal rights types. Jesus,
pretty soon you won't even be able to swat bugs!
What's the world coming to? Women's rights, animal
rights, these rights, those rights! I tell you, J.W.,
pretty soon the rest of us won't have any rights left
at all."

"Oh, I don't know," I said. "I want women to have
any rights that I have."

"Don't rile me, now. You don't rile a man when you're drinking his coffee."

"You don't look too riled to me. As I remember Joan, she and you didn't play slave and master."

His wife had been dead for several years, but even now Nash's eyes seemed to sadden for a moment when I mentioned her name. Then he gave a little shake of his head, and grinned. "Well, Joanie wasn't any ordinary woman, remember. She was special. Did you know that we left out that obey part when we got hitched? Now'days everybody's doing that, I guess, but back then it was pretty rare. Had to talk the priest into it. Joanie's idea, and it seemed all right to me. Later on there were a couple of times that I sort of wished we'd left it in, Joanie being strong-minded like she was, but . . ." He sipped his coffee. "But these animal people, they're something else. They're like those crazy tree people I read about out west. Want to save the trees, so they blow up sawmills and burn down offices, and like that. Pour sand into people's Caterpillar tractors and wreck the engines! Why, I just read about some rancher got thirty of his cows shot dead by somebody who doesn't think he should be grazing them on government property! Damn dirt and trees and wild animals are more important to these people than people are, for God's sake! Nuts! All of them!"

There was a knock on the front door. Nash yelled, "Come on in!"

But no one came. Grunting, Nash got up and disappeared toward the front of the house. A moment later I heard a muttering of voices. Then I heard Nash's voice rise angrily, and could catch his words.

"Oh, he doesn't, eh? Well, tell him that if he doesn't like it, to keep those women home where they belong!"

Low, indistinct speech, then Nash's angry voice again:

"Is that a fact? And just what's he plan on doing about it? This is a free goddamn country, and I'll say what I think and do what I want to do when and where I want to!"

More muttering. I stared at my coffee cup and shook my head. Nash was at it again. He was making enemies faster than any man needed to, I thought.

Then I heard a sodden sound from the living room. A piece of glass shattered and a weight thudded against the floor, causing the coffee in my cup to vibrate. I heard a groan as I was going out toward the front of the house.

I came into the living room and saw Nash on the floor. There was blood on his lip and he was trying vaguely to get up. Beyond him the end table on the far side of his sofa was overturned, and there were broken pieces of china on the rug. I remembered a figurine that had stood on the end table. One of Joan's collected works. Beyond the broken china, just inside the front door, stood a lean, pale-faced man about my age. As I came into the room, he looked up at me and frowned. He wore neat but nondescript clothes. His hands hung by his sides. He wore black gloves. I had seen gloves like that before, when I was a cop in Boston. In fact, I had seen the man before.

"Joey Percell," I said. "You're a long way from home. I heard that after they kicked you off the Boston P.D. you found a job in Providence, working for the mob. What are you doing down here on the Vineyard this time of year?" I gestured toward Nash, who was trying, in slow motion, to make his arms and legs work. "I can see you're not here on vacation."

He stared at me, trying to remember my face.

"I was just coming on the force when you were leaving," I said. "I doubt if you remember me. But I remember you. Tough guy. Liked those gloves with powdered lead on the knuckles. Good for knocking people around and not leaving much in the way of marks. I see you still favor them."

"Who are you? I thought this poor sap lived alone."

"You're the sap. You just assaulted a man in his own house. Now your lawyer's going to have to bail you out of jail, and your name will be in the papers. Your boss is not going to be happy, Joey."

Percell made a fist out of his right hand and smiled at me. "As your friend on the floor asked me a minute ago, is that a fact?"

He didn't look frightened.

I walked across to the fireplace and picked up the poker. "I don't happen to have my pistol on me, or I could just shoot you where you stand," I said. I hefted the poker. "I don't have a baton, either, but I think this will do."

Percell looked a little less comfortable. "Wait a minute," he said, holding up an open, gloved left hand.

"We can do this with trouble or without," I said. "It's up to you."

He glanced behind him. Through the window I could see a car at the curb. It had Rhode Island plates.

"This is Martha's Vineyard," I said. "Even if you get to the car, you can't go anywhere. It's not like home. There's water all around you. And we've got more police forces on this island than you can count. Sit down while I call the local cops."

"Who the hell *are* you?"

"My name's Jackson. Sit down."

He unbuttoned his jacket with his left hand. "I've

had enough of you," he said. "Put down that god-damned poker before I blow a hole in you."

I took the poker in both hands and stepped toward him. "I'm scared stiff," I said. "I don't think you've got a gun, but if you do, you'd better haul it out, because I'm about to break both of your arms."

He stepped back. "Wait a minute."

But I kept coming.

"All right," he said. He moved to the couch and sat down. His face registered annoyance.

Nash had rolled over and was trying in a punch-drunk way to get up onto his hands and knees. Having been knocked silly a couple of times myself, I knew how he felt. You didn't hurt, but your head was ringing and your body seemed far away and out of your control.

"Look," said Percell, "maybe I made a mistake. Maybe I owe this man an apology. I think I do."

Nash was up on his hands and knees, looking as if he was made out of rubber.

"You made a mistake, all right." I picked up the telephone, called 911 and gave my message. Then I pointed my poker at Percell. "Leave your gloves on. I want the cops to see them, so they'll know what kind of a guy they've got on their hands."

Nash looked up at me, focused and looked some more. Then he bent his head and threw up on the rug.

Percell leaned forward. "When you have the rug cleaned, Mr. Cortez, send me the bill. You're going to be fine, sir. Awfully sorry about this. Let's settle this thing. No hard feelings, eh? Why cause trouble when we don't need to? You know what I mean, Mr. Cortez?"

Nash looked at him.

"Hey, I'm really sorry," said Percell, leaning toward him. "I was wrong, and I apologize. What do you say? A hundred bucks and we call it square." Then he gestured at his own chin and put a grin on his face. "Or you can take a swing at me, too. A swing and a hundred. What do you say?"

Nash's eyes glazed and he fell in his own vomit and lay there.

"You pack a good punch," I said. "You had it back in Boston and you still have it."

I heard sirens. Percell studied me with cold, irked eyes. "I think I can take you," he said.

"We have about one minute to find out," I said, as the sirens grew louder.

His face made me think of a snake. His head thrust out of his shoulders like the head of a coiled rattler. I tightened my hands on the poker. Then, having changed his mind, he settled back.

"Later," he said.

Two squad cars pulled up outside and four policemen, including Tony D'Agostine, got out. I went to the door and waved them inside. I told them my story while two of them worked on Nash.

When I was through with my tale, they looked at Percell.

"He's lying," said Percell.

"I like your gloves," said Tony D'Agostine, getting out his cuffs. "Put your hands behind you, please. Mark, take Nash up to the emergency ward and make sure he's okay. Nash, you okay?"

Nash looked vaguely at him. When you're hit just right, it takes a long time to get your brain working again. Sometimes you never do. I thought it might be hard to tell with Nash.

Tony and another cop took Percell and led him out

to their car. Two other cops took Nash off to the hospital.

I put the poker away, cleaned up Nash's vomit and straightened up the living room, washed up the coffee stuff and went out to the garage. I opened Nash's scallops and put them in his refrigerator, then went home and called the hospital.

Nash was being held overnight. I could see him in the morning.

It was barely noon, and already I'd had a full day.

Down at the county jail, Joey Percell made his phone call and went to his cell. About the time Nash was getting out of the hospital the next morning, Joey's lawyer had showed up in Edgartown, bailed him out, and Joey was headed back to America.

I had thought that sooner or later somebody might take a swing at Nash Cortez, but I'd never guessed that it might be someone like Joey Percell. Why was the Providence mob mad at Nash Cortez? I thought I'd ask him, as soon as his brain stopped spinning, if it ever did.

Nash needed to be told that if he kept making enemies the way he seemed intent on doing, somebody might really get hurt. The next time Joey might use a lead pipe or a knife, or Mimi might use a real gun, or maybe somebody would get so mad that they'd beat or murder an innocent third party—a lover or spouse or friend or child. Anger is often misdirected.

As things turned out, nobody got killed until just before Christmas.

— 10 —

The hurricane went out to sea after brushing Bermuda. Nash Cortez, his prediction of a big blow on the Vineyard having been absolutely wrong, crawled out of his hospital bed before I had a chance to talk to him, and went bow and arrow hunting with considerable fanfare, making sure that everyone, especially Mimi Bettencourt and her crew, knew all about his plans. This may have been a mistake, because Mimi's gang arrived on the hunting grounds just before dawn on the first day of the season, as I was driving past on my way to West Tisbury to see if I could talk Zee into having a coffee and doughnut breakfast with me at Alley's store.

Nash and his fellow bow and arrow hunters, no doubt dressed in camouflage, as such hunters are inclined to be, were already in the woods as I was driving by Carl Norton's fifty acres. Nash's pickup and a couple of other trucks were parked off the pavement, and Mimi and her animal rights followers were parking their cars right beside the trucks. Hers was a motley crew of women, children and men dressed in bright colors and wearing intent looks. I saw Heather Manwaring, but I didn't see her mother. I wasn't surprised, since Phyllis Manwaring wasn't the type to go wading through the woods before dawn. Her heart and pocketbook might be all with the animal rights people, but she was a bit too proper for such stuff as this.

I pulled over and stopped to watch the action.

Mimi's people unloaded their weapons: old pots and pans, tin whistles, one battered trumpet and a variety of other noisemakers. Mimi saw me and waved. "Come on, J.W.! Join the party!"

I got out and walked over. "Mimi, did you bring your gang here just because you know Nash Cortez is in these woods? There are a lot of other places where people are hunting, you know."

She lifted her chin, and colored slightly. "We have other people in other places doing this same thing. There aren't enough of us to be everywhere, but we're trying to hit the most popular spots. Here, join in." She thrust two old frying pans toward me.

"No thanks. You're going to make some people pretty mad, Mimi. And some of them have got bows and arrows."

"Phah! A pox on their bows and arrows! Here. Take these pans."

"No thanks. If I was out there trying to get my deer, I wouldn't be very happy if somebody like you came by and scared all the game away."

"But you're not out there. You're here with the good guys."

"Those hunters probably think that they're the good guys."

"Ha! Well, if you don't want to whack pans together, come along with us anyway. Do you good to watch us save some poor animals from all those brave men hiding in the bushes. Might make a better man out of you."

I had on my red down vest and my red baseball cap with the little helicopter on the front of it, so I figured I wouldn't be mistaken for a deer, but on the other hand, Zee would just about be waking up now, and the prospect of seeing her was a lot more appealing than walking with a bunch of pot bangers into a wood full of furious hunters.

"You'd better get started," I said, nodding to the east. "The sun's almost up and it won't be long until it's light enough for good shooting. Nash Cortez may get his deer before you bang a single pot. You wouldn't want that to happen."

"That's for damn sure!" She raised her voice. "All right, everybody, you know what to do. Make a line. Stay in sight of the people on either side of you, and we'll walk through the woods making as much noise as we can. When we get to the far side, we'll meet in the field back there and turn west. Now, remember: don't be frightened if any hunter says anything or threatens you. You've got as much right in these woods as he does! Let's go!"

Pans banging, trumpet tooting, whistles cutting the cool morning air, her company started into the woods. They were soon out of sight, but the cacophony could still be heard when I finally pulled away, shaking my head.

Zee, sleepy-eyed and clutching her woolen robe together with one hand as she answered my knock, pointed out that Alley's wouldn't even be open for an hour, so I had best come in. Just what I had hoped she'd say. I placed a leer on my face, licked my lips and reached for her.

Later, at Alley's, as we ate breakfast and shared the *Globe*, she agreed that the Celtics needed some new legs and a stronger bench if they were to make it far in the play-offs next spring. In New England, nobody ever doubts that the Celtics will make the play-offs; the only question is whether they'll win the championship. Zee also agreed that Nash Cortez was going to be furious with Mimi Bettencourt.

"No more than she's mad at him," I said.

"I'm afraid that somebody's going to get hurt. There are probably a lot of angry people out there. On both sides of the issue."

"Most of it is just talk."

"It only takes one person who isn't just talking."

True.

The next day the Dock Street Coffee Shop was abuzz with gossip about the pot bangers.

"I guess that old Nash just about had a heart attack when those do-gooders came crashing and banging through the woods. Claims he had a two-point buck lined up at thirty feet when everything went to hell. Buck ran and Nash never even got a shot."

"You know Nash. He can tell a tale. Does he even know how to shoot a bow?"

"Doesn't make any difference. I hear that Mimi Bettencourt has lined up a bunch of her people just to stay with him for the rest of the bow and arrow season. If he goes into the woods, one of them will be right with him banging pans."

"Ain't that illegal?"

"Nash says so. Says he's gonna sue."

"Damned lawyers'll have everybody's money before this is over."

"Just hope nobody loses his head and does something that can't be fixed."

There were general murmurs of assent to this bit of wisdom. But I sensed a secret hope that things would not quiet down too quickly. Winter is a slow time on the Vineyard, and scandal is always a popular entertainment.

After he failed to get his deer with his bow and arrow in November, Nash Cortez reportedly consulted his lawyer. When asked about those consultations, he would raise an eyebrow, give a slow wink and, with an enigmatic smile, would say, "No comment."

Mimi Bettencourt consulted in turn with Heather Manwaring, who turned out to be the animal rights group's lawyer, just in case Nash really had some plan. But Mimi was of the opinion that Nash's eyebrow, wink and smile were pure theater. "That's what he does every time anybody asks him what he's got up his sleeve. That eyebrow, that wink, that sneaky smile and that 'No comment.' It's just an act, part of a script he probably wrote himself. Damned fool!"

"Now, Mimi," I said, "calm down."

"I'll calm down when I'm good and ready, J. W. Jackson! More tea?"

I pushed my cup forward.

Nash went hunting with his shotgun in early December, but had no better luck getting his deer, even though he had figured out a way to escape the watchdogs Mimi had set upon him. On hunting days he no longer drove his own pickup, but simply walked through his own woods to one of several neighboring driveways, and caught rides with sympathetic fellow hunters. Mimi's hounds were too few to cover every escape route, and so Nash was free to hunt.

In vain.

Mimi was sardonic. "Why don't you try a cannon or an atom bomb next time?" she asked Nash when they happened to bump into each other at the A & P.

"It's not the getting that's important," yelled Nash. "It's the principle of the thing! Can't you get that through your head?"

"You should get yourself a bowl of goldfish and shoot at them," snapped Mimi. "You might be able to hit one of them, and even if you didn't you'd break the glass and the fish would die, and you could call in your gun-happy buddies and take pictures of your kill!"

"People have been hunting since the beginning of time, goddamn it! You and your milksop crowd are fighting nature itself! That gang of yours should just pack up and go to Boston or some place and leave us normal humans alone!"

"That'll be the day, you bloodthirsty bird shooter! I'd never leave you alone in the woods. You'd kill everything you saw!" Then she hooted, "If you could shoot straight, that is! I hear you buy your deer and geese and ducks off island and tie them to trees so you'll be sure to hit them! Sounds just like something you'd do, you big-mouthed buffoon!"

He turned red and stuck his face down into hers. "Why, you little twerp, someday some normal-sized person is going to step on you by mistake and when it happens the last thing you'll hear is me laughing! Har! Har!"

"I'll outlive you, you . . .!"

Then suddenly Vincent Manwaring was there. Large, florid, cold-eyed, he glared at Nash. "Cortez. I know you and your bullying ways. I'll not have you harassing my wife and her friends. You shut your mouth, sir!"

Nash's eyes flared. "Or what? You'll shut it for me? Try it, you overstuffed city slicker!"

"Please, folks," said the manager, taking a chance by stepping between them. "You're disturbing my customers. Quiet down, please!"

"I'll quiet down when I feel like it!" bellowed Nash.

Mimi, on the other hand, nodded primly to the manager, shut her mouth into a firm line, put her chin in the air and pushed her carriage off down the aisle.

With her gone, Nash glowered at the manager, then at Manwaring, then snorted and pushed his carriage off in the opposite direction. Manwaring glared after him, and the crisis was past.

This scene was related to me by the chief of police as we stood, collars turned up against a cold south wind, outside of the bank at the four corners, where Main and Water streets cross. I had caught him coming out of the bank as I was going in, and since he wanted a pipe more than warmth, and the town had recently decided to ban smoking in most buildings with public access, we were outside instead of inside.

Now he was stoked up and enjoying the homey comfort that only an old familiar pipe can give you. There is almost nothing more alluring than the smell of pipe smoke. I inhaled the fumes.

"Nash is stepping on a lot of toes," I said, when the chief had finished his tale.

"That Joseph Percell fella is a case in point," nodded the chief. "We don't get mafiosi strong arms down here very often, unless they're just riding along with their bosses on holiday. If Nash has got Providence up in arms, he really must be hurting somebody. Damned if I know who, though. Wish I did."

"Well, he must have told you something."

"Not much. Percell shows up, tells Nash to stop hassling the animal people or else, then flattens him. Just to show he means business, I'd guess. I imagine Nash might have gotten worked over some more if you hadn't been there." He squinted at me. "This Percell used to be a cop, I hear. Boston P.D. You knew him?"

"Not really. He was kicked off the force about the time I was joining it. Too handy with those gloves. Too many complaints. The kind of cop that gives cops a bad name. Went to work in Providence. Muscle."

"Got a good lawyer. The best that money can buy."

"A lot of good lawyers work in Providence. What did Nash know about Percell?"

"Said he'd never seen him before and didn't know anybody in Providence. Said next time he sees Percell, he's gonna talk to him with a shotgun."

"You've known Nash longer than I have. Has he always been like this? Big talk, and all?"

"No. Only since his wife died. Oh, he always liked a joke and a tall tale, but when Joan died it did something to him. Seemed like nothing meant anything to him anymore. He began to talk in these wild ways. He never actually does anything too crazy, but he says things as if he wants you to think he just might do something as wacky as his talk." The chief blew a smoke ring. "Ten-cent psychology. You get it for nothing. A bargain."

"So you don't think he'd actually take a shotgun to Joey Percell?"

"I wouldn't be surprised if somebody shoots Percell someday, but I don't know if it'll be Nash Cortez who does it. I've been in this business long enough to keep my mouth shut about who'll do what to who. You never know."

"You never know, eh? Gosh, that's pretty smart. Can I quote you on that?"

"Absolutely not. I'm saving that for my memoirs."

"The long-awaited *Wit and Wisdom of a Small-Town Police Chief?*"

"That's the one. Then I'll be able to quit working and loaf like you do. Speaking of which, while you hold up this wall I must go forth to protect and serve."

"What with the shootists and the animal rights people at each other's throats, you shouldn't be bored," I said.

"Tell me about it. It's getting so wintertime on this island is almost as bad as summertime. Well, only black powder season left. If we can get through that, maybe we'll all last until spring." He knocked out his pipe on the curb and walked up Main Street.

The primitive firearms deer season allows black

powder hunters to ply their craft for a couple of days in mid-December. Nash Cortez, I recalled, had looked over Manny Fonseca's Hawken rifle, so I imagined that he would be in the woods once more, just to make the animal righters mad, if for no other reason. What a guy.

On the second day of the black powder season I was in the shed behind my house ignoring both the hunters and the pot bangers who were contesting for supremacy in the woods. I was opening scallops and listening to my tape of Beverly Sills singing arias from *La Traviata*. Beverly was retired now, but her recorded voice could still make you weep for joy. It gave me pleasure to know that Beverly also lived on the Vineyard. Now, if I could get Pavarotti, Willie Nelson and Emmy Lou Harris to retire here, too, maybe we could all get together and have a band.

Beverly was between songs when the extension phone in the shed rang. I turned down the tape player.

"Guess what," said Manny Fonseca, excitement in his voice.

"What?"

"They just found a body up at Chug Lovell's place."

You can be surprised and not surprised at the same time. I paused before asking. "Who was it?"

"Chug Lovell himself! Got an arrow right in the chest. Imagine that!"

— **11** —

I read the details in the *Martha's Vineyard Times* on Thursday, and in the *Vineyard Gazette* on Friday. Their stories gave pretty much the same information. Lawrence Lovell, age thirty-eight, had been found dead in the living room of his house on the Edgartown-West Tisbury road. An anonymous telephone call had informed the police of the body. Lovell's death was apparently the result of a wound caused by a hunting arrow that had entered and lodged in his chest. Near the body were a bow and similar hunting arrows, such as are used for large game, like deer. Because of the nature of the death, the state police had assumed responsibility for its investigation. The authorities were awaiting the medical examiner's report.

I noted that the *Gazette*, whose style sheet obliges its writers to use titles of address when referring to people, had not strayed from its policy but had consistently identified Chug as *Mister* Lovell. The *Gazette*, which devotes itself only to matters concerning the Vineyard, and is one of America's great newspapers, is probably the only entity that ever referred to Chug as *Mister*.

For what it was worth, I also noted that Chug's body had been found on the last day of the black powder hunting season.

I wondered if Chug had any relatives to mourn him. None had been mentioned in the *Gazette* or the *Times*. I thought back to the last time I'd seen Chug, and remembered seeing a bow in the next room. And now Chug was dead of unnatural causes. Maybe from one of the arrows that presumably went with the bow

I'd seen. Life was an odd proposition. As the jazz man said, "One never knows, do one?"

When the Friday mail had arrived, I had been making kale soup and listening to Linda Ronstadt sing so heartbreakingly about how a woman could never trust a man that I had found myself wanting her to know that she could trust *me*. I could be true to Zee and Linda at the same time.

Why not? Linda obviously needed a man who was straight and true. A perfect description of me. Zee also needed that kind of guy. Me, again! I could be perfectly faithful to them both. And maybe to some other women as well. Emmy Lou Harris came immediately to mind. I could be true to Emmy Lou, too. I could be true to all of them at once. With one arm tied behind my back.

Or would being true to all of them just prove Linda's point: that men were no-good two-timers who were nothing but grief? I thought I might ask Zee's opinion. I would begin by explaining how difficult it was to be traditionally true when, as a rare example of a truly manly man, there were so many women in need of me. I would put forward the notion that maybe for special men like me a new definition of being true should be developed, one that let us be true to a lot of girls at once. I was sure she'd understand.

I had lifted the lid of the pot and inhaled the fragrance of the soup. Kale soup is a soup that is a meal. You boil a shinbone in water, then add a pound of cubed and braised stew beef and simmer that for an hour or two. Then you take out the bone and add onion soup mix (one of the really great packaged foods), chopped kale and a couple of chopped onions. You simmer everything until it's tender and then add some sliced linguica and cubed potatoes. When that stuff is tender, you add kidney beans and chili powder and maybe some pesto, and whatever leftover cooked veggies or soup you have around. A bit of salt and pepper and *violá!* Anything you don't eat right away, you freeze for future reference. With kale soup in the freezer, you can withstand an atomic attack.

I decided to not ask Zee's opinion about a new definition of being true.

By four o'clock, everything was in the pot, and I had gone up my long sandy driveway to the mailbox on the highway. The *Gazette* and a number of green and red folders advertising Christmas sales made up most of the mail. The sun was very low and the air was chilly. I was glad to have the fire in my new stove waiting for me when I got back.

Christmas was coming, and the local merchants were again promoting the idea of a Vineyard Holiday. The streets of the island's villages were strung with lights and Christmas trees, and the stores, some of which had closed after Labor Day and then reopened for the holiday, were displaying miniature houses, toys, bright winter garb and other attractions to lure a tourist's wallet from his pocket. For several days there had been a suggestion of snow in the air, and people were feeling festive. I read my mail in front of the fire and sipped a Sam Adams out of a brass mug I'd found in a yard sale last summer.

I like the rituals of Christmas. It's my favorite pagan holiday. Every culture is glad when the long nights start to get shorter and the promise of a renewal of life is made once more, and every culture therefore has a happy midwinter celebration of some sort. Ours is Christmas, borrowed and modified by the Christians from those who preceded them. Since one set of renewal rites and symbols is as good as another, I play my tapes of carols, decorate a tree in my living room and mail a package of presents to my sister and her family out near Santa Fe. I am even sometimes enticed into church by the promise of a good choir. It seemed an unfortunate time for Chug Lovell to have been shot by his own arrow, but then death takes no holidays.

I hadn't known Chug well enough to be more than slightly moved by his departure and relieved to learn that he had no close family. He had indeed shared his venison and a couple of laughs with me, but aside from that, I had seen little of him and was, probably like most people, more interested in the curious way he had died than in his death itself. To be shot by a hunting arrow in your own living room is an unusual way to go, to say the least, and I, again like most people, I imagined, was quick to wonder who done it, and why. Not that it made any difference to Chug, who was just as dead one way or another.

I was warmed by my fire and soothed by my beer. Old folk songs and seasonal myths turned in my brain. Had someone taken Chug for a swan? Had someone decided to make him a symbol of the old year and sacrificed him so some new god could start the cold world turning once again toward the light of life?

Chug was no role model or idol of the people, but who had disliked him enough to shoot him? And why use a bow and arrow? If bows and arrows were as efficient as guns, Robin Hood would still be in business, and Manny Fonseca's ancestors would have sent the Pilgrims packing.

All in all, I was glad it was a problem for the state police and not for me. Homicide was not in the spirit of the season.

I phoned Zee and invited her to a supper of kale soup.

"Tomorrow night. I'll bring the jack cheese and wine," said goodly Zee, who was knowledgeable in the ways of kale soup and knew that a bit of grated jack cheese was the proper topping for your hot bowl.

"Not tonight?"

"My last day on the evening shift. Tomorrow morning I'm sleeping in, and by evening I'll be ready to boogie."

"You could drop by here after work tonight and practice your boogie just so you'll be sure to have it right tomorrow."

"I need some *sleep*, my testosteronic friend."

"Testosteronic? Is that a real word?"

"It is now. Thanks for the invitation. I'll see you in twenty-four or so."

I lifted the lid of the soup pot and inhaled. Ah! I cut some thick slices from a loaf of yesterday's homemade white bread, broke open another Sam Adams, grated a bit of cheddar and had a kale soup supper. Delish. Zee had a real treat in store.

The next afternoon, I was downtown looking for a *Globe* after selling the day's scallop catch. The scallops were getting harder to find, and there were only a few boats still out there after them. Dave Mello and I had gone out early and done a lot of cold, hard work for our limits, and after we were in Dave, who was seventy-something, had told me he was going to take a Christmas break so he could spend some time with his grandchildren, who were coming from off island. I was cold enough to agree that he had a good idea and that I'd take a vacation, too.

"You don't have to quit on account of me," said Dave. "Hell, you do all the muscle work as it is right now. You want to go out alone, just go ahead and do it. I'll probably start again after New Year's."

"I'm not quitting on account of you," I said. "I'm quitting on account of it's miserable out there on the water and I want a Christmas vacation."

"Makes sense to me," nodded Dave.

So to celebrate, I looked for a *Globe* to read in front of my fire while I waited for Zee to arrive. I found a last tattered copy of the paper at the Midway Market, and was climbing back into the old Land Cruiser when someone touched my arm. I turned and found myself looking down at Heather Manwaring. She was wearing her lawyer clothes: a tweed coat over a wool suit, a white blouse, medium-heeled shoes. Her long yellow hair was neatly combed and held in some sort of knot by pins I couldn't see. She looked very professional, but a little pale around the gills.

"I need to talk to you," she said. "I've been calling you all day, but you've been out."

"I've been scalloping."

"Are you going home now?"

"Yes."

"Can I follow you, so we can talk?"

"Sure. Are you all right?"

"No. Yes. My car's over there. I'll follow you."

I hadn't seen Heather since that day when I'd discovered her in Chug Lovell's canoe. She'd been boozing and as giggly as a schoolgirl then, but she didn't look giggly today. She followed me out of town and down through the winter trees to my house. Inside, we stripped off our outer coats and I poured two vodkas, a straight one for me, one with orange juice for her. She drank hers right down while I stoked up the fire. I got her another.

She put down about half of that one. "I want you to do some work for me," she said.

I felt a frown on my face. "I just quit working. I'm on vacation for the holiday season."

"Good. Then you'll have some free time. I want you to find out who killed Chug Lovell."

She'd gotten right to the point. No messing around with preliminaries for Heather. I hedged. "You're a lawyer. You know that the authorities are pretty good at their work."

She leaned forward. "If the police find out about me and Chug, they're going to come asking me questions. They're going to think that I might have killed him."

She tossed down the rest of her second drink.

"Did you?" I asked.

She held out her glass.

"Maybe I wanted to sometimes, but no, I didn't. One more?"

I finished my own drink and made each of us another one.

I pointed at the couch and she sat there while I sat across from her in the easy chair I had gotten from the Edgartown dump before the environmentalists seized control of it and made it harder to get into than Outer Mongolia.

"Why me?" I asked.

"Because you know this island. You know everybody. You can talk to people and they won't get suspicious. If I hire a private detective from off island, people won't talk to him. Or they'll lie to my detective just like they'll lie to the police. At least some of them will."

"The police expect people to lie to them," I said. "People lie when they feel in danger or when they want to protect someone. Sometimes they lie just because they don't like having people ask them damn fool questions. It's normal. The police take that into account when they do investigations."

"I know all that. But pretty soon they may be trying to ask me questions. I'll be a suspect."

"Then they won't be surprised if you lie too."

"Do you think I'd lie?"

"I don't know. It doesn't make any difference because I'm not judging you."

She leaned forward. "I want someone working for me. And not just to prove that I didn't do it!" She made a fist with the hand that wasn't holding the drink and brought it down on the arm of the couch. "I want you to find out who did it! I don't want that person to get away!"

I looked at her wild eyes and her flushed face. "I probably wouldn't find anything the police wouldn't find," I said.

"If you don't find anything, well, that's the way it will be. But I want you to look! Everywhere!"

I remembered how happy and silly she'd been in Chug's canoe. There was none of that to be found in her now. I felt a flicker of pity for her.

Her voice was sharp. "You were a policeman yourself. You know how to ask questions."

I had liked being a Boston cop at first, but my wife had not liked being a cop's wife. Her constant worry had exhausted her, and after seeing me through a recovery from that shooting that had left a bullet near my spine, she had left me for a quieter life. Not too much later I had decided that I would let other people solve the world's problems from then on. I had taken my disability money and moved to the Vineyard, where felonies and I would not meet.

But no island is an island. And even the Eden of Martha's Vineyard was a garden where the weed of crime bore its bitter fruit.

"There's something you should consider before you start this ball rolling," I said.

"What?"

"I may find out something you don't want to know

or don't want the police to know. Have you thought of that?"

She looked at me with her fierce eyes. "Just find out who did it!" She opened her purse and put some money on the coffee table in front of her. "There. Is that enough?"

It was enough.

"You'd better get yourself a lawyer, too," I said. "You know the old saying about lawyers being their own lawyers."

"I know it," she said. "I'm getting one."

Whether you're guilty or innocent, some lawyer always gets your money. It's one of the laws of the universe. Could it be that God is a lawyer? What a revoltin' development that would be, as Riley might have said.

She looked at me. "I want to know everything. How will you begin? Where will you start?"

"I'll start with you," I said.

— 12 —

She stared at me. "What do you mean?"

"I want to know what you'll tell the police if they come to see you."

Her face got stiff. "Why? You're working for me. I'm not guilty of anything."

"You're a logical suspect," I said. "You said it yourself."

"But you know I'm not guilty!" The expression on Heather's face could have been anger or fear. Or both.

"I know you told me you're not. Look, if you want me to do this job, you have to work with me, not against me," I said.

"You're the one who's working against *me!*"

"No. I saw you with Chug Lovell, remember. The two of you weren't just meeting by chance. Killings are often committed by people who are close to one another. Any cop can tell you that. If I was a real cop, and I knew you and Chug had the hots for one another, you'd be one of the first people I'd question."

"But no one knew about us!"

Her blush indicated that that was an unsurprising lie. I never knew a woman who could actually keep a secret about an affair. Sooner or later, she had to tell someone. I wondered who had heard Heather's story.

"Heather, this is a little island. It's twenty miles long and seven miles wide at the most. It's only got about ten thousand people on it this time of year. It's a small town. Do you really think that nobody knew about you and Chug? And remember, you've hired me because you think that the police *will* find out."

She reddened, but still held on to her lie. "Who . . .?"

"Well, there's me, for one. And there's whoever you confide in, for two. And there are probably your confidant's confidants and their confidants and their friends. You get the picture."

She was now recognizably angry and frightened. "But I didn't do it! I couldn't have hurt Chug! You have to believe that."

I didn't have to believe anything. "Where were you when Chug was killed?"

"I don't know. I don't know when he was killed."

I wondered if she'd thought of that answer when imagining what questions the police would ask her. It was true that information hadn't been made public, but it irked me that she was choosing to play games with me. I put my irritation aside. Frightened people often do irrational things. On the other hand, maybe she was just trying to be precise in her answers.

"They found him Wednesday morning. You can start by telling me where you were on Tuesday and Tuesday night."

"I was in my office on Tuesday. My secretary can verify that."

"And Tuesday night."

She drank from her glass, and I wondered if she was going to be clever again. "I was at home. Alone."

"Can anyone verify that?"

"No. I told you, I was alone. I don't like this."

"Did you talk to a neighbor? Did you get any telephone calls or make any?"

"No. I was tired. I went to bed early and I read."

"Did you watch any television?"

"What if I did? What's that got to do with anything?"

"Maybe you could prove you were watching TV when Chug was killed."

"Well, I didn't watch television, I read."

"How long does it take you to get from your office to your house?"

"I never thought about it. Ten minutes, maybe?"

Heather's office was on Circuit Avenue in Oak Bluffs. I thought she lived over on East Chop someplace, but I wasn't sure. Five or ten minutes seemed about right.

"Did you see anybody you knew on the road?"

"I don't remember seeing anyone."

"When did you leave the office?"

"A little after five."

"And your secretary can verify that?"

"No. She left at five. I worked a while longer."

"Do you know how to use a bow and arrow?"

She paled and stared at me. "No! What an awful thing to ask!"

"You never took archery lessons at the Y, or in gym class?"

"No!"

"When I was a kid, I made slingshots out of leather boot laces and old shoe tongues, and bows out of yews and arrows out of willows. You never did anything like that?"

"No."

"I'm almost done. Do you know anyone who had a grudge against Chug?"

"No . . . Well, my mother never approved of him, but . . . But, that was just because he wasn't . . . her sort, her class. He wasn't like the people she and Daddy know, and he was never on her side when it came to the animal rights issue. She didn't like the way he smiled at those meetings. She said he was dirty and that he smirked. Daddy wouldn't have liked him, either, for the same reason. Neither of them would have wanted me to be his . . . lover, but neither of them knew about it! And even if they knew, neither of them could have killed him!"

That was probably true. Parents rarely killed the young men their grown daughters dated. It did happen occasionally, of course.

"Can you think of anyone else? Did he ever mention anyone he was afraid of? Somebody associated with him in his business? Somebody off island, maybe? Anybody he was worried about?"

"No. He didn't talk much about his private life. I know that lately he's had to go off island on business every now and then, but he never talked about it.

Something to do with his inheritance, I always thought."

I didn't think so. "He never mentioned anyone he disliked?"

"Chug liked everybody." Tears appeared in her eyes, and she dabbed at them with a tissue. "No one could have hated him enough to do this awful thing."

That was possibly true. I still didn't know whether Chug's death had been a murder or an accidental shooting or maybe even some other sort of accident. Rifle hunters killed themselves, each other and innocent parties with a certain regularity. I remembered my father joking about whether he should wear red or buckskin during hunting season, since red made him a better target. Children accidentally killed their friends and family members with guns they found where Dad thought they were safe, and I imagined the same sort of accidental shootings might involve bow and arrow people. Maybe some friend of Chug's was just playing around with the bow, and the thing went off . . .

I had one more question. I wasn't sure she was up to answering it, but I didn't see how it could hurt to ask. Besides, the police might ask it sooner or later.

"Did you know that Chug was seeing Helene Norton over on the Cape?"

She lifted her teary face. "What? What are you saying? Helene has a boyfriend. They're probably going to get married!"

"I hear that Helene was thinking of switching men, and that Chug had the inside track. Do you know anything about that?"

"No! That's a lie! What dirty-mouthed person told you that?"

The fury on her face caused a little light to flash in my brain. I thought I now knew who her confidant was. It was Helene Norton. Helene had been told all about Heather and Chug, but Heather had been told nothing of Chug and Helene. I raised a hand, wondering if I thought that gesture would ward off her rage.

"It's just a bit of gossip," I said.

"It's a nasty, mean lie!"

"But the police may hear about it, and they'll ask you about it if they find out about you and Chug, because it gives you a motive for murder. Hell hath no fury, and all that."

Her eyes blazed. "I'd like to murder the wicked witch who's spreading that story! That's who I'd like to murder! I swear to God, half the people on this island have nothing better to do with themselves in the wintertime than to tell lies! Where did you hear that awful story?"

"I won't tell you that. It was just another story on the grapevine. I don't want you to go punch out the tale bearer. You've got enough troubles as it is. Who's your lawyer?"

"Percy Goodman."

Of the island's ten-thousand year-round residents, nine-thousand are lawyers, it seems. The other thousand keep them all busy with suits and countersuits over anything and everything. You can't do anything on Martha's Vineyard without having somebody sue you or threaten to. Try to build a house, and someone will sue you. Try to take a house down, and somebody else will sue. Do this or that, and be sued. Don't do this or that, and be sued again. It's a game played all year round, and Percy Goodman was one of the players. I had probably seen him on the courthouse steps, wearing a suit and carrying a briefcase, or, on weekends, standing in front of Midway Market, drinking coffee out of a Styrofoam cup and wearing a golfing cap while waiting for his foursome to show up, but I didn't know who he was.

"You go see him and tell him everything. Tell him I'll be in touch with him if I learn anything. Meanwhile, don't worry too much about not having a good alibi for Tuesday night. Most of us can't prove we were any particular place at specific times. Of course, if you happen to remember anything that will prove you were somewhere else when Chug died, whenever they decide that was, let your lawyer and me know about it."

She was still angry. "Why should I let you know about it? You don't trust me anyway!" Betrayed by Helene, she now saw deceivers everywhere.

I said, "Maybe that's a good reason to tell me. So I won't waste my time and your money trying to find out where you were when Chug bought it."

She looked down at the money on the coffee table.

"You can still pick that up and hire yourself a real private eye," I said. "Maybe you should do that."

She emptied her drink down her throat and put the glass beside the money. She seemed to pull herself together. I could almost see it happening physically. "No. You're the one. I just hope you're as tough with other people as you've been with me."

I followed her out to her car.

"I want to know everything you find out," she said, repeating what she'd said earlier.

"Go see Goodman. Do what he says."

I watched her drive away. People don't really want to know everything. They think they do, but they don't. Only a god could stand knowing everything that people do to themselves and to one another.

I went back inside, rinsed out Heather's glass and

put it in the drainer beside the sink, and put the money in a bureau drawer where it would keep until Monday when I could put it in the bank.

I put some wood in the stove and got out silverware, plates and bowls for supper. Midwinter darkness was beginning to settle over the house. Out to the east, beyond the mostly brown and viny remains of my garden, I saw fishing boats moving toward harbor across the cold, dark waters of the Sound. Above them the sky was gray and chill. I flicked on the lights and was glad once again that I didn't live in the good old days before electricity and internal combustion engines. No king or prince of yore had ever lived or traveled as comfortably as I did. None of them had had as beautiful a woman as Zee Madieras coming to supper, either.

I thought of Chug Lovell's reputation of living a return-to-nature lifestyle, and of his admission that he actually used electricity and his car like everybody else. Chug, like most of us, was not what he appeared to be. I wondered if that had anything to do with his death.

I rinsed a martini glass with vermouth and thriftily poured the unused vermouth back into its bottle. From the freezer I took the bottle of Tanqueray vodka and filled the glass. Then I returned the bottle to the freezer and set the glass beside it. I would add two black olives when Zee appeared.

She arrived bearing the promised cheese and a bottle of cabernet sauvignon. I exchanged these for the perfect martini, and placed Zee before the fire while I busied myself in the kitchen. When the cheese was grated and the soup warming nicely, I came back and sat beside her, a Sam Adams in hand. She had made quite a hole in the brie and smoked bluefish hors d'oeuvres.

I helped her finish them off and told her about my new job.

"You always did have a long nose," she said. "And speaking of noses, mine is twitching. Isn't that soup about ready?"

I filled bowls from the pot on the stove, and sprinkled cheese over the contents of each bowl. I cut thick slices of bread and poured glasses of wine, and we sat down to eat. There wasn't much talking for a while. When Zee and I sit down to eat, we sit down to *eat*. After a while I filled our bowls again and we ate some more. At last we pushed our chairs back.

"Viva Portugal, said Zee, smothering a ladylike burp with her napkin. "I tell you, Jefferson, life could be worse. Being married to you is not going to be all that bad."

Fine words. I cleared away the dishes and we took coffee, brandy and some Pepperidge Farm mint cookies back into the living room.

Beyond the dark windows we could hear a winter wind moving through the trees, blowing brown oak leaves along the ground.

"Do you know anything about bows and arrows?" I asked.

"I've seen both Kevin Costner and Errol Flynn as Robin Hood. Does that count? Kevin is more my kind of guy."

"When I was a kid, I used to make bows and arrows and shoot the arrows into bales of hay in a neighbor's barn, but since then I haven't pulled a string, or whatever it is that you call it when you shoot a bow."

"Go see Manny Fonseca," said Zee. "He's a mighty Nimrod. He'll probably be able to tell you anything you need to know."

So the next morning Zee and I went by Manny's

place and found him in the gun shop he had built in his basement.

"Hail, Red Cloud," I said. "I've come to find out all there is to know about modern bows and arrows."

"You've come to the wrong Wampanoag," said Manny. "I'm a gunpowder guy. Doug Wooten is the man you want to see. He bow hunts all over the place." He smiled at Zee. "Hi, Zee," he said. "Nice day."

When a man looks at Zee, he always thinks it's a nice day.

We went off to find Doug Wooten.

— 13 —

Doug Wooten is about the size of a moose and favors camouflage clothing in the woods, at home and on the job. He is one of those guys who reads catalogues about paramilitary and outdoor equipment (lots of knives, boots, old west cavalry hats and shirts, videos about deadly weapons, etc.), magazines about soldiers of fortune and paperbacks by Louis L'Amour. His wife, Gladys, takes all of this in stride since he's a gentle father to their kids and husband to her even though he looks like he just got out of the woods after being lost there for several years. His sole diversions from family life and his work at his building supply place are his trips around New England to go bow and arrow hunting. Since he brings home the meat as often as not, Gladys does no complaining about his hunting, either.

Doug lives out on the great plains, that flat hunk of land between Edgartown and South Beach. The Katama airport is there, and what was once farmland is now thick with new houses. Once, long ago, Doug decided to learn how to fly and bought himself an elderly airplane which he planned to fix up and keep at the little airport. Gladys wouldn't put up with that idea, but he wouldn't give up the plane, either, so it sits in a homemade hangar behind his house, unused but well maintained for the past decade or so. Doug's shop is out there beside the hangar, and that's where we found him at his workbench doing something incomprehensible to a complex-looking bow. A fire in an old potbellied stove was keeping the place warm and comfy.

"Howdy, J.W.," he said to me. "Howdy, Zee." He smiled at her. "Nice day," he added.

Predictable.

"Doug," I said, "I need to know something about bows and arrows and how you hunt deer with them."

"Ah," said Doug, nodding his big, shaggy head. "That business about Chug Lovell, eh? I seen that in the papers." He looked up at me from under his thick, prickly eyebrows. "Tell you one thing. I'd sure like to know who put that arrow into him. I liked old Chug."

"Did you?" I was surprised. I'd never have imagined Chug and Doug being buddies.

"Hell, I sold Chug that Browning bow and them Zwickey heads and that there Loc-On of his . . ."

"Stop," I interrupted. "You're talking to ordinary English-speaking human beings here. What are Zwickey heads? What's a Loc-On?"

He gave me an impassive look intended to disguise his sorrow at my child-like ignorance, then shook his head slightly. "Well, the Zwickeys are broadhead points, of course, and the Loc-On's a treestand. Damn shame him buying it the way he done. What's this here island coming to?"

A question worth asking, but one I could not answer. "So you knew Chug was a bow and arrow hunter? Until earlier this month, I thought he was a vegetarian."

"Vegetarian, my eye." Doug allowed himself a bull-like snort. "Chug liked his meat as much as the next feller. Yeah, I knew he was a bow hunter. Far as I know, I taught him most of what he knew about it. Tried to get him to join the BOA, but he didn't want nothing to do with any organizations. Just liked to hunt by himself. Funny fella."

"What's the BOA?" asked Zee, looking at bottles and containers of substances on shelves behind Doug's workbench. "And what's this stuff?" She picked up a bottle and read the label. "Buck rut? What in the world is buck rut?"

Doug smiled indulgently. "BOA, that's Bowhunters of America. And that there stuff you're holding is an attractant scent. Sex scent to pull in the bucks." He pulled down some other bottles. "This here's one that smells like a cow elk in heat." He ran a finger along the label. "See here. Contains cow elk urine and extracts from musk glands."

"Terrific!" said Zee. "I can see why you guys love this sport so much. You get to roll around in female elk urine all day long."

Doug nodded approvingly. "Stuff works great. And this one here's got skunk musk in it. Deer'll come right up to you and never smell you at all. Good stuff."

"I'm sure."

"Thing is," said Doug, "You got to get your game

up close if you're gonna get a killing shot. The closer, the better. No more than thirty yards. Ten or so, if you can manage it. Don't want to hit and lose your game, so you don't shoot till you got a good shot."

I was looking around. Nothing I saw looked like the bows and arrows I'd made long ago. "What's all this high-tech gear?" I asked.

Doug brightened and told us. These were his Wasp broadheads, that was his moose call, this was his range finder, those were two of his sights, these were his brand-new graphite arrows, these were his equally brand-new Pucketts Bloodtrailer Broadheads with blades that were closed in flight but opened on impact even if your bow wasn't tuned right; over there hung various camouflage masks, jackets and nets, this was his hunting release, that was a stabilizer and those little spidery-looking things were silencers for your bowstring.

He went on for some time before taking up the complicated-looking bow he'd been working on.

"PSE Phaser compound bow," he said. "Just ordered myself a new Martin, but it ain't come yet. "Here." He put it in my hands.

I turned it as I looked at it. I had seen such weapons, but had never held one. "This doesn't look like the one Robin Hood used."

"Nope. But I got one of them kind, too, if you want to see it. Traditional bow. Lots of guys like to use them. Different kind of shooting."

"Chug had this kind. I saw it in his house." I lifted the bow. the bowstring ran back and forth through pulleys, and the grip fit my hand comfortably. I pulled the string experimentally.

"Go ahead," said Doug. "Pull her all the way."

I did and felt the resistance of the bow suddenly give way so that I could easily hold it fully bent.

"Let her go," said Doug.

I did, and the string snapped forward off my fingers.

"That's the advantage right there," said Doug. "You pull one of them traditional bows, say an eighty pounder, and you got to hold it eighty pounds' worth till you let her go. These compound bows let you hold without hardly no effort at all. Hell of a lot easier, if you ask me, but them traditional bow hunters seem to like to suffer when they hunt, so what the hell, I say . . ."

I handed the bow to Zee. "Here, try this."

Zee is in good shape. She's one of those nurses who can toss a two-hundred-pound patient around in bed as if he's a piece of cloth. A lot of little nurses can do that, for some reason.

She tugged on the string, gritted her teeth and hauled back some more until, suddenly, she was holding the bow fully drawn.

"Hey," she said, grinning. "I did it. For a minute there, I didn't think I could, but I did!"

"Let her go," said Doug, and she did.

"That bow is set for sixty pounds," said Doug admiringly. "You did good."

"Hard on the fingers," grinned Zee, shaking her hand.

"Be easier with this." He handed her a small device with a pistol grip and a trigger. "Now'days you use a release like this instead of your own hand. Pull the trigger and the arrow goes. Nice and straight. Course this being Massachusetts, naturally these is illegal for hunting here, but you can use them in other states."

I thought about the bow and looked at some of Doug's arrows. He had a lot of different kinds, including some in camouflage. Camouflage arrows?

Why would you camouflage an arrow? And how would you ever find one if you lost it? I remembered often losing arrows when I was a kid. I picked up one of Doug's. There was a needle-sharp point on the arrow. I touched it with my finger and could feel its razor-like edge.

Doug was watching. "Got a sharpener there." He gestured. "A dull broadhead is like a dull knife. Not worth a damn."

"If you shoot a deer with the kind of bow and arrows Chug had, would the arrow go through or just go in partway?"

"Well, that depends on a lot of things. Whether you hit a bone, how far away you are, whether you hit leaves or something before you hit your deer. Even with these broadheads, you hit a bone, your arrow might just lodge there. You don't hit a bone, she might go right on through. Old Chug shot at sixty-five pounds, as I recall. That should put your arrow through most game, even if you did hit bone."

"Why do you want to know that?" asked Zee.

I put down the arrow. "Because the stories I read about Chug said that he had an arrow still in his body, and I was wondering if an arrow would normally stop there or go on through."

Doug grunted. "If the arrow was one of Chug's, it had a Zwickey broadhead on it. And if Chug did like I told him to do, he kept them Zwickeys razor sharp. I figure that a Zwickey like that should have gone on through. Funny it didn't. Maybe it hit his spine or a rib or something."

I took the bow from Zee and the release from Doug, and using the release pulled the bowstring again. Much easier. I pulled the trigger and the string snapped away. "You say this bow is set for sixty pounds. Does that mean that you could adjust it to pull at some other weight?"

"Oh, sure. Higher or lower. I hunt with a seventy-five-pound pull, myself, but right now I'm doing some experimenting."

Just like a rifleman or a fisherman. Always trying something different, something new. I knew about the impulse for experimentation, having given into it myself often enough with various rods, plugs, lines and reels.

I had learned about as much about bows and arrows as I could handle at one sitting. Before I knew more about archery, I needed to know more about some other things.

I gave Doug his bow and my thanks.

"You wanna shoot, I got a target range set up back of the hangar. Anytime."

"I may take you up on that," I said.

We got back in the Land Cruiser and drove toward Edgartown. The road was empty, a far cry from the congestion of cars, bikes and mopeds that makes summer driving on the Vineyard such an adventure.

"Now what?" asked Zee.

"Now we go by the police department and see if we can get some information from the chief."

"Why should he give you any information?"

"I can't imagine."

Neither could the chief, who was in his office at the almost new station on Pease Point Way. "Why should I give you any information?" he asked. He smiled at Zee. "Hi, Zee. Nice day."

Ye gods.

"I have a client who wants to know everything," I said.

"You can't have clients. You don't have a license to investigate."

"If I did have a license, would you tell me any-thing?"

"Probably not."

"Exactly. On the other hand, I'm a citizen who helps pay your salary. You owe me access to all public information."

"Ha!" He looked at Zee. "It's not too late to call off the wedding, you know. I don't think you really want to marry this guy."

"You're my real love," said Zee, "but you're taken, so I have to settle for a lot less." She batted her lashes and smiled sadly.

He looked at me. "You brought her along on pur-pose, didn't you? Just to soften me up. Well, what do you need to know? Remember that the state police are handling this. They don't trust us small-town cops to take care of anything as serious as a possible murder. Who's your client, by the way?"

"If I were a real detective, that would be confidential information. Since I'm not, it's Heather Manwaring."

He dug out his pipe and put it in his mouth, but did not light up. Instead, he munched on the pipe stem. "Now why would a nice lawyer like Heather Manwar-ing hire the likes of you for a job like this?"

"Why don't you ask Heather?"

"I might just do that. Well, what do you want to know?"

"A few things. Was Chug killed by the arrow that was found in his body? Was it one of his own arrows? Was his bow there, too? Was the arrow fired from his bow or by some other one?"

The chief sucked on his empty pipe and answered the questions in order. "Yes. Yes, we think so, since there were others like it in the quiver we found and on the floor. Yeah, there was a bow lying there, too. I don't know." He sucked some more.

"Could it have been an accident?"

"They haven't said it wasn't. Ergo, maybe it was."

"*Ergo.* I like that. And people say that you ain't got no education! Do you *cogito* and *sum*, too?"

"I'm telling you," he said to Zee, "you don't want to marry this guy!"

"All right, you two," I said. Then, "So someone shot him either by accident or on purpose. Right?"

"Maybe," said the chief.

"Any suspects?"

"Well, I'm suspicious of your client for hiring you . . ."

"I mean besides her?"

"You'll have to ask the state cops that question. While you're at it, you might ask them if they found anything interesting in Chug's house when they searched it."

"Did they?"

He smiled. "You should ask them. You really should."

In Massachusetts, the state police handle most homicides and are sometimes overly secretive about what they find. A lot of small-town cops don't like being shut out of the circle of those getting inside information about such crimes when they occur in their territory, so there's often a rivalry bordering on dislike between the state and local cops. A similar dislike often exists between local, state and federal cops.

Corporal Dominic Agganis, not my favorite policeman, headed up the state police contingent on the Vineyard. I had about as much chance of getting information out of him as the Red Sox had of winning a World Series.

"You've been a big help," I said. "A couple more things. When did Chug die?"

"About 9 P.M. the night before we found the body. What else can I do for you?"

"Who called in the tip? A man or a woman?"

"A woman, we think. Whoever it was talked through a muffler or a kerchief or something. Just said there was a body at Lovell's house and hung up. That was about eight the next morning. Car went out and by God she was right."

"Did the bow on the floor belong to Chug?"

"Hmmm," he hummed. Then he looked thoughtful. "I don't know. You can ask the state police that one, too."

"Just in case nobody knows," I said, "you might ask Doug Wooten. He says he sold Chug his bow hunting gear and taught him all he knew about how to use it."

"He says that, does he?" The chief brightened. "I'll check into it."

"Tit for tat," I said. "We small-town folk must act in the common good."

Outside, I admired Zee. "I'll make the same deal with you. Tit for tat. What do you say?"

"I say let me have a look at your tat first, and then I'll decide."

What could be fairer? We got into the Land Cruiser and drove right to my place.

— 14 —

The island contingent of the state police is headquartered in Oak Bluffs, just up the road from the Martha's Vineyard hospital. The building was painted an odd blue. I had never been there before. Corporal Dominic Agganis was actually in, and seemed surprised that I had come for a visit.

"Uh oh," he said. "What brings you here?"

"I just came by to see my tax dollars at work. I see you're using your share of them for coffee and doughnuts. I'm hoping they'll also buy me some information about the Lovell killing."

"You can read all about it in the newspapers," said the corporal, putting down his coffee cup.

"The island papers won't be out again till the end of the week. I'd like to know some things before that."

"That's tough," said the corporal.

"When's the medical examiner's report going to be ready?"

"Ask the medical examiner."

"It should be ready by now. You mind if I have one of your doughnuts?"

He snatched the bag and hauled it out of my reach. "You're damned right I do. Buy your own doughnuts."

"Do you have any theories about who done it?"

"None of your business."

"Did that bow belong to Chug Lovell?"

"We're finding out."

"You might ask the chief down in Edgartown. He may know a guy who sold Chug archery equipment."

Agganis frowned. "He never told me that."

"Maybe he didn't know about the guy when you two talked. You know, you have a terrific frown. Do you practice in front of a mirror?"

Agganis put his coffee cup gently on the table and stood up. His eyes and mine were on the same level. "I've got nothing to say to you about this case. Goodbye."

"I know how you must feel," I said. "You're out of sorts because you don't know much yet."

"You don't know what I know and you aren't going to find out."

"Gosh, I thought we might trade information."

"What information?"

"I just gave you some. The chief in Edgartown knows about a guy who sold Chug Lovell his bow and arrows."

"I'll soon find out what that's all about."

"What it's about is that I told the chief about the guy, and now I'm telling you. I'm doing your work for you, Dom, and look at the thanks I get. You won't even share your doughnuts with a fellow sleuth."

"You gotta have a license to be a sleuth. You got a license?"

"Hey, you're the professional cop. I'm just one of the folks who pays your wages. I hear you found some interesting stuff in Chug's house. I'd love to know what it was."

"I'll bet you would. Who's the guy who sold the bow and arrow stuff to Lovell? You might try to keep in mind that it's a crime to withhold evidence in the Commonwealth of Massachusetts."

"Who's withholding evidence? I already gave that information to the chief in Edgartown."

"Now I want you to give it to me."

"Can I have a doughnut or not?"

"No! Oh, all right!"

He pushed the sack toward me, and I selected a honey dip. "Thanks, Dom. Doug Wooten is the guy. How about some coffee, too?"

"No goddamned coffee! Wooten, eh?" He scribbled on a notepad.

"Aside from that tidbit of information, I'm afraid I don't know much of anything that'll help you, Dom."

"That's no surprise. Goodbye. I've got work to do."

"So you aren't going to tell me what you found in Chug's house, eh?"

"No, no and no."

"I mean aside from that freezer full of venison and scallops."

Agganis narrowed his eyes. "What do you know about that?"

"How about some coffee? I see you've got a couple of extra cups over there."

He pointed to a coffeepot. "All right. Get some coffee. What do you know about that freezer?"

"Don't bother with the cream and sugar. I like it black." I poured a half cup. I didn't really want any coffee, but now I had to drink some. I sipped from my cup. The coffee wasn't bad. "I was in Chug's house once. That's how I know about the freezer."

"For this I gave you a cup of coffee?"

"Hey, Dom, I know you're a sensitive guy, and I don't want you to think you got the short end of this stick, so I'll toss in another thought for free. Okay?"

"What?"

"Whoever killed Chug, if Chug didn't somehow do it himself, which I guess he might have, didn't plan on it much before it happened and wasn't very good at the work."

"Chug didn't do it to himself," said Agganis. "So you can get that idea out of your head. He didn't stab himself with the arrow or fall on it on purpose or by accident or any crap like that. Somebody put it into him. What makes you think it wasn't planned in advance?"

"Probably the same thing that makes you think it wasn't. Most killings happen when people have a falling-out that they never expected, and are committed with some weapon that just happens to be there. A kitchen knife or a fireplace poker or a baseball bat or some such thing. In this case, it was Chug's bow and arrow. If whoever killed Chug had planned it in advance, he, or to be fair to the ladies, she, would have brought a more dependable weapon. A gun, for instance. This killing looks like your spur-of-the-moment thing."

"That's not anything we didn't think of ourselves," said Agganis. But he nodded toward a chair. "Sit down. What's this about the killer not being good at his work?"

"Or her work, as the case may be. Because the arrow was still in the body, as I heard the story."

"So?"

"So if somebody who actually knew much about these compound bows had decided to shoot Chug with a hunting arrow with a broadhead point from close range, using Chug's sixty-five-pound-pull bow, the arrow would probably have gone right through the body. But the arrow was in the body, right?"

He nodded. "Right."

"But maybe it wasn't fired into Chug. Maybe the killer grabbed the arrow and used it like a sword and ran him through, as they used to say in the old swashbuckler movies. All I'm sure of is that it was a spur-of-the-moment thing. There wasn't any sign of forced entry, was there?"

"No. And don't think you're getting any inside information, because that'll all be in the mainland papers tomorrow. Any ideas about who did it?" Dom didn't actually think that I knew, but it didn't hurt to ask.

Heather was the only person I could think of. I shook my head. "No. I hear you found some stuff up in Chug's house. I mean besides the freezer and the hunting equipment. I don't suppose you'd like to tell me what it was."

"No, I wouldn't. Why are you prowling around this case?"

"Come on, Dom. It's a free country. I can prowl anywhere I want."

"You get between me and my work and we'll see how free you are. Somebody put you up to this, didn't they? Who is it?"

"'They' is a plural pronoun, Dom."

"They is? Well, I'll be damned. Who are you working for?"

"You might ask Percy Goodman."

Dom leaned back. "Ah. I know Goodman. Public defender, among other things. So he's hired you, eh? Does he know you don't have a license?"

"I didn't say he hired me, I just said you might ask him who did. Well, if you don't want to talk to me, Dom, I guess I'll mosey on my way. If you learn anything, let me know, will you?"

"One more thing," said Agganis. "That guy Joey Percell, the one who slugged what's his name, Cortez. You know much about him?"

"I know he was a Boston cop and that they say he works for the Providence mob."

"You got any idea what he was doing down here?"

"The last I heard, he was telling Nash Cortez it was all a mistake."

"Yeah, that's what he told the judge. Cortez didn't show up to press charges, so they let Percell walk. Did you know about that?"

"No, I didn't." But I wasn't surprised. People have a lot of reasons for not pressing charges. They're paid off or they're afraid or they don't trust the courts enough to make the effort. Or they might want to take care of things themselves. For example, the last time I'd seen Nash, he'd had a shotgun solution to his problem in mind.

"Do you think it was all a mistake?" asked Agganis.

"I don't know. What do you think?"

Agganis rubbed his big square chin. "There's talk about some sort of gang hookup between Providence and Hartford. Joey Percell has made a few trips to Connecticut. That ring any bells?"

"None at all. I don't pay much attention to crime in America. I came down here to get away from all that."

"Well, maybe some of it followed you down. Anyway, you might be a little careful about your health. I don't know if Joey Percell is a certified psychopath, but I do know he's dangerous as hell."

We looked at each other across the table. Dom was not kidding.

"I'll be careful," I said. "Thanks for the coffee and doughnut."

I went out and got into the Land Cruiser and drove away, thinking. I wasn't too surprised that Dom might not know more than he did, since the chances were that some off-island state guys had come down to do the actual investigation, and they might not have kept him as informed as he would wish. Similarly, the corpse had probably been taken off island for the autopsy since the local medical examiner normally only would handle pretty obvious cases—heart attack, automobile accidents and the like—and mainland medical examiners would handle possible murders and other unusual deaths. Still, Dom had told me a couple of things and obviously knew more that he had not told me. In his place, I wouldn't have told me either.

The only information I had that he didn't have consisted of the names of some of the people who knew Chug. Since we usually get killed by someone we know, and since whoever had killed Chug had not forced an entry into his house, it seemed logical that he had let the killer into the house himself. Ergo, as the chief might say, Chug knew the person and didn't expect to get killed by him. Or her.

It seemed reasonable to start talking with some of Chug's acquaintances. The police, of course, were probably making up their own list of names and already asking people questions, but there was no reason why I couldn't do it too. Mimi Bettencourt was Chug's nearest neighbor, so I drove to her house.

There was a car in her front yard, a gray four-door Caddie that I recognized as belonging to Phyllis Manwaring. It was impossible for me to imagine living on Martha's Vineyard as much as Phyllis did without a four-wheel-drive vehicle. But Phyllis was not the four-wheel-drive sort. A Caddie was just her style. Besides, her husband would probably be embarrassed to have her drive anything less expensive. Mike Dukakis used to ride the subway to work, and look what happened to him when he ran for President. Vincent Manwaring was not interested in appearing financially modest. His election road would be paved with dollar bills, the symbol of success in America.

I parked and knocked on Mimi's door.

It opened and Mimi smiled at me. "Come in! Merry Christmas!" Then she instantly sobered. "Of course it's not as merry as it should be. Poor Chug Lovell. What a terrible thing." She lowered her voice. "And poor Phyllis. She isn't very brave, and she's very upset. She came down to spend the holidays on the island, and this killing had to happen. Vincent won't be down until next weekend, and she was alone in that big house with a murderer on the loose! So I'm having her stay here with me for the week. We'll both have each other. She's in the living room."

I walked into the living room and saw Phyllis Manwaring. She looked pale, and her makeup had run a bit around the eyes. She did not look as polished and proper as usual. And no wonder. Her house was only a half mile from Chug's, and the winter winds made wild sounds at night. A tough place to be alone when a killer is wandering around.

Phyllis smiled weakly, and waved a hand clutching crumpled Kleenex. The other hand balanced a cup and saucer upon her knee.

"We're having tea," said Mimi. "I'll get you a cup." She pushed a plate of cookies at me.

When I had my teacup in hand, I said, "I'm nosing around this Chug Lovell business. You both knew him, so I'd like to talk with you about him."

Phyllis's cup jerked in her hand, and tea spilled on her dress.

"Terrific!" said Mimi, giving me a hard look as she rolled to her feet and headed for the kitchen. "I told you that Phyllis was upset! You're as bad as Ignacio Cortez, I swear!"

Phyllis dabbed at herself with her Kleenex. "Oh, it's all right, J.W., it's all right. It's just that this whole thing has been so . . ." To my dismay, she burst into tears.

Well done, Jackson. Teacup in one hand, cookie in the other, I sat there in that stiff, awkward way that men do when they've said something stupid and insensitive. It was once again clear that I had been wise to forgo a career in politics.

— 15 —

Mimi's Christmas tree was set up in the corner of her living room. The tree was decorated with small electric lights and colored balls, and an assortment of little figures and decorations she had collected over the years. She had told me once that whenever she and Gus traveled anywhere, they bought little souvenirs that they could hang on their tree in remembrance of the places they'd been and the good times they'd had. There were candles and greenery on her mantle and more greenery woven up the banister of the stairs leading upstairs. In each of her windows was a single electric candle. The room smelled good, and there was a fire in the fireplace.

Mimi came back with paper towels, and she and Phyllis dabbed at the tea stains on Phyllis's skirt and blouse. Stain removal not being a specialty of mine, I stayed where I was.

"Phyllis, you go upstairs and change," said Mimi finally. "We'll have to attack these spots later when you're not wearing them."

"That wicked man!" choked Phyllis, getting up.

"J.W.'s not wicked," said Mimi. "He's just not too sensitive sometimes. Go on, now."

Phyllis put her hand to her mouth and looked at me. "Oh, dear! I didn't mean you, J.W.! I know you didn't mean to . . . I mean . . . Oh, I hope you didn't think . . . Please excuse me. I'm a wreck. I think I'll lie down for a while, Mimi." Dabbing at herself, she fled upstairs.

Mimi sighed. "She's a dear, but she can be a trial, too. I've known her since we were at Buckingham School together, and she's always been too easily upset. She came flying in here the day they found

Chug's body. Couldn't bear to be alone. I'm not sure I blame her."

"Well, her husband seems to be the kind of guy who might like that sort of a wife. Somebody he can boss around."

"Oh, she's been a good wife to him. Better than he deserves, I sometimes think. I don't think he's really capable of loving anybody except his daughters. He dotes on them. On the other hand, he and Phyllis stay together as a matter of form, more than anything else." She shrugged. "You figure that out. I'll tell you one thing: down underneath all her surface propriety and nerves, Phyllis isn't as flighty as you might think. Look how she's stuck with the animal rights group, in spite of all the rancor that goes with that work. Don't be too quick to judge her."

That was good advice with regard to most people. I lifted my cup. "Nice tea. I know it's the season to be jolly and that we should probably be singing Christmas carols to each other, but I really would like to talk to you about Chug Lovell."

"I barely knew Chug," said Mimi. "And all I know about his death is what I read in the papers."

"You're his closest neighbor."

"That's what the police said when they came by. I couldn't tell them a thing, though. I didn't see any strange people lurking about, or any cars acting oddly, or anything at all."

"Did they tell you anything?"

"Policemen don't tell people things. They just ask questions." She looked at me over her teacup. She had keen eyes with laugh wrinkles at their corners. "But you're a civilian. What can you tell me?"

"Wait a minute, Meem. I'm the one who's trying to get you to tell me something. Not the other way around. Besides, I don't know anything."

"You're thinking about something," said Mimi. "I can see it in your face. You get a wrinkle in your forehead. Angie told me about it when you two were going out together. She said that whenever you were thinking about something you didn't want anybody to know about, you got that wrinkle, and that whenever she told you about it, you ironed it out and said you weren't thinking about anything."

I ironed out the wrinkle and said, "Well, I'm not thinking about anything."

"There," said Mimi. "You did just what she said you do. What are you thinking about?"

"Nothing."

"See. You men! It'll be good for you to be married. You learn to tell Zeolinda everything, because I'm going to tell her about that wrinkle."

"I'm not worried about wrinkles in my forehead. Have you heard anything about the police finding something, some sort of evidence or something, maybe, in Chug's house?"

"No. What have you heard?"

"I know he had a freezer full of venison and scallops and that he was killed by somebody who shot him with a hunting arrow. Do you know any of his friends? Anybody who might have been a close acquaintance?"

"No. I only saw him in meetings when he showed up to try to get people to let land go back to nature. I never saw anybody with him. What are you thinking about?"

"Who's the wicked man?"

"What?"

"The wicked man Phyllis mentioned. Who is he?"

"I thought it was you. You are a little bit wicked sometimes."

"No, it wasn't me." Who was it? Chug? Her husband, Vince? Somebody else? "Did the police question her?"

"Yes, they did. Her house is not far from Chug's, after all. She was here with me when they came by. I think that everybody along the road has been questioned."

Maybe it was some cop who had rubbed Phyllis wrong. Maybe not.

Mimi gave me a piece of mince pie with my tea. Then she gave me another one. When I finished that one, she ignored my hopeful look and the plate I was picking clean of crumbs and waved me toward the door. "Off you go. I've got work to do. The grandchildren are coming for Christmas and I've got to start making cookies."

"I could help you make room for the cookies by getting rid of the rest of this pie."

"No, you couldn't. Phyllis and I are having that for dessert this evening."

"Cheez, Meem, this is the Christmas season. We're supposed to share our goodies with those less fortunate than ourselves."

"I already shared my pie with you. Go cook your own pie."

"Rats." I got up and took my plate and cup into the kitchen.

"There is something useful you could do," said Mimi, when I got back to the living room. "Keep an eye on Phyllis's house while she's here with me. Here. I keep a key to her place." She handed me the key.

"You're a tough customer," I said. "More work but no more pie."

"You got it." She tipped her head back and I kissed her, then went out to the Land Cruiser.

The December sun hung far to the south and the

air was clear and chilly. I drove past Chug Lovell's house and saw that the reflective police ribbons and crime scene cards were still up, but that there was no policeman on duty. That probably meant that the state police had already given the place a good going-over, and had whatever evidence they thought that they'd find.

I drove on to the Manwaring place, turned in and felt a sudden chill at the sight of a car in back of the house and a man at the front door, his nose against the window as he peered into the house. I felt a rush of adrenaline and was instantly skittish and alert, thinking "Joey Percell."

Hearing my car, the man straightened quickly, and turned toward the driveway. Of course it was not Percell. Why should Joey Percell be peeking into Phyllis Manwaring's window, after all? (On the other hand, why had Joey Percell punched out Ignacio Cortez?)

I stopped and got out of the Land Cruiser, and the man came toward me along the walk. I had seen him here and there over the years and knew who he was, but he didn't know who I was.

"Dr. Williams," I said.

Dr. Cotton "Shrink" Williams was wearing a knit wool cap, a thick sweater and wool pants over his Bean boots. He was a graying, fit-looking man pushing fifty, who was now simultaneously smiling and frowning.

"You have the advantage of me, I'm afraid." He put out a strong, slender hand and shook my bigger one.

"J. W. Jackson. I'm sort of looking after this place. Can I help you?"

His eyes, behind round, gold-rimmed glasses, were blue, keen and, by practice or nature, unrevealing.

"Well, yes, perhaps you can. I'm looking for . . . the

Manwarings. I was told they'd be down for the holidays."

"I understand that Vince Manwaring is on the mainland chasing money or votes or maybe both."

"Oh. Ha, ha! Yes, I believe he does have political ambitions. And, ah, is Mrs. Manwaring with him?"

"You a friend of theirs?" I was thinking that most friends would have parked in front of the house.

"A friend. Yes."

"We had a murder just down the road the other day. I'm told that Mrs. Manwaring got spooked."

He abruptly revealed emotion. "Yes! I was at a conference in New York when I heard! I came right back . . ." He paused, and the invisible veil once more fell into place behind his shining eyes. I watched him place a caring smile upon his face. "That is to say, I was concerned about the Manwarings' well-being, what with the killer still not being apprehended. You understand."

"It could be spooky for a person alone in a big house like this," I agreed.

Again a hint of feeling. "Yes! Poor Phyllis, all alone . . ." Then the veil again. "I would very much like to speak with her. Do you know where she is?"

I had a thought. "Is she a patient of yours, Doctor?"

He looked at me, instantly very composed, but with that smile still on his face. "I'm afraid I don't discuss my patients with other people, Mr. Jackson."

"I don't want you to discuss her. I just want to know if she's a patient of yours. Is that confidential information?"

He pursed his lips. "Some still attach a stigma to people who seek assistance from psychologists, psychiatrists and others in the field. I therefore have made it my policy to neither confirm nor deny the existence of a professional relationship between me and any other person."

"Just like the U.S. Navy will neither confirm nor deny the existence of atomic weapons on their ships, eh?"

"I'm afraid I know nothing of the navy, Mr. Jackson." His smile faded. "Do you or do you not know where I can get in touch with Mrs. Manwaring?"

I didn't think he was going to tell me much more. "Call me J.W. Everybody does." Actually, that wasn't true. Zee called me other things.

"J.W. Well?"

"I'll tell you what I'll do. I'll tell Phyllis that you want to see her, and let her get in touch with you."

He frowned. "I assure you that she'll want to see me."

"In that case, she'll probably call you right away. Where'll you be? At home, or at your office?"

He pushed at the frown until it left his face. "You're being very careful, but I can appreciate that. All right, have her call me at either place. I have answering machines on both phones, in case she misses me."

"I'll give her that message," I said, then gestured toward his car. "You find anything odd while you were out back?"

He looked surprised. "No. What do you mean?"

"You know, a broken window, a door ajar, any sign of vandalism or somebody trying to get into the house?"

"No. No, I didn't."

"The back door? A broken lock or anything?"

"No. No, the door was fine. Why do you ask?"

"Just my job. Christmas is a busy time for housebreakers. Lots of expensive presents around. You know. Well, I guess I'll check back there myself. Walk you to your car?"

"What? Yes, of course."

When he was in his car, I leaned down. "The last time I saw Phyllis, she was going to lie down for a while. I think she needs a rest, but I'll leave your message so she'll have it when she gets up. It might be a while before she tries to contact you." I straightened, stepped back and raised a hand. "Merry Christmas."

"Merry Christmas, Mr. Jackson."

"Call me J.W."

But he drove away without another word. I noted his license plate, then walked around the grounds and through the house, checking things out.

Phyllis had apparently abandoned the house in a hurry. The thermostat was still on seventy. I turned it down to sixty, not because Vince Manwaring couldn't afford to heat a big house with no one in it, but because the idea of doing that offended my economic principles. Some of Phyllis's clothes were tossed over a chair in the master bedroom, a closet door was half open and the bed was unmade. In the master bathroom, a thick towel I would have loved to own lay on the floor where it had fallen from its hook. I hung it back up. There was some soot on it and in the washbasin.

In the living room fireplace I found the source of the soot: the remains of a badly made fire. A couple of pieces of thick cardboard lay amid the ashes, and more ashes had blown out onto the floor because Phyllis had neglected to shut the screen and the still open damper had allowed the wind to blow down the chimney after her fire had died. I thought that Phyllis was lucky she hadn't burned her house down. I closed the damper and the screen, but left the scattered ashes to someone else. Phyllis clearly needed lessons in fireplace management if she ever expected to be a true island woman, which I didn't imagine she did.

Shrink had been right about the back door. It was fine. So was everything else. I used Phyllis's phone to call Mimi and give her Shrink's message, and went out.

I got into the Land Cruiser and drove back past the late lamented Chug Lovell's house and past Mimi's house. I drove on by Carl Norton's fifty acres until I came to a narrow dirt road that led through Carl's land south to the great pond. Duck hunters used it during the season. I drove down the road a hundred yards and parked in a wide spot. I rummaged in the glove compartment and found my lock picks. My rusty Toyota blended nicely with the winter-bronzed oak brush. You had to look carefully to see it. I walked through the trees to Chug's house and, after another check to confirm that no one was on guard, ducked under the police ribbon and went to the back door. There I got out my picks. It was illegal entry all the way, but I didn't think that Chug would mind.

— 16 —

I have far to go before I am a good lock picker, but the ancient lock on Chug's back door didn't offer much of a challenge. When I felt the bolt slide, I eased inside.

Homicide detectives hate having other people coming around crime scenes, messing up evidence. Onlookers, relatives, souvenir collectors and just plain thieves cause enough trouble, but other cops and officials of various kinds trying to help are an even bigger problem. Fortunate is the detective who is able to secure the scene from such people. Here, the cops had had a week to look things over, so I didn't feel a bit guilty about breaking in.

I was pretty sure that any movable evidence had probably been taken away, but not all interesting stuff can be moved, and there was always a possibility that something had been overlooked. Actually, I didn't hope to find much, but the chief's hint that something interesting had been found in the house, and Dom Agganis's refusal to tell me what it was, if indeed he knew, had stirred my curiosity. I don't trust people who think they can be trusted with information that I can't be trusted with. I normally don't want to know personal secrets, like the details of your sex life or your choice of wallpaper, but I'm different about public ones. Them, I want to know. And what is a more public matter than murder?

There was a brownish bloodstain on the floor surrounded by an outline indicating the configuration of Chug's body when they'd found it. I wondered how long the blood and chalk would stay there. Forever? Who would remove it?

I moved around carefully, so as not to disturb anything unnecessarily. I went through the rooms of the house, checking windows as I went, just to make sure that none of them had been forced. None had. In the pantry off the kitchen, Chug's freezer was still full of venison and scallops. In what had probably been intended as a bedroom, but had been roughly converted into a workroom with a bench and the sort of tools you find on such household workbenches, I also found bow hunting equipment. Aluminum arrows, points and other paraphernalia, some of which I recognized from my visit to Doug Wooten's shop. Chug had not been the complete bow hunter that Doug was, but he'd had enough gear to keep himself happy. Until last week, at least.

In Chug's bedroom I found what the cops had found. I couldn't have missed it. A mirror on the ceiling over the double bed. Other mirrors on the walls. Also on the walls, between mirrors, were painted scenes depicting imaginative sexual activities which I found rather educational, once I got over my surprise, since I had never even thought of some of them. Stodgy me. Against a wall were two dishes such as are used to feed and water pets. I had not seen any dog or cat when I'd visited Chug and gotten my venison. There was a bit of liquid in one of the bowls. I sniffed it. White wine. On a hook behind the door was a silk bathrobe. Under it was a dog collar with a chain attached. There was a single long, blond hair tangled in it. I coiled up the hair and put it in my shirt pocket. The collar looked like it would just about fit a woman's neck.

Bondage? Voyeurism? Masochism? Sadism? What sort of paraphilia appealed to Chug? I would have to ask Heather if she knew. And if his partner consented, what complaint did anyone have?

I wondered if Chug's sexual preferences and his death were connected. Had his lover, man or woman, killed him as part of some ritual activity gone wrong? Or killed him in a quarrel bred of passion? Had Chug said it was over between them and his partner had made sure that it was?

In a hallway I found one of those attic ladders that comes down when you pull on it, then folds back up into the ceiling. I went up into the attic and found a light switch. The attic wasn't much more than a crawl space stuffed with dusty boxes and abandoned gear. I worked my way toward Chug's bedroom and found, sure enough, that I could see through the ceiling mirror over the bed. There was a fitting that looked like it might once have held a camera, but there was no camera. The cops or someone else had been there before me.

I went through the rest of the house, then returned to the workroom, and looked around. Maybe Chug made some of his own sexual apparatus. I didn't find any. Then I looked some more, and had better luck. Like a lot of us, Chug had cans of stuff pushed against the back wall of his workbench: nails, stray bolts, keys without locks, and other odds and ends you might find a use for someday. I dumped the cans and refilled them one by one, and found, mixed in with two rusty outboard motor spark plugs and some roofing nails, a key to handcuffs. Having once been a cop with handcuffs of my own, I had no trouble recognizing it. I put it back into its tin can and left the house through the back door, locking it behind me.

I went back to the Land Cruiser, thinking about Chug. He had liked to laugh, he had liked wilderness, he had liked unconventional sex (if there still is such a thing), he had liked to jack deer and he had trusted somebody enough, or had been careless enough, to let that person into his house that night. Jesse James, and a lot of other people, had made the same mistake.

I drove downtown and went into the town hall, which was newly refurbished and looking good. As I went upstairs I could not but muse once again on the fact that Edgartown had a new police station and a practically new town hall, but it still couldn't manage to build public toilets for the thousands of visitors who poured into town each summer. Since before I was born, there had been great debate in Edgartown about when and where and whether to build public toilets. People had been born and had died in those thirty years, wars had been fought, political and financial dynasties had risen and fallen, but there still were no public toilets in Edgartown. Why, even Gay Head had public toilets, although, Gay Head being the way it is, they were the kind you have to pay to use. I hold that pay toilets are an abomination in the eyes of God, but the Wampanoags and other Gay Headers, with pockets open for tourist dollars, disagree. As a citizen of toiletless Edgartown, I had trouble holding high moral ground in the great toilet debate.

Upstairs I smiled my best smile and asked Norma Quintana if Chug Lovell had gotten his shellfish license that year.

"I don't think Chug Lovell ever had a permit," said Norma. "I don't think he did any shellfishing. I don't think I ever saw him in here for any permit of any kind."

"How about a hunting license for deer?"

"Nope." Norma was old enough to be my mother. She raised an eyebrow. "What's got your nose sniffing, J.W.? Tell Norma." The murder was the current topic of island gossip. And why not? We didn't get many murders on Martha's Vineyard.

I lowered my voice. "My spies tell me he got shot with his own bow and arrow. It was a broadhead hunting arrow, they say. They say there's a freezer full of venison and scallops up at his place. I just wondered if he had a license for the venison and shellfish."

"Maybe somebody gave him the meat. Hey, this is good stuff, J.W. You got any more inside dope?"

"Nope. You have any for me?"

"Not a bit. Nobody tells me anything." She grinned.

"But now I've got some stuff to tell everybody else!"

I went down Main Street, past the Christmas trees, past Tashtego, which has the island's most interesting Christmas decorations, to the Wharf pub, where, in the summer, they once served draft Commonwealth Brewery beer, the best beer in America. The Wharf claimed to be the only place outside the Commonwealth Brewery itself where you could get Commonwealth Brewery beer. Unfortunately, the pub ran out of this beer, so I settled for a bottle of Beck's dark while I thought things over.

I wasn't surprised to learn that Chug had no licenses. He was the kind of guy who apparently liked being outside the law. I wondered if he had stepped too far outside once too often, and if that had gotten him killed. The only other guy I knew offhand who consistently operated outside the law was Joey Percell. I wondered if they were hooked up somehow. Had Joey killed Chug?

Thinking of Joey, I thought of Ignacio Cortez. Now, if I'd been told that somebody on the island was going to get murdered, my money would have been on Nash Cortez as either victim or killer. Passions ran high around Nash. He had made a lot of enemies and seemed to enjoy making them. There were several people who probably wouldn't have shed a tear at the news of Nash's death. But Nash had not died; chubby, grubby Chug Lovell had.

I wondered if Nash might have killed him. The only problem there was that I'd never heard Nash say one thing, good or bad, about Chug. Nash's venom was all focused on the animal rights people, seemingly on Mimi Bettencourt in particular. What was the tie between Nash and Joey Percell? I didn't believe for a minute that Joey had slugged Nash by mistake, even if Nash didn't know why he'd done it. Joey Percell was a

guy who did not get paid for hitting or shooting people by mistake. One thing was clear: if Joey had hoped
to get Nash to lay off the animal rights faction, he'd
failed to do the job. Of course, that might be because
I'd interrupted him before he could work Nash over
some more.

I ordered another Beck's, and as I was testing it to
see if it was as good as the first one, who should come
in, looking very seasonal with a pin in the form of
green holly leaves and bright red berries on the lapel
of her gray wool blazer, but Angie Bettencourt.

"Well, hello," she said, smiling. She flickered an eye
around the place and pulled out a chair. "Just Ted said
he'd meet me here for a bit of Christmas cheer, but
he's late, so I'll sit with you."

"Just Ted will have to learn to show up on time if he
doesn't want you to cozy up to the first other man you
see. You want a little something while you wait?"

"Is the Pope Polish? I'll have white wine." She
waved at a waitress and gave her order.

I was glad to see her. "You and Helene Norton are
pretty close, aren't you?"

"What do you want with Helene? You've already
got more women than you can handle. Jeez, you're almost a married man, and here you are interested in
another woman who isn't even me."

"I don't want to handle Helene. I want to know if
it's true that Chug Lovell was seeing her."

"'Was' is the word. Poor Chug. Helene was pretty
shaken when she got the news." Her wine arrived and
she sipped it. "Why do you want to know about Chug
and Helene?"

"Who's the guy Helene was seeing before Chug got
into her act? Some real estate guy, I hear. You know
him?"

"You have more questions than answers. No, I don't know him. I guess he's been on the island a couple of times, but all I know about him is what Helene tells me."

"What does she tell you?"

"That he likes money and is willing to do a lot to get it, like maybe marry her. She was pretty hot for him for a while, but things were cooling when Chug started going over to see her. The guy's name is Mike Yancy. Office over on the Cape."

"Is he comforting poor Helene in her hour of sorrow?"

She looked at me over her glass. "How'd you know that?"

"If he really likes her, that's what he'd do. And if he really likes her daddy's land, that's what he'd do. Strong shoulder and pats on the back and all that."

She smiled. "What a cynic. I thought you were too sentimental to harbor such realistic thoughts. But you're right. Good old Mike is back at her door, being comforting."

"Do you know anything about Helene's sexual preferences?"

"Goodness, what kind of a conversation are we having? Isn't it enough that you know Zee's preferences? To say nothing of mine! Are you becoming some kind of kinky old man, Jefferson?"

"Is Helene's hair still long and brown?"

"Curiouser and curiouser questions! This is becoming interesting. What *are* you trying to find out? Yes, her hair is still long and brown. Tell me what's going on! Wait. I need another glass." She waved her glass at the waitress. "I do hope that Just Ted doesn't come too soon, because I want you to tell me everything!"

"It's simple enough. Word has it that Chug had some offbeat sexual practices. Nothing unheard of, mind you. Maybe handcuffs and stuff like that. Helene ever mention anything like that?"

"No! But then I don't think that she and Chug ever got that far. He was still in the roses and candy stage, I think. Gosh, you mean that Chug was into domination? I never would have guessed. Ah, that's why you asked about her hair. Somebody must have seen him with a woman with long brown hair!"

"Something like that. Chug was quite a ladies' man, according to your mom. He ever date you?"

"None of your business, but no, he didn't. Which did he like, do you know? Was he dominant or submissive? I might be willing to try dominant, but I don't think I'd be very good at submissive." She batted her eyelashes. "Except with you, of course."

"Oh, of course. Women come from miles around and beg me to dominate them. It's exhausting. Aside from liking money, what kind of a guy is this Mike Yancy?"

"She showed me a picture of him once. About thirty-five, plump, not bad-looking. Why?"

"I'd like to know where he was the night Chug got killed."

Angie's wine arrived, and she took a quick sip. "You mean you think he might be the killer?"

"I doubt it, but Chug was moving in on his woman and her money."

"Well, you're wrong. Helene and Mike were together that night. They went to the movies in Hyannis. She told me that when she heard about Chug. It made her feel twice as bad when she thought that while Chug was getting killed, she was at the movies with Mike and having a good time even though she thought they were breaking up." She raised a forefinger adorned by a Christmas-red nail. "Ah, but maybe he hired a hit man to do the job! The perfect alibi. At the movies with a reliable witness. Perfect! What do you think?"

I knew that no hit man had killed Chug. It was an amateur job, like most killings. I pointed over her shoulder. "I think that Just Ted just came in."

"Oh." She turned and waved, and Just Ted came over to the table.

I had finished my beer. I got up and waved at my chair. "Take over. I have places to go, things to do and people to see."

"What a busy fellow you are," said Angie.

"Thanks, J.W.," said Just Ted. "Sorry I'm late, sweets." He and Angie kissed, and he sat down.

Sweets? Shades of Chug Lovell!

Angie leaned across the table and took his hands in hers. "J.W. has just been telling me the best stuff! Wait till you hear this!"

I didn't mind having the gossip getting around. Maybe somebody would hear it and add more to it and I would eventually learn more than I now knew. But I had learned something: I could scratch Mike Yancy and Helene off my list of suspects. Unless Helene was lying about having gone to the movies, of course.

I went outside. Somewhere a radio or CD machine was playing Christmas carols. "It Came upon a Midnight Clear." There was a nip in the air, and the sky was getting gray as the short winter day began to fade. Red and green lights were shining from storefront windows.

I walked up Main Street past the four corners, past Tashtego, past the hardware store, the only useful store left on Main Street, the other once practical stores all having long since been replaced by tee shirt shops, gift shops and stores catering to the tourists, whose money was the grease that lubricated the island's wheels.

There were some people strolling the street in winter coats, hands in pockets, cheeks a bit red, looking in windows. They looked quite happy. They liked being in lovely Edgartown for the holidays. I didn't blame them. I liked being there, too. I wondered if Chug's poor ghost was spending the holidays somewhere, and whether his killer was humming a carol, or wrapping a present or otherwise enjoying the season.

Then I thought a bit about Heather confiding with Helene about her affair with Chug, and Helene confiding with Angie about Chug's romance with her, but nobody confiding in Heather. The circle didn't seem complete, but then it's an imperfect world.

I got into the Land Cruiser and went home.

— 17 —

The next morning I awoke to the hush of falling snow. Great, soft flakes were falling silently out of a gray-white, windless sky. The ground was covered, and the leafless limbs of the trees and oak brush were powdered white. I got up, wrapped myself in the woolen robe Zee had given me last Christmas, and fed wood into my new stove, where the embers of last night's fire were still banked red and glowing.

The silent snow blocked my view of the sea, shut me

off from the world beyond my yard and created an undefiled white fairyland out of the dark woods around my house. Pure, cool, cleansing, the snow fell gently and steadily, covering the hard and barren land of winter.

I made coffee and put together blueberry pancakes as the house warmed. I got out the maple syrup, then devoted myself to a large and leisurely breakfast while I looked through the kitchen window at the lovely, secret snow. I felt incredibly Christmasy.

Surrounded by water pushed north by the Gulf Stream, rarely does the Vineyard get a harsh winter. Rather, its infrequent snows tend to melt and disappear in short order. Occasionally, of course, a really cold spell does set in, and the harbors freeze, and the ferries must break through ice to get to their docks. In years past, for reasons known only to the gods of storms, the weather was apparently much more harsh. There are photographs of square-rigged ships lying offshore, being unloaded onto horse-drawn wagons and sleds which had traveled out to them over ice. And someone once told me that the news of Lincoln's inauguration reached the island via a messenger who traveled over ice.

When I was a boy of five or so, my father brought me to the island on an unfortunately timed winter visit. We arrived with a major-league snowstorm which marooned us for a few enjoyable days. During that time the highway departments of the towns were kept busy shoveling snow and the sea froze so solidly that when my father put me on his shoulders at the beach at the bend in the road, I could see only ice all the way to the horizon. It occurred to me that maybe we wouldn't ever be able to leave, and that seemed like a fine stroke of luck. In not too many days, of course, the ice broke up and melted, and my father and I were obliged to go home. There hadn't been an island winter like that since.

I wished that Zee were with me, but if she was looking at the snow, it was from somewhere else. Her house or the hospital, depending on when she was working. When *was* she working? I couldn't remember. Not a good sign for a guy who was scheduled to be her husband. I thought that maybe we should get married on my birthday, which is one of the few dates I can remember, so I would never forget our anniversary. Why take chances when you don't need to?

I went to the phone and dialed her number. She was there. "I love you," I said, and hung up.

A minute later the phone rang. "Not so fast, Jefferson! I love you, too."

"What do you think about getting married on July 13?"

"July 13? That's your birthday."

"I'm a romantic guy. Don't you think that would be romantic, to get married on my birthday?"

"I'm looking out at this beautiful snow and you're planning a July wedding date. You are indeed a romantic chap. July 13 sounds good to me. Now that that's settled, have you bought me my Christmas present yet?"

"None of your business, but I'm going to get my tree today. Do you want to help me decorate it?"

"You bet. I'll be by after work. I'll see you then. I gotta go. I go on duty at eight. Bye!"

I got dressed and got my axe from the shed and walked into my winter woods toward Felix Neck. I'd been watching the growth of a little fir tree back toward my property line (or maybe a little over it, if you insist on being strictly honest, which I don't), and this was its year to be my Christmas tree. The woods were hushed and white with the falling snow, and I came across the slowly filling tracks of deer, rabbit, skunk and other little critters whose footprints I did not recognize.

I felt like a woodman in a Grimm fairy tale, and would not have been surprised if Hansel or Gretel or maybe a gingerbread house or an elf in a red hat had suddenly appeared.

My tree looked very fine with its mantle of soft snow, and I knelt beside it and lifted the axe. The ring of my blade biting home seemed the only sound in the forest. Clear as the sound was, the silent snowflakes seemed so muffling that I had the impression only I could hear it.

Axe in one hand, dragging the tree with the other, I followed my filling tracks back home. Another deer had crossed my trail since I'd come out. Dasher? Dancer? Rudolph? Bambi?

I leaned the tree against the house and brought my Christmas stuff from the shed to the house: the tree stand, the boxes of decorations, some of which I'd had since I was a little kid, and some of which my father and mother had had when they were little kids, the lights, the candles for the windows, the old sheet that I put under the tree, the wooden Santa Clauses that my father had carved when he wasn't carving duck decoys, the crèche that went on one side of the tree, and the little ceramic town that went on the other.

I brought in the tree and set it up in its stand and put on the star and the lights. That was it for now. Nothing else would happen until Zee got here to help with the real decorating.

Zee would have been pleased to know that it was now Christmas shopping time. I got into my red down vest, put on my green wool watch cap and drove down to the animal shelter, where I went in to check out the kittens. The shelter always has more cats and kittens than it has homes for, so there was a nice selection. Just what Zee wanted, although she probably didn't know it: two little kittens, who could keep each other entertained while they grew up. I knew what kind they should be: a black half-Siamese and a short-haired tiger kitten. No fat, long-haired, flat-faced, potential lap cats, but real, part alley, kittens, tough enough to catch mice when they got big enough, and to keep the rabbits out of my garden after Zee and I tied the knot and her kittens became our cats.

There wasn't a black half-Siamese kitten on hand, but there was a gray tiger kitten with big feet, a kink at the very end of his tail, a scraggly meow and a bad need for a human in his life. He was obviously a very sentimental guy, so I started looking for another kitten who might toughen him up a bit before he turned into the softy he obviously would otherwise become. There were a lot of kittens who deserved Zee as their human, but I could only take one more, so I was picky, and finally found one that fit the bill: a whacked-out little white female about half the tiger's size, but full of piss and vinegar. I paid the adoption fees for the kittens and took them next door to the vet for checkups and shots.

When the vet had done her thing and I had made arrangements to bring the kittens back for follow-up exams and more shots, I put them in their boxes and the boxes in the Land Cruiser, and went shopping: litter, a litter box, a couple of little balls with bells inside them, some wide-bottomed dishes that kittens couldn't spill and some kitten food. The kittens were rapidly becoming expensive propositions. I didn't even have them home yet, and already they had set me back a pocketful of cash.

No matter. 'Twas the season, after all. Now where could I keep them until Christmas Eve?

At Angie's place? I didn't think that Zee would go for that. At Heather's house? Maybe. She owed me a favor. At Mimi's? No, she already had Phyllis on her hands. Then I knew. I drove to Nash Cortez's house.

"What do you have there, J.W.?" he asked, looking at me standing on his porch with a cat box in each hand.

"I have a couple of kittens here that I'm going to give to Zee for Christmas. I need a place to keep them until Christmas Eve. I remember you said your cat ran off and never came back, so I know you're a cat man. What do you say? I've got a litter box and food and everything else you'll need, out in the Land Cruiser."

"Well, don't just stand out there in the cold. Come on in." I put the boxes on the living room floor and he shut the door. He leaned over the boxes. "Let's have a look at 'em."

I opened one of the boxes and the white kitten jumped out. "There is one thing," I said. "You can't let them get together until I find out for sure that neither one of them has feline leukemia. The vet says that we should know by tomorrow, at the latest."

"Tomorrow, eh?" He rubbed a gnarled hand on his hard, bony chin. A little smile floated across his face, and his eyes were soft. "I guess I can manage that. I'll put one of them in the extra bedroom, and keep the other one out here."

"I've only got one litter box. I can go get another one."

He knelt and touched the kitten, who immediately

galloped off. "Independent little cuss, aren't you? No, I still have Horatio Hornblower's old box. I can use it in one room. By tomorrow, they can be together, so I won't even need that."

"It's only for a few days, Nash. I really appreciate this."

He was watching the white kitten start to play with the fringe on the couch cover. "No problem, J.W." He leaned forward, and the kitten scampered away. "Cute little character, ain't you. Got a lot of zip."

I went out and brought in all my kitten gear. By the time I got inside, Nash had the other box open and the gray tiger cat out on the floor of the bedroom. He was rubbing against Nash's leg and meowing pretty well for a little kitten.

"This one is going to be a shoulder cat," said Nash, picking him up. The kitten immediately produced a cat-sized purr. "Feller likes to be held. There, there, little guy. There's plenty of attention in the world. You don't need to try to get it all right now."

The kitten buzzed and Nash's big, rough hands stroked it gently.

"They're going to call me as soon as the results of the leukemia tests are in," I said. "I'll let you know as soon as I do."

"That'll be fine," said Nash. "Just fine. Come on, Stripe, and I'll get you something to eat and drink, then go feed your pal in the other room. You're a friendly little guy, you are."

I went out into the snow, feeling happy, and soon discovered that I was whistling carols as I drove home.

Zee arrived just before five, and I had a hot toddy waiting for her: cinnamon and rum and a bit of honey in hot cider.

"Sweet, but just the thing for a winter evening," I said. "Just like you."

She kissed me. "I love this snow. We must have six or seven inches on the ground. It just keeps falling."

Indeed it did. Great, soft flakes that piled on tree limbs and would blow into gentle drifts when the wind came up. It was a dry snow that would pack down to almost nothing, and would melt as soon as the sun hit it. I hoped it would stay around until Christmas, because I love and rarely get the white Christmases I remember (or imagine) from my youth.

Zee went into the spare bedroom where she kept her stay-over clothes, and changed out of her white uniform into dungarees and a checkered shirt.

"There," she said. "Tree decorating clothes. Shall we get at it?"

I put the high stuff on the tree—tiny balls, small ornaments, little things for the highest, smallest limbs—and Zee worked her way around the lower branches. I had a lot of decorations because I never threw anything away and over the years had, like Mimi Bettencourt, liked to buy doodads that I thought would look good on next year's tree: a miniature lobster pot, a little fishing boat, a tiny fire engine like my father used to ride, a little carved figure I'd gotten in Vietnam, a miniature policeman from my days in the Boston P.D. I'd collected a lot of stuff, and I always put it all on the tree.

"If we keep adding decorations after we get married," said Zee, "you're going to have to cut a hole in the ceiling so we can set up a tree big enough to hold everything."

"No problem. I'll just jack up the ceiling. Have you bought my Christmas present yet?"

"None of your business. Besides, I don't buy you presents. Santa brings them."

When the tree was done, Zee put the electric candles in the windows and I put the carved Santas on the fireplace mantel. Then I turned off the overhead light and turned on the candles and the tree lights. The room danced in the light of the flickering fire, while the lights of the tree and the yellow window lights glimmered gently at us.

We sat on the couch with new drinks and admired our work. Zee snuggled against me, and we were happy. After a while, I went out into the kitchen and whipped up some spaghetti to go with the meat sauce I'd had heating. We ate and snuggled some more. I had a sudden thought. All the scene needed to be perfect was a couple of children. Nice, clean children, of course, but children nevertheless. I was shocked, but also fascinated. I watched the nice, clean children in my imagination. They looked happy as they played in the gentle light. Did Zee see them, too?

Then for some reason I found myself wondering if Joey Percell was sitting at home with his wife, watching his children play near his Christmas tree. I didn't know what to make of this sudden vision, but I remembered that Dostoyevsky was not the only one to suggest that even violent criminals were like the rest of us in most ways, and that even Hitler was fond of dogs, children and opera.

In my mind, then, I watched the Führer lift a wassail cup and smile as a colorful party of formally dressed civilians and men in uniforms with swastikas joined in a Christmas toast. Behind him, a giant, decorated tree glowed with lights as an orchestra began to play "*Stille Nacht.*" The Führer and his guests raised their voices in song. They sang with feeling, and faith and sentiment, and their voices were strong and sweet.

"What's the matter?" asked Zee, lifting her face up toward mine, and bringing me back to this room in this time.

I tightened my arm around her. "Nothing," I said. "I love you." I put a smile on my face and kissed her forehead. "Snug back down there," I said.

She did and I stared into the fire.

— 18 —

The snow stopped sometime during the night, and lay glittering on the ground the next morning. The sky was winter blue and cloudless, and the air was chill and clean. There had still been no wind, so the trees and oak brush were fairyland white. When Zee left for work, the wheels of her little Jeep cut blue eight-inch furrows in the snow that lay in my long driveway.

"No problem," she'd grinned, putting the Jeep into four-wheel drive before she kissed me and drove away.

I washed up the breakfast dishes, got my snow shovel and dug out a path from the driveway to the front door, then got into my red vest and green hat and drove down to the animal shelter. The highway was plowed and already the thin spots of snow left behind by the plow were beginning to melt.

My kittens' tests had come back. They did not have feline leukemia. I drove to Ignacio Cortez's house and gave him the news.

"Good," he said, and opened the door between his spare bedroom and the living room. The white kitten and the tiger kitten stared at each other. Then, with a bound, the white kitten attacked the tiger and both went tumbling across the floor. A second later, the tiger tore out of sight down the hall, with the white kitten right after him.

Nash smiled. "Would you look at that! The little one is all over the big one!" He laughed.

The kittens came back in a mad gallop and disappeared into the kitchen. A moment later they reappeared, end over end.

"My gosh," laughed Nash, as we got our big feet out of the way. "If that tiger doesn't figure out pretty soon that he's bigger than she is, she's going to beat him clear to death! Look at that!"

There was no doubt that the little cat was putting it to the bigger one, who seemed a bit confused about what was happening to him and refused to fight back other than to wave an ineffective paw at his attacker as she got to him with tooth and claw. His principal contribution to the fray was to run away whenever he could manage it, and this he now did with her in hot pursuit.

"Damned good," said Nash. "Only had Horatio Hornblower before. Never had two cats at the same time. Should have, though. Those two will entertain each other all day. Entertain me, too. Gets lonesome around here, sometimes." He laughed as the kittens tore back through the living room into the kitchen. "Mimi'd get a real kick out of you guys," he said almost to himself as they went by.

Mimi? Had I heard right? Mimi Bettencourt? Could it be that Nash . . .?

I watched the kittens go tumbling by. Well, why not? The Cortezes and the Bettencourts had been friends back when both couples were intact, after all . . . Nash and Mimi were of an age, after all . . .

I took the bull by the horns. "Nash, what do you mean Mimi'd get a kick out of these cats?"

Nash looked startled. "What?"

"You heard me. You said Mimi'd get a kick out of these cats. Why'd you say that?"

"You must have heard wrong."

"No, I didn't hear wrong." I narrowed my eyes. "Come clean, Nash. What's going on? I thought Mimi was your number-one enemy, what with all the grief you give her."

"None of your business, J. W. Jackson." But his voice had no ring to it.

"Tell me the truth, Nash. What's with you and Mimi Bettencourt?"

"Well, damn it all, J.W., a man doesn't like to talk about his feelings with just anybody!" He thrust his hands into his pockets and stalked across the room, giving me a glance over his bony shoulder.

"You can't fool me any longer," I said, "so you may as well tell me everything."

The kittens were suddenly rolling and tumbling at his feet. He reached swiftly down and extracted the tiger from the melee. The white kitten pranced away and the tiger immediately began to purr. Nash stroked the kitten with a big, rough hand. "Friendly, aren't you? I'm gonna miss you little fellers when you're gone." He looked at me. "That woman drives me crazy. She doesn't even know I exist unless I get in her face about that nutty animal rights stuff she's always going on about. You understand what I'm saying? Hell, we were friends, her and Gus and Joan and me. And even after Joanie died. But after Gus died, she didn't even know I was alive, seemed like." He stroked the buzzing kitten.

"You mean you've been giving her all this grief just to get her to look at you?"

He frowned. "Well, no. Hell no! Those animal rights people are all crazy as loons! You let them take over and pretty soon a man won't be able to swat flies! Somebody's got to face 'em down!"

"Mimi swats flies, Nash. She just doesn't eat meat and doesn't think you should either."

"There! You see what I mean? Damned woman thinks we should all eat goat food! It's not natural. A man's got to have some red meat now and then, some fish, some chicken, and like that. Hell, she probably doesn't like lions and tigers eating deer, either. It's not natural, what she thinks, you have to admit that."

Omnivorous me had no problem with admitting that. "But it isn't just that, is it, Nash?"

He sat down, and the tiger kept purring. Nash sighed, and looked at me. "No, it's not just that. Joan and I were married for over thirty years. Our kids turned out okay, and we were happy. All that time, we were close to Gus and Mimi. Now there's only me and Mimi, and I think about her all the time, but she never once thinks about me."

"How do you know?"

"Because she never told me so."

"Did you ever tell her?"

He looked indignant. "Well, of course I didn't. I mean, Gus is barely in the ground. You know?"

I couldn't believe what I was hearing. I counted back the years. "Nash," I said, "Gus Bettencourt has been dead for four years. Mimi stopped mourning at least two years ago. You don't have to be afraid to talk to her."

He rubbed the kitten absently. "Oh, I know that, I guess. But what if she just sticks her nose up in the air like she does? Or what if she laughs?" He gritted his teeth. "God, I don't know what I'd do." He looked suddenly pitiful. "Hell, J.W., I'm not a kid, I'm damned near sixty years old. I haven't wooed a woman for nearly forty years. I don't know how to do it anymore. I'm not sure I ever did."

"Well, you may not know how to woo her, but you sure know how to piss her off. You haven't forgotten how to do that."

"It's like being a clown," he said. "You act like a fool and she may hate you, but at least she knows you're there."

I remembered what Zee had said about braid pulling. Nash was like your average junior high school male experiencing his first crush and trying to explain why he acts like an idiot whenever the girl shows up. But he had my sympathy. I wasn't sure how to woo a woman either, and was just glad that I had managed it with Zee.

My skills as matchmaker were strictly limited, but as I watched the white kitten spot the tiger in Nash's lap, flatten on the floor with only her tail waving and then begin her stalk, a little light bulb went on in my head. Before I could tell Nash about it, the white kitten attacked, leaping into Nash's lap and landing on the tiger with all four feet. Nash looked astonished and then roared with laughter. He got a kitten in each big hand and pulled them apart.

He looked at them, then put them together on the floor. The tiger fled, with the white right behind him. "I just got an idea," he said.

I knew it was the same one I had. "You're right. It's perfect. Two kittens for Mimi. Nobody worth a damn can resist two kittens. You can get them at the animal rescue shelter, then give them to Mimi on Christmas Eve."

His eyes were bright. "I'll do it!" Then he frowned. "But where can I keep 'em till Christmas Eve? I've got your kittens here, and I haven't got room to keep two others away by themselves till their leukemia tests are done."

"No problem," I said, thinking fast. "We'll keep them at my place. Zee'll love them. And at Christmas you can deliver hers to my house and pick yours up."

"And deliver them to Mimi. And if she takes 'em . . ." said Nash thoughtfully.

"That's right. You'll have a chance to show her you're not just a mad animal killer."

Nash and I looked at each other with satisfaction.

"How about a cup of coffee?" asked Nash. "We'll drink to two kittens for Mimi."

"The animal shelter is going to love us," I said, following him into the kitchen. "We're taking cats off their hands faster than they can bring them in."

The kittens roared into the kitchen and roared out again. I thought they seemed to be slowing down a little, though. Even kittens have to get tired sometime.

"What do you think about this Chug Lovell business?" I asked.

Nash looked at me over his cup. "Don't know. Never knew Chug well. Saw him at those meetings, but that's about it. We didn't end up at the same places very often. Rotten way to die, that's for sure. And I don't like the idea of some murderer running around right here on the island. What do you think about it?"

"Not much more than you. You ever out at his place?"

"Not once. Drove past it often enough, though. I remember when that place looked pretty good. Been falling down ever since Chug bought it. More like a dump every day. Shame."

Nash's house was well maintained and neat as a girl on her first date. "You ever hear anything about him jacking deer or shellfishing without a license?"

He shook his head. "Can't say that I did. But then I've got no objection to a man taking a deer out of season if he needs it to eat. Same with shellfishing. Man needs the food, I don't hold it against him if he goes and gets some. Hell, the ponds and the shellfish were here before the licenses were, just like the woods and the deer were."

It was an attitude shared by me and a lot of people I knew, including a couple of shellfish and game wardens. Most of us got our licenses, but we didn't care if a poor man with a family didn't have his.

Of course Chug didn't have a family. I wondered if he was a poor man. He had enough to live without a job, at any rate. Or at least not a job I knew about.

"What did Chug do for work?"

Nash got us more coffee. "Hell, I never saw Chug work at anything. I thought he was supposed to be a tobacco heir or some such thing. Money from down south. Something like that."

"My idea of being a tobacco heir doesn't include living in a shack that's rotting out from under me."

"Mine neither, but then I never was an heir of any kind. Maybe that's how they all live."

"You ever see anybody hanging around with Chug? A girlfriend, maybe? Or maybe some guy? Maybe you saw somebody with him sometime when you were driving up past Mimi's house?"

"You're mighty curious about Chug Lovell."

"Dave Mello and I gave up scalloping for the holidays. I'm filling up my time by nosing around in Chug's business. He might not have been a tobacco heir, but he got some money somewhere or other. I wonder where. I hear he went off island now and then. You know anything about that?"

"Not a thing. Why are you asking me all these questions? Like I told you, I don't know a damned thing about Chug Lovell."

"I guess you just happen to be the guy sitting in front of me." I changed gears. "You ever figure out why Joey Percell slugged you?"

Nash's face grew cold. "Just that nonsense about laying off the animal rights ladies. I'll tell you one thing. Mr. Percell had better not come around this way again. I'll fill his ass full of bird shot!"

"Who'd he say sent him here, anyway?"

"Didn't say. Just said his boss didn't want any more out of me. Just about then is when he must have belted me. I don't remember a thing about it. They say he was wearing gloves with lead in them. Sort of like getting hit with a sap, I guess. Glad you were here, I'll say that."

I finished my coffee and got up. "When you get your kittens, just bring them by my place. There's a good deal of snow in my driveway . . ."

"Don't worry. I've got four-wheel drive."

Everybody on Martha's Vineyard has a vehicle with four-wheel drive. I went out and climbed into mine.

Downtown, everybody was working to get rid of the snow. Merchants were shoveling sidewalks and the highway department was busy with a scoop loader and dump trucks, hauling snow down to the harbor and dumping it. The snow made Main Street look even more Christmasy than before, and the window shoppers looked quite Dickensish as they dodged snow shovelers and peered into windows, their breaths making clouds in the air.

I drove down to the Reading Room, and put the glasses on the *Mattie* and the *Shirley J.* Their cabins and decks were covered with snow, but there was no ice to be seen, and the boats swung easily from their stakes between the Reading Room and the yacht club. Still, I dug my dinghy out from under the snow that covered it, rowed out to the boats and cleaned off the snow. On the off chance that we might get a real freeze, I didn't want two ice-covered boats on my hands.

About the only other boats in the harbor were fishing boats—scallopers, conchers and draggers. A fisherman's life, like a farmer's life, is a tough and chancy one in the best of times, and a very tough one during the winter. Not many people were up to it. Scalloping all winter in the Edgartown ponds was hard enough. I didn't want anything to do with going outside into the deep water. I thought about Joey Percell as I rowed ashore. Then I drove to the police station on Pease Point Way.

I found the chief holed up in his office. He had a little Christmas tree sitting on a file cabinet.

"Merry Christmas," I said.

"Well, it was until just a second ago," he said. "What brings you out of the snowy woods?"

"The eternal search for truth."

"Are we talking about the late Chug Lovell? If so, I don't know any more than I knew last time."

"But I do," I said.

"I'm not involved in the case. The state police are handling it. Nobody tells me anything." He leaned forward. "What do you know?"

I told him.

—— **19** ——

When I was done, he looked at me. "How do you know about this sex stuff?"

"How do *you* know about this sex stuff?"

"I'm an officer of the law."

"Yeah, but I'm a civilian. There are more of us than there are of you. I've got contacts out there among the normal humans."

"Listen to me," said the chief. "If you've been breaking and entering or interfering with a murder investigation or anything like that, your ass is in a sling. You understand?"

"What? Me break and enter? I'm shocked that you'd even think such a thing."

"Sure you are. So you think there was kinky sex going on. What do you make of it?"

"I don't know. Personally, I don't care what kind of sex goes on if it goes on between grownups who both agree . . ."

"I believe they're called consenting adults," said the chief.

"Okay. Consenting adults. Whatever."

"But what if they don't both agree?"

"That's something else."

"That could be a motive. A lover who didn't like being loved that way. You know the joke: sado-masochism is okay as long as the sadist and the masochist agree about who's doing what to who. But if they don't agree . . ."

"Yeah, unhappy lovers kill each other every day."

"So who was Chug's lover?"

My client. Perhaps among others. I shrugged. "A good question. Well, now that I've been so helpful to you, maybe you can be helpful to me."

The chief narrowed his eyes, leaned back and put his hands behind his head. "I'm a cop. Cops are always helpful."

"Sure."

"What do you want?"

"I want to know who Joey Percell works for and why he came down here to tell Nash Cortez to lay off the animal rights gang and then flattened him to underline the message. You're a cop, so you might have some contacts over in America who keep an eye on people like Joey. What are the chances of you asking them some questions about him and his boss's business interests?"

The chief smiled his thin smile. "As a matter of fact, I already did that. When a guy like Percell comes to my town to punch somebody out, I like to know why. So I called some people I know in Providence. What's your interest in Joey Percell? I mean, aside from the fact that he might decide to come back down here and break you into little pieces for interfering when he was delivering his message to Nash."

"The animal rights people and Nash Cortez and Chug Lovell were all interested in what happens to Carl Norton's land. Joey gets tied in because he slugged Nash. Joey's boss is tied in because he told Joey to slug Nash. I wonder if maybe Chug got killed for some reason tied in with Joey slugging Nash."

"It's almost Christmas. The season to be jolly. Why don't you go home and sit in front of your fire with Zee and string popcorn and leave the police work to the police?"

"I'd sure like to know who Joey works for and why he cared enough to send the very best to keep Nash from jawing with a bunch of animal rights people way down here on the Vineyard." I arched a brow. "I'll bet Quinn could find out, now that I think of it."

"Who's Quinn?"

"You may have met him. A reporter from the *Globe*. Down here a while back on that drug bust that went sour. Friend of mine from when I worked on the Boston P.D. I take him bluefishing once a year or so."

The chief frowned. "Oh, yeah. I remember that bastard. Dumb cops, smart drug ring story. Some reporter!"

"Quinn is good, all right. You know, I think I will give him a call. He'd probably like another cops and robbers story, and this one has all the ingredients: small-town murder, Providence mob enforcer, cops who won't talk to each other. Quinn will love it." I put my hands on the arms of my chair. "Well, thanks, chief."

"Wait a minute," said the chief. "We don't need any hotshot big-city reporters nosing around where they don't belong." He pointed at my chair. "Sit." He leaned forward. "This is off the record. Nothing anybody can take to court yet . . ."

"Yet?"

"Yet. There are some people working on a case in Rhode Island and Connecticut, but so far that's all they're doing, working. Some reporter gets his nose into it, everything could fall apart. You understand?"

"Yeah. Are you telling me that this case they're working on has something to do with Joey Percell coming down here and dinging Nash Cortez?"

"I'm telling you that there's an important case being investigated up in Connecticut and Rhode Island, and that's all I'm telling you." He sat back, dug his pipe out of his pocket and stuck it, empty, into his mouth. He looked at me.

I thought awhile. "Are you telling me that Joey's boss has interests in Connecticut that are tied to the animal rights people here on Martha's Vineyard, and that that tie is important enough for him to send his enforcer down here to quiet Nash down?"

"I'm not telling you any such thing," said the chief, sucking on his pipe.

I thought some more, putting names I knew into different configurations. Phyllis Manwaring emerged from the animal rights group. "Are you telling me that the Providence mob has an interest in Vince Manwaring's political campaign? And that they don't want any embarrassing stories coming out about the candidate's wife fighting with island hunters? And that Joey came down here to make sure there wouldn't be any?"

"I've never said one word to make you think that," said the chief, getting out his tobacco and stuffing it into his pipe.

I ran things through my mind for a while. "Okay," I said, finally, "but how did Chug fit into all this? He went off island every now and then. Was he tied to the mob? Did he make his money doing business with the wise guys? Did he cross somebody up there, maybe, and get himself killed?"

"My little bird never said anything about Chug Lovell."

"Well, if you talk to your bird again, will you ask him?"

The chief sucked his pipe. It was his policy not to smoke at his office. If he wanted to puff, he went outside to do it. "I might, but we both know he wasn't killed by a hit man. Some amateur did it."

True. "Did you find any long-lost relatives? Any family?"

"If he had any, we haven't found them yet. I used to hear that he was from down south someplace."

"The tobacco heir rumor. But if he had tobacco money coming in, there should have been paper in his place to show it. Check stubs, receipts, some such thing."

"The way I hear it, all they found in that line was a bankbook and some checks for an off-island bank. Chug had a couple thousand in savings and another thou or so in his checking account. Not much, for a tobacco heir."

"Don't be condescending, chief. That's more money than I have. So he didn't do business with island banks, eh? I wonder why."

"He was a private sort of a guy. Didn't tell people much of anything about himself. At least I don't know much about him, and I'm the police chief. Maybe he figured that bank people gossip just as much as other people, and that he didn't want the locals talking about him and his money."

"Maybe he was trying to hide his money from his ex-wife, or something."

The chief peered over his pipe. "He has an ex-wife?"

"No, no. I just made that up. Or maybe he did have one. I don't know." I got up. "I'm not even making sense to myself. Time to go home."

The chief nodded agreeably. "Past time, some might say." He got up. "I'll walk out with you. I feel the need to stoke up this briar."

"You just want to make sure I actually leave."

"That too."

A light wind had come up, and there were snowflakes in the air, blown from the trees. The air was still nippy, and the snow crunched under my feet as I walked to the Land Cruiser. It was lunchtime, and I wondered if food would improve the blood circula-

tion in my brain. Things were a little sluggish up
there right now, for sure.

I went down to the coffee shop on Dock Street and
had two portuguese mcmuffins, coffee and pie. Delish, high-cholesterol American food. Just what the
doctor ordered. When I got out on the street again, I
was ready to face the world with a smile.

I drove along the beach road to Oak Bluffs, past
the empty, snow-covered beaches where not too long
before I would have passed an unending line of
parked cars and hundreds of summer people lying
on the yellow sands or splashing in the blue water of
the Sound, the mothers, sitting with their backs to the
road, watching their small children playing in the water, and the teenagers wishing that they could be at
South Beach instead, so they could play in some real
surf and flirt with each other out of their parents'
sight.

And in not too long, the beach would be that way
again. But not now. Now it was white and lonely and
coldly beautiful, and the frigid gray Sound was no
place for swimmers.

I passed the statue of the Confederate soldier, the
northernmost such statue in the country, I've been
told, and drove up Circuit Avenue until I found a
parking place not too far from Heather Manwaring's
law office.

I went in and confronted Heather's answer to Effie
Perine. Effie said she'd see if Ms. Manwaring would
see me, went into an inner office and came out again
and said that I could go in. I went into Heather's office and closed the door behind me.

It wasn't the world's champion office, but it was
good enough. Very businesslike. A desk, file cabinets,
bookcases with law books and other thick, well-bound

tomes, a couch against one wall fronted by a coffee table and two stuffed chairs, two plain wooden chairs in front of the desk, a couple of standing lights and a large, slightly beat-up oriental carpet under everything.

Heather got up as I came in and pushed some papers off to one side of the desk. She was wearing a silk blouse with a sort of ruffle at the neck, and a gray skirt. I wondered if she was wearing those uncomfortable shoes that professional women seem to think they have to wear when they're doing business, or whether, hidden by the desk, she'd kicked them off and was wearing either no shoes at all or the running shoes a lot of women wear to and from the office, or maybe even slippers. I hoped it was slippers, but I doubted it. Heather didn't seem to me to be the slippers-in-the-office type. Too stiff. Too proper. Too much like her parents.

"J.W. How nice to see you." She smiled, but there was a question behind the smile.

I poked a thumb at the door. "Does much sound get through there?"

She looked at the door, then back at me. "No. Anything you say will be strictly between the two of us. Why? Have you learned something?"

I sat down in one of the wooden chairs.

"Do you want some coffee? I'll have Harriet bring some in . . ."

"No thanks."

She sat down and posed her hands together on the desk. "Well then . . ."

I looked at her yellow hair. It was pinned in a neat bun, but it was the right color and looked long enough. I got the strand of hair I'd found at Chug's house out of my pocket and laid it on her desk. "I

think this is yours," I said. I told her where I'd found
it, and told her about the handcuff key and the dishes
on the floor, in one of which was still the smell of white
wine.

As I talked she first blushed, then turned visibly
pale. Her eyes grew blank and strange, and she took
her lower lip between her teeth. Her hands tightened
against each other, but she didn't look away.

"How long were you two lovers?" I asked.

She stared at me without saying anything.

"How long?"

She put a hand to her throat.

"Look," I said. "I don't care about what went on between you. But I need to know some things. How long
were you two seeing each other?"

Her voice was small and tight. "Since midsummer. I
don't want to talk about this."

"You'll be talking about it to somebody. To me or to
the police or maybe to both of us. Chug wasn't a very
dominating guy out in the real world, but I take it that
at least some of the time he liked to play that game
with his women. Or was he the one on his hands and
knees?"

"No." She put both hands to her throat and curled
her fingers as if grasping a dog collar that was still
around her neck. "He wasn't the one."

There are houses in Boston where very wealthy and
powerful men pay a lot of money for the privilege of
dressing in panties and bras or diapers or nothing at
all and being spanked until they cry by women wearing leather clothes and spike heels. They pay to be
handcuffed, and tied in strange ways. They pay to be
whipped and abused, and to whimper and bleat and
become babies again. And the next day, they go back
to being wealthy and powerful men who walk the cor-

ridors of political power and whose faces appear regularly on the financial and social pages of the *Globe* and *Herald*.

And there are also houses where Brahmin women and women of lesser castes can find people who will play similar games with them. And of course, since there is a lot of money to be made in such business, there is a very professional group of people, male and female, who make a good living catering to their customers' desires. There seems no limit to the varieties of human sexual activity, as many Boston police officers can tell you from either professional or personal experience.

"He wasn't cruel," said Heather. "But he liked to have me . . . do things I'd never done before. I didn't mind, really. And it pleased him. I never knew about such things . . ." She seemed suddenly glad to talk. "He liked to call me Asta. That was a dog in some movie. He put my food and wine in dishes and fastened my hands behind my back with handcuffs and made me eat and drink there on the floor, with my face down in the dishes. He held the leash. We had sex that way too, sometimes. The doggy way. There's nothing wrong with that." This last came with a quick defensive energy, and she looked right at me as if in anger.

"Did he take pictures?"

"Yes."

That meant the police probably had them, and I wondered why they'd taken so long to come knocking at her door. It didn't make any sense that they hadn't come. I began to get an idea.

— 20 —

"Did you ever look at the pictures?"

A small blush. "Yes."

"Did he ever show you other pictures? Of other women?"

She tossed her head. "Yes. So what? I never really looked at them."

"I hope that you did. Did you?"

"No." She lifted her chin. "I told you they didn't interest me. He had them in albums. I didn't really look at them."

"Did you recognize anyone? If you did, I want you to tell me who it was."

"You're nastier than I thought you were." She was getting her gumption back.

"Could be. Look, you're not the first woman Chug ever had out at his place. You were just the latest in line, and if rumor is correct, he was planning to replace you with Helene Norton . . ."

"That's a lie!" But her face said she didn't believe it was, and her voice no longer had the rage in it that I'd heard when I'd first told her of Helene and Chug. I wondered if she'd had a talk with Helene, and if their friendship had survived.

I shrugged. "Maybe so, maybe not. The point is that all of his earlier women are potential suspects. So if you know any names, give them to me."

"I didn't really look at them . . ." She touched the papers on her desk, then touched her hair. "Well, I did think I recognized one face . . . I'm not sure . . ."

I thought she was sure. "Who?"

"A woman named Kittery. Christine Kittery. She teaches at the high school, I think. Her husband did some business with me once. Real estate. She came in with him to co-sign some papers. I think I saw her in some pictures."

"Doing the same sort of thing that you did later?"

"Yes. Look, we didn't do that all of the time. That wasn't the only thing we did . . ." She looked at me with fiery eyes, and leaned forward. "You're working for me, and I expect you to keep this confidential. My private life is no one's business, and I want it kept private. Do you understand?"

I was glad to see that she was replacing her fear with anger. "I don't care about your personal life one way or another," I said, "and I don't plan on telling anyone about it. Do you know what happened to the photographs?"

"No." The anger that had stiffened her spine seemed to abruptly disappear, and she sagged back into her chair.

"In that case, somebody else besides me knows about you and Chug, because the photographs aren't in Chug's house anymore. I looked around pretty carefully, and there were no photographs."

"Oh, God, the police have them!" She fumbled open a drawer of her desk and brought out a box of Kleenex. She took a tissue and blew her nose, then stared at the desktop. "I knew they must have them. I knew it right away, as soon as I heard about Chug being dead. I mean, they couldn't have missed them. Chug kept them right there in his closet. He never even locked the door." Tears began to form in her eyes. "Oh, God, why did I let this happen to me?"

"I don't think the police have the pictures," I said. "I think that if they had them, they'd have come to talk with you before this. Something else happened to the pictures. I think that whoever killed Chug has them."

She stared at me with her watery eyes. "The killer has them? The killer?"

"Or maybe Chug hid them away somewhere. Maybe he gave them to somebody to keep for him. But I think that the most likely thing is that the killer took them away after the murder."

Heather dabbed at her eyes. "But why? Why would he do that?" Then she frowned at me. "Blackmail? Is he going to blackmail me with the pictures?"

"Maybe. When we find the killer, we'll know. Has anybody tried to blackmail you, Heather?"

"No." She wiped at her face with clean tissues. "I'm a mess. I must look awful." She wiped some more. "So the police don't have them . . ."

"That's how it looks to me. If anyone talks to you about having the pictures, I want you to play along and then call me right away. It would be better if you called the police, but I don't imagine you want to do that, do you?"

"No."

"You might be smarter to play straight with them."

Her eyes grew strange and wild. "No. I don't want them to know about this."

"They'll probably find out anyway."

Her anger was there again. "Not if you don't tell them!"

"I won't, but there are other people who might. The cops aren't fools. Don't make the mistake of thinking they are."

"Who would tell them? Who?"

Fear makes us stupid sometimes. It can transform a bright person into a fool. I counted on my fingers as I spoke.

"The killer might send the albums to the cops. An anonymous contribution to the investigation to give them a suspect. Or whoever you talk to about your love life may get nervous and go to the cops so she can't be accused of withholding evidence. And then there's whoever *she* talks to . . ."

Heather's face was stiff. "You're a wicked person to say such things."

"I'm just telling you how things are. I still think you should give some thought to going to the cops yourself."

"Well, I'm not going to! This is my life, damn you!"

In her place, I wondered what I would do. I was glad I wasn't in her place.

"All right," I said. "Have it your way. Now, were there any men in the pictures you looked at? Or were there only women?"

She seemed almost shocked at the question. "Women. There were only women. Why, Chug didn't . . ."

"Did Chug borrow any money from you?"

"What? Yes. I gave him some. A little . . ."

"How much?"

"I don't know . . ."

"How much?"

"Two or three hundred dollars. Why do you want to know?"

"After he showed you your pictures or before?"

"What are you asking me? Oh, all right. It was afterward, but the one thing never had anything to do with the other. He never threatened to show them to anybody. He never did that. It was just that he was a little short of money. You have a really filthy mind, do you know that? Don't you ever just think the way normal people think? Maybe you should go to a doctor."

"Maybe." There was a door in the side wall of the

office. I pointed to it. "Is that a bathroom? Okay, why don't you go in there and get yourself fixed up? I'll wait."

She opened her mouth as if to say something, then shut it again. She took a purse out of the same drawer where she'd found the Kleenex, and went into the bathroom.

I sat and wished that Heather had looked at Chug's albums more carefully and could tell me whose pictures were there. I wondered if she was lying to me about not having recognized anyone but Christine Kittery. I wondered if she really had seen Christine Kittery's picture at all. I wondered how many women had their photos in the albums and whether Chug's killer just had a fancy for such pictures, or had taken them for some other reason. Blackmail was a possibility, of course, but not the only one. If one of Chug's women was the killer, she might have taken the albums so she could destroy them. Or maybe one of the women had a husband or a boyfriend who, learning of Chug's sexual adventures, did in Chug and took the pictures to protect the woman's reputation. Or to provide entertainment for himself and his friends. Or to become a blackmailer in his own turn.

There were a lot of possibilities. The longer I worked on this case, the longer my list of suspects became. It wasn't supposed to work that way. An investigation was supposed to narrow the list. Could it be that I had been right to quit the cops when I had?

Heather came out looking pretty good. Her eyes were a little red, but aside from that, the damage had been controlled. She looked at me and made a vague gesture with one hand. "I'm sorry I said those things about you. I know you're just trying to do your job."

I got up and let her look at me look her over. I nodded. "You look okay. I'm going now. I'll let you know if I learn anything. If the cops come or you have to talk to somebody, talk to Percy Goodman first. Keep a level head and a closed mouth with everybody else and you may come out of this without any scars."

"I've already got scars."

"I mean the kind that other people can see."

"I know. You won't . . .?"

"No," I said. "I won't tell anybody."

She took a deep breath and exhaled it. "Thank you. I . . . What kind of a person am I?"

I didn't know what sort of expression was on my face. "A fairly ordinary one, I think. Brighter than most, probably. Not the kind you should worry about. I've got to go." I gestured at her desk. "You've got work to do."

"You'll stay in touch?"

"Yes."

I went out into the cold afternoon air. Snowy Circuit Avenue was decorated with red and green and silver adornments, and people were strolling the sidewalks and looking into windows, their faces red and happy. The street itself was slowly turning to slush. From Circuit Avenue I took a right and drove through the narrow streets of the campground, past the Victorian gingerbread houses, including my favorite, the particularly cute pink one whose picture graces so many postcards. When I fetched the main drag again, I drove to the blue-painted headquarters of the state police.

There was a cruiser in the driveway with a chunky young officer about to get into it. He told me that Dom Agganis was not in but that he liked to grab a cup of coffee about this time up at the Black Dog.

Both the Black Dog bakery and the Black Dog restaurant are in Vineyard Haven, near the ferry docks, which makes them popular with people waiting for their boats. They are also near the infamous five corners road intersection. Along with other traffic, almost all of the Vineyard Haven ferry traffic and the traffic going to and from the A & P parking lot passes through the five corners intersection, but Vineyard Haven has no interest in improving it, although its summer-long traffic jam could be eliminated pretty easily by the installation of a traffic circle. In midwinter, on a snowy weekday, things weren't too bad, and I even found a parking place by the A & P.

Both Black Dogs serve up excellent food at good prices, and are favorite island eating places. The bakery also makes a pretty good buck selling hats and sweatshirts with black dogs on them. Rumor has it that the black dog hat is the most coveted one in the whole U.S.A. Could be. In the restaurant, you can sit by a window and look out at the ferry boats coming and going, and the only possible complaint you might have is that, Vineyard Haven being a dry town, you can't get a beer to wash down your food. Whenever Vineyard Haveners are invited to vote on whether to go wet or stay dry, they stay dry, their reasoning being that as long as Edgartown and Oak Bluffs are the only wet towns on the island, that's where most of the rowdies will hang out and most of the fights will happen. Five corners apparently provides Vineyard Haven with all of the excitement it wants.

I found Corporal Dominic Agganis sitting in a window seat having coffee and staring out at the harbor. Vineyard Haven harbor has a fine collection of schooners, and a lot of them swing on their moorings

all winter long. I sat down across from him and asked,
"Are you fevered with the sunset? Are you fretful with
the bay? Is the wander-thirst upon you? Is your soul
in Cathay? If so, I want to remind you that this is the
middle of the day and you're still on duty even
though you're hiding away in here trying to escape
your responsibilities while you indulge in romantic
fantasies."

"Fuck you," said Dom.

A waitress came by and I ordered a coffee, black.

Dom sucked at his coffee. "What do you want?"

"I have a friend who's a reporter up in Boston. He
has other friends in other places. I understand that
the cops found some kinky stuff up in Chug Lovell's
house."

Dom's eyes were dull and bored. "No comment."

"I understand that there was some other stuff that
the cops didn't get."

Dom opened his mouth, then shut it when the waitress brought my coffee, then opened it again.

"What are you talking about?"

"Pictures."

"What kind of pictures?"

"What kind do you think?"

"I think you better tell me what you're talking
about."

"I hear that there were pictures to go along with the
other stuff you found. I hear that you guys might
have found some cameras, but you didn't find the pictures."

Dom lowered his voice and pushed his face across
the table toward mine. "If you know something, you'd
better damn well tell me about it."

"I just told you. Chug had pictures."

"Who told you that? I want his name."

"I'll bet you do."

"I'll haul you in on this."

"Sure you will. For what? Repeating rumors? So it's true, eh? You guys don't have the pictures."

"Do you?"

"No."

Dom sat back. "But there are pictures? You're sure?"

"So I hear. I never saw them."

Dom thought awhile. "It would be interesting to see those pictures. You know how that might be done?"

"No. All I know is what I told you. There were pictures . . ."

"Of what went on up there at Lovell's place?"

"Yes. Albums of them, I hear."

"Albums, eh? And you don't know any more about it than that, eh?" A lazy smile crossed his face. "You know, I think I might just haul your ass over to the office so we can talk."

"The jail's in Edgartown, if you really want to be a tough guy."

"You ain't seen tough, yet. Who gave you this information?"

"You're scary. I can see that I'd better tell you the truth, the whole truth and nothing but the truth. All right, I'll confess. I've been kidding. Nobody gave it to me. I just made it up."

I drank my coffee and we looked at each other.

"We can get this out of you," said Dom.

"Maybe. But if you lock me up, who's going to do your detecting for you?"

Dom looked out of the window. Out by the breakwater, a fifty-foot schooner hung on her mooring, her bowsprit pointing into the cold winter wind. "You know," said Dom. "Sometimes I think I should just get on one of those things and leave all this shit behind me and sail south until I find myself a tropic island with some coconut trees and some wild pigs and some good fishing, and then just stay there."

"I did something like that several years ago," I said. "I left all the law and order crap behind and went south to an island. I ended up on this one. There isn't any away."

"I guess not," said Dom. He lifted his cup. "Well, here's to crime."

We drank to that, then walked outside together. Dom's cruiser was parked just outside. He got into it and looked up at me.

"Peace on earth, good will to men," he said, and drove away.

— 21 —

I went home and fed some wood into my stove, then got out my Vineyard phone book. I found one Kittery. M. Kittery, North Road, West Tisbury. I glanced at my watch and figured that school should be out by now. I dialed and after two rings heard a woman's voice say, "Merry Christmas."

"Mrs. Kittery?"

"Yes."

"My name is J. W. Jackson. Is your husband at home?"

She had a cheerful voice. "No, Matt isn't here. He should be home a little after five. Can I take a message?"

"No, it's you I want to talk to. Do you have a few minutes?"

"I've already done my Christmas shopping, and besides, I don't buy things sold over the phone. Sorry."

"This is about Chug Lovell."

There was a silence.

"I'm investigating his death, and your name came up."

The once cheerful voice was strained. "I haven't had anything to do with Chug Lovell for years. I don't know anything about his death."

"There were some photographs . . ."

"Oh, God . . ."

"Do you want to talk on the phone, or should I drive up there?"

"Oh, I don't know . . ."

"I'll be up. Is your name on your mailbox?"

"I don't want my husband . . ."

"We could meet somewhere."

"No. The sitter just left, and the baby has a cold . . ." Her voice drifted away.

"This won't take long. I'll leave before five, but I need to ask you some questions."

"Who are you?"

"We can talk on the phone, if you'd rather."

"No, no . . ."

"Tell me how to get to your house."

She did, and I drove up there.

She lived in the woods not far from Fisher Pond. A neat house with a goodly supply of fireplace wood stacked out back beside a shed. Smoke was rising from the chimney, and there were Christmas candles in the windows and a green wreath with a red ribbon was hanging beside the front door. Through the living room window I could see a Christmas tree. I parked in the driveway and walked to the door. It opened before I got there.

Christine Kittery was a pretty woman. Slim, brown-haired, wearing jeans and a green wool shirt. A little Santa Claus pin was fastened to her collar. Her face was strained.

"Mrs. Kittery? I'm J. W. Jackson," I said.

"Come in. You don't look like a policeman."

"Policemen don't always look like policemen, I guess. Are you all right?"

"I've got myself glued back together, I think." She waved at a chair beside the fireplace and I sat down. She sat across from me. The fire danced in the fire-place and its warmth felt good after the long ride in the Land Cruiser, which had a heater that didn't work too well. "My husband will be home soon. He doesn't know anything about me and Chug Lovell. That was all over before I met him. Does he have to know about it?"

"Maybe not. This won't take long. When was the last time you saw Chug?"

Her eyes were wary. "I saw him a month or two ago. At the market."

"Not since then?"

"No."

"When were you and Chug together?"

"Four years ago. Just after I came down to the is-land. The summer before I started teaching, I had a job waitressing. Chug and I met then."

"How long were you together?"

"Almost a year."

"What split you up?"

"A lot of things. I'd met some other men. I got tired of some of the things he liked to have me do. And he probably got tired of having me do them. He found a new girl. He was good at that."

"I'm told that women found him attractive. Something about him being roly-poly, childish and lovable, and liking women, as I remember."

"Oh, he liked women, all right. He liked to have them humiliate themselves for him. Part of the time, at least. Usually, he was just soft and sweet and cuddly. You've seen the pictures, haven't you? How many other people have seen them? I imagine that I get to spend the rest of my life wondering who's seen them. What a fool I was."

"Did Chug Lovell blackmail you with those pictures?"

"Of course he did. He didn't get much, because I'm a schoolteacher and I don't make that much, but he got some."

"Can you tell me how much?"

"A hundred a month. That was as much as I could hide from Matt. Chug wanted more, but he settled for that."

"Cash, of course."

"Of course. I mailed it to him."

"When you were together, did he ever show you the pictures he took?"

"Yes. At first they were a shock. Then I got over being shocked. He liked them, but I didn't think they were interesting or titillating or anything else. Later, they were just embarrassing. Do you have them?"

"Did you ever see pictures of anyone else? Any other women?"

She nodded. "Yes. He liked to show them to me. I can't say I was very interested in them. Why do men like such things?"

"Did you recognize anyone in the pictures?"

Her face got harder. "If I did, I wouldn't tell anyone."

"This is a murder investigation. Maybe Chug's

killer was one of his women. I have to talk to everyone who knew him."

"You mean maybe it was me!"

"Do you know how to shoot a bow and arrow?"

"No."

"Then it wasn't you. Did you recognize anyone in Chug's pictures? I need to know."

She looked into the fire, then at her watch, then back at me. "There was one face . . . I was new to the island, you understand. I didn't know very many people . . . But there was one. She works in the bank in Vineyard Haven. I have an account there . . . I see her often. Her name is Hazel Fine." She gave me a cold stare. "She's very nice. A very nice person."

"I'm sure she is. Were there a lot of women in the pictures? Had Chug been doing this sort of thing a long time?"

"Yes," she said, nodding. "There were a lot of women." Then she caught on. "You don't have them, do you?" She stood up. "If you had them, you wouldn't have to ask how many women were in them. How did you know about me?"

"Someone recognized your picture. Another woman."

"And now I've given you another name. And she'll give you another. And she'll give you another. My God!"

"I hope you're right. I want as many names as I can get." I got up. "If you think of anything that might help me, give me a call. I'm in the book."

"If you don't have the pictures, who does? Who'll be coming for money next time?"

"I don't know. Probably nobody. But if somebody does, let me know." I went to the door. "I think it's over as far as you're concerned. I think you can start stowing that hundred a month away in a special account so you can buy something for yourself that you've always wanted."

She followed me to the door. "I want you to know something. I want you to know that I was happy when I heard about Chug Lovell. I was happy. It was like a rock had been rolled off my shoulders. I have a good man and a beautiful little girl and I think I'm a good person, and I was glad when I heard he was dead."

She shut the door behind me, and I got into the chilly Land Cruiser and drove home. I thought I had spread enough good cheer for one day. As I drove, I wondered if Christine Kittery had lied about not knowing how to shoot a bow and arrow. A bit of verse got stuck in my mind:

> "I," said the sparrow,
> "with my little bow and arrow,
> I shot cock robin."

That verse went around and around in my head. Finally, to make it go away, I sang Christmas carols. By the time I was back in my living room, good King Wenceslaus had sent the sparrow packing. Good riddance.

I thawed some frozen chowder makings, stirred in milk and cut some thick slices of bread. I found a tape of Pavarotti singing Christmas songs with a Canadian choir, and put that on. I like Luciano's opera arias better, but he can sing a wicked "Ave Maria," too. That grand voice filled my house while I first had a martini, then washed down the chowder with a couple of bottles of Sam Adams, America's finest bottled beer. For dessert, I sliced up an apple and a pear and some cheese, and poured myself a cognac. I sat in front of the fire and looked at my Christmas tree. Its little lights glimmered in the round colored balls, and glittered off the other ornaments. Beyond it, in the windows, the yellow candles looked warm and comforting. I let Luciano carry me away into Christmas as it ought to be.

The next morning I looked up Hazel Fine's telephone number. Hazel was a little harder to find than Christine Kittery had been. There were more Fines than one on Martha's Vineyard, and I called two wrong numbers before I got the right one. The right Fine, it turned out, lived on West Chop. Convenient. She could walk to work. A woman's voice said, "Hello."

"Hazel Fine?"

"No. She's gone to work. Who's calling, please?"

"J. W. Jackson. I didn't think bankers went to work this early."

"The bank may not be open, but bankers go to work like everybody else. Can I give her a message?"

"It's personal. Would her boss be mad if I went by the bank to see her?"

"That's probably not the world's best idea."

"It's important."

"What did you say your name was?"

"J. W. Jackson. What's yours?"

"Mary Coffin. We share this place. Maybe you can give me some idea what this is all about. Hazel and I don't have many secrets."

"I don't know if this is a secret, and if she wants to tell you what we talk about, she can. I won't have any objection. But I think she should make that decision. When does she have lunch?"

"Twelve-thirty. She eats it here."

"I'd like to see her then. I'll call her at the bank and see if she's agreeable."

"Tell you what," said Mary Coffin, coolly. "Let me call her, so she'll know I'll be here, too. Okay?"

"Sure. Tell me how to find you, and I'll see you at twelve-thirty."

She told me, and I rang off. So Hazel Fine had a defender. I wondered what she was like.

Hazel and Mary Coffin lived about a block from the library, always one of my favorite places in any town. A little before noon, I drove by their house, then parked in front of the library and went in there to wait.

Libraries are full of lore and people who will help you find it. I had nothing particular in mind, and ended up reading about modern Israel, a place I'd never been nor ever expected to be. The book had lots of pictures and not too much text. It looked to me like the Israelites had picked themselves a tough hunk of dirt to live on. Desert and more desert; buildings built of stone and cement; a shortage of water and trees. What made that hard land so important to so many people that they'd soaked its sands with blood since the beginning of history? I couldn't tell from the pictures. On the other hand, it looked like a place the Navajos and Zunis and Hopis might like, so maybe there was some magic to it that I could not see in the photographs. I decided I preferred Martha's Vineyard.

That important decision made, I walked to Hazel Fine's house and knocked on the door.

A woman wearing what I immediately recognized as a housedress opened the door. I felt an instant pleasure. My grandmother had worn housedresses, but I hadn't known women even had such things anymore. The women I knew who did housework wore jeans or shorts or sweats, depending on the season.

"A housedress!" I said. "I haven't seen one of those in years! You must be Mary Coffin."

"And you must be J. W. Jackson. Come in."

"Of the Nantucket Coffins?" I asked, stamping my slushy Bean boots on the porch before stepping through the door.

She nodded. "Distant kin. There are a few of us here on the Vineyard, too, these days."

Mary Coffin's housedress was blue, and matched her eyes. Her dark hair was touched with gray and was cut in a sort of Prince Valiant bob. She wore comfortable black shoes and rimless spectacles. Now, she raised her voice. "Hazel, your visitor is here." To me she said, "Let me have your coat. I'll stick it here in this closet."

Another woman came into the room. Very attractive. Just this side of forty. Wearing banker's clothes: white blouse, woolen skirt (I saw the matching jacket folded on a chair across the room), low-heeled black shoes. Fair skin, thick curly dark hair, an inquisitive expression.

"How do you do? Mr. Jackson, is it? Have we met?" A pleasant voice with a lilt to it.

"No, we haven't met."

"Please sit down. I only have a short lunch period, so I'm afraid we don't have a great deal of time."

I took a chair. "I don't need much time." I looked at Mary Coffin, who looked back at me.

"Mary and I have no secrets," said Hazel Fine.

"I'm investigating the murder of a man named Lawrence Lovell. They called him Chug."

"Are you a policeman?" asked Mary Coffin.

"No."

"Then I don't think we have anything to say to you," she said. "I'll get your coat. Hazel, why don't you go back into the kitchen and finish your sandwich. I'll show Mr. Jackson out."

— 22 —

I stood up.

"Before I go," I said to Hazel Fine, "I should tell you that there were photographs of you in an album in Chug Lovell's house . . ."

"We know all about those photographs," said Mary Coffin. "If you've come to try blackmailing Hazel with them, you'll have no better luck than that wretched little Lovell man had. Now, you be on your way before I call a real policeman in here and have him arrest you."

I looked at Hazel's retreating back. "So he tried to blackmail you, too? He had better luck with some other women." Hazel paused, and I said, "The police know there were photographs, but they don't have them. I think the killer has them."

Hazel turned back toward me. I looked at Mary Coffin. She stood by the open closet door, my coat in her arms.

"I was a cop once," I said. "A woman who was also in his book has asked me to help her. So far, I don't think the police know about her or any of the other women he photographed, but that could change anytime. When it does, all of those women will be suspects. The police have already collected Chug's paraphernalia, so they know what went on in his house. They just don't know who was involved."

"Hazel hasn't been there for years," said Mary Coffin. "She was only a girl. She didn't know who she was, then."

"I was more than a girl," said Hazel, "but you're right. I didn't know much about myself then." She looked at me. "It was a long time ago. It seems almost like a dream."

"Well, it was a dream caught on film," I said. "I found you because someone remembered seeing your face in Chug's album, and if I can do it, so can the police. There were a lot of women, apparently, and the police will be interested in every one of them."

Hazel placed an immaculate hand on her chest. "You mean that I could become a murder suspect?" She wore an amused little smile.

"You could." I looked at Mary Coffin. "Or you could. On balance, I imagine you'd be a more logical choice."

Mary came into the living room and put my coat on a chair. She nodded her head. "Yes. I could have done it. I nearly did it a long time ago, in fact. That disgusting little man came here and tried to get money from Hazel. Threatened to show those filthy pictures to her boss, to get her fired, and to tell other island men about her, and to sell the pictures to those pornographic magazines that publish such things. I told him to do his worst, that it wouldn't make any difference to me, but that if he did I'd kill him. I got a butcher knife from the kitchen . . ."

"Yes," nodded Hazel, catching my eye. "She did. She actually got a knife. Chug went out and never came back. We never heard from him again, did we, dear?"

"No." Mary Coffin smiled at her, then looked at me. "We never did. Since then, if I happened to see him in the store or on the street, he'd go the other way or cross the road. I think he believed that I always carried that butcher knife in my purse, just for him."

"And he never did any of the things he threatened?"

"Not that we know of."

"And you never paid him any money?"

"Not one red cent."

I looked at Hazel. "While you were with Chug, did you ever look at the pictures in his albums?"

"Oh, yes. He'd get them out and we'd both look at them. He enjoyed them, and wanted me to enjoy them, too."

"Did you recognize any of the other women in his pictures?"

"No. It all happened a long time ago," she said. "Besides, I really didn't like pictures of women doing those things, so I didn't look at them very closely. To be frank, right now I'm not really sorry, even though I know you'd like to interview some of the other women."

"Why do you say that?"

"Because maybe one of those women did kill Chug Lovell. And if she did, I want her to get away with it."

She and Mary exchanged looks of complete understanding. I felt a crooked smile form on my face.

"Well," I said, "thank you both. I guess I'd better . . ."

"We're having sandwiches and soup in the kitchen," said Mary Coffin, who had been studying me. "If you haven't eaten, maybe you'd like to join us."

I hesitated. "Sounds good."

"Perhaps you'd like something to drink?"

"Beer?"

"Oh, dear. Will white wine do?"

"White wine will do just fine."

We went into the kitchen.

"Would you like to buy a ticket to a Christmas concert?" asked Hazel, as soon as we were seated at the table.

"Oh, Hazel," said Mary. "Have a little couth. Don't put the poor man on the spot."

"I want him to be on the spot," said Hazel. "The church needs all the money it can get. Well, Mr. Jackson? I assure you that it will be a very enjoyable evening for you. We have both an orchestra and a chorus, all island people—we have some very talented musicians, you know. Mary will be playing the oboe and recorder, and I will be singing. It's the night before Christmas Eve. Early and Baroque music, and traditional carols. We'd love to have you."

The turkey sandwich was moist and good, and the Graves was clean and refreshing.

"Is it really going to be as good as she says?" I asked Mary.

She nodded. "As a matter of fact, it is."

"In that case, I'll take two tickets."

"You're a shameless person," said Mary to Hazel. "Exploiting a guest like this. Well done. More wine, Mr. Jackson?"

I drove home with ideas moving around inside my skull. They were taking shape, for a change. I thought about them, turning them this way and that, until I came to my driveway.

The paved roads and streets were pretty much melted and free of snow, but there was sandy slush beside them. Beyond the slush, the ground was still white, but the once fine light snow was settling and becoming heavier as the winter sun worked on it. The snow had melted from the trees and bushes, and was beginning to melt in my driveway where the car tracks had cut through it to the sand beneath.

There was a new set of tracks among the old ones.

I turned in and stopped and looked at the tracks. Zee was working and I didn't get many other visitors. I felt tingly. I shifted into four-wheel drive and eased halfway down the driveway, then stopped and got out.

I walked down the driveway until I could see my house. There was smoke coming from the chimney, and Nash Cortez's pickup was in my yard. I walked back to the Land Cruiser and drove on in.

Nash was sitting on my couch watching a kitten drinking milk out of one of my saucers. "Look at that little fella," he said. "Hungry as a bear in the springtime." He pointed at the closed door of my spare bedroom. "Got his sister, well, not his sister, but a little girl cat looks just like him, in there. Should know the results of their leukemia tests tomorrow."

The kitten was black with one white paw.

"Only way you can tell 'em apart without turning them over and having a look, is this one's got a white front paw and the other one's got a white back paw. What do you think?"

"I think Mimi is going to love them."

"Boy, I hope so."

"How are my cats?"

"Terrific. Named 'em already. Oliver Underfoot and Velcro. Oliver's the big one. Always wound around your ankle when the two of them aren't sleeping or tearing around the house. And Velcro, she likes to hang on screens or your chest or the side of the couch. Like if you threw her against anything, she'd stick. Course Zee'll get to name 'em again, if she wants." He looked fondly at the kitten, which was now washing its face. "These two, I haven't got names for them yet. Haven't had them long enough."

"How about coffee?"

"That'd be good." He glanced around. "Place is looking good, J.W. Real homey. Zee'll like it."

"I hope so."

"Course she'll change things to suit her fancy. Women do that."

"I imagine."

"She'll say don't you think we might do this or that, or don't you think this or that would look nice, and what she means is she wants to do it. But that's all right, because she'll probably be right."

"As long as I have a place for my stuff, she can do anything she wants to."

The kitten had followed me into the kitchen and now followed me out again. I put coffee, milk and sugar on the table. Nash sampled his cup, stared at it with a wrinkled brow and sampled it again.

"Cinnamon," I said. Cuts the acid."

"It's good," he said. "Smooths out the brew. Worth remembering. I brought up two Kitty Litter boxes. One for each cat. I put their food out there by the stove."

"I saw it. She's going to love these kittens."

"Thought I'd put a red ribbon on one of them's neck and a green one on the other one. What do you think?"

"Great idea."

"Christmas colors, you know. Sure hope she likes 'em."

"She will."

"You think I ought to give her some candy or something, too?"

"I think the kittens will be enough, but you do what you like."

He rubbed his bony hands together. "Nice fire. New stove, isn't it?"

"Yep." I poured more coffee.

The kitten ran into the kitchen, then came bounding out again. Nash got down on his hands and knees and dug under my overstuffed chair. He brought out a small ball of tightly wound yarn. "Made 'em each one of these. Training mouse. Made a couple for Oliver and Velcro, too." He rolled the ball toward the kitten, which immediately attacked it. "I'll make a couple more for when I give these guys to Mimi."

"Good idea. Now, stop worrying. This is going to work out all right. I admit that Mimi may not exactly greet you with open arms when she comes to the door, but she'll have family there so she won't be able to make too big a fuss. The thing is, you give her the kittens before she can say anything. Just say merry Christmas and give them to her. Once she's got them, she'll love them. Besides, her grandchildren are going to be there. They'll love them, too. It'll be great."

"I don't know," said Nash, picking up his cup and putting it down again. "I don't know. Look, I got this idea. You and Mimi are friends. Maybe you could be there to sort of tell her what's going to happen. Tell her that I'm coming and not to get all worked up. You know, so when I get there, she'll be ready . . . What do you think?"

"Oh, no. I'm J. W. Jackson, not John Alden Jackson. You're on your own on this one, Nash. You have to bite the bullet sooner or later, so you may as well do it Christmas Eve. No, I'm not going to do it, so forget it."

"Yeah, yeah, okay. Maybe you're right."

"I know I'm right," I said. "Trust me. It'll be fine. It'll work out just fine."

But when Nash drove away, he didn't look like he was sure it was going to be fine.

I called the hospital and left a message inviting Zee to supper, then set about making it. A *fruits de mer* pie made out of stuff in my freezer: scallops, some pieces of flounder and some lobster meat, covered with Aunt Elsie's pie crust (which has helped me win a couple of blue ribbons at the county fair up in West Tisbury) and baked at 350 until the crust is just the right color. On the side, baby peas and mashed potatoes drooling with butter. Everything washed down with a jug of chenin blanc and topped off with coffee, cognac and Pepperidge Farm mint cookies. What fair maiden could resist such a feast?

Not Zee, who afterward sat on the couch and unzipped her uniform. "Oh, my. Fat city. Why does it feel so good to be so bad?"

When I had introduced her to the kittens and told her about Nash's plan to give them to Mimi, she had proclaimed that not only were the kittens sweet, but that I was sweet and Nash was sweet. Now I told her about Nash's notion that I should be at Mimi's house to smooth his arrival on Christmas Eve.

"Naturally, I told him that I absolutely wouldn't do it," I said.

She lay inside my curled arm and was looking at the kitten sleeping in the overstuffed chair off to our right. "Well, I think you should," she said. "Nash may bungle it, or Mimi might run him off before he can give her the kittens. It's best that you be there."

"I want to be here with you."

"You can come right back here as soon as Nash makes his delivery. I'll be waiting." She snuggled against me. "There. That's settled. So we're going to a concert, eh? That will be nice. I love Christmas."

— 23 —

The next day there was even less snow. Was my white
Christmas going to melt away before the Great Day
actually arrived? As I drove out along the West Tisbury road, I hoped that most people were feeling
more cheerful than I was, and I had a flashback to
Christmas in Edgartown.

Enterprising owners of Vineyard shops and inns,
always eager to extend or add to the island's tourist
seasons, offer *Christmas in Edgartown* in hopes of luring
prospective visitors down to enjoy what is called "an
old-fashioned Christmas." This idea, stolen more
or less whole hog from Nantucket, which had begun a
similar holiday practice for similar reasons some years
before, is manifest in exhibits of crafts and arts—
ornament making, wreath making and tree trimming,
among other things—bazaars, holiday movies and
songfests, wine tastings, skating parties, a variety
of tours, meals ranging from pancake breakfasts to
chowder and chili feasts, and other entertainments.

I had stood in the chilly wind long enough to watch
the Christmas parade go down Main Street, and then
gone up to attend Santa Claus's official arrival at the
park. Rudolph had not made an appearance, but a lot
of other red noses were there, including mine. These
noses and the mouths below them had been puffing
solid-looking clouds of steam into the winter air, but
their owners' cheerful hats and scarves and happy
faces were in sharp contrast to the thin gray sky which
lay over us, and the cold gray sea that surrounded us
and reached from horizon to horizon. We'd all felt
pretty good.

I hoped that everyone was still feeling as jolly, because I now was not. I had some more snooping to do,

and I was not sure I enjoyed the thinking that went with it.

I drove past Mimi Bettencourt's house, which looked quite Christmasish and cozy, then past Chug Lovell's house, which looked sad and abandoned amid its overgrowth of bushes and slushy-looking snow, then came to Vince and Phyllis Manwaring's house, which just looked empty. I drove in and parked behind the house. I opened the rear door of the Land Cruiser and got out the plastic bucket and the piece of coarse screen that I'd brought from home. Then I made a circumnavigation of the house, checking windows and doors as I went. There was no sign that anyone had been there since I had been there days before.

I stamped the snow from my boots on the porch, then got out Mimi's key and went inside. The house had that chilly feel that an empty house can get during the winter, and I turned the thermostat back up to seventy, so Vince and Phyllis would find a warm nest waiting for them when Vince came down for the holiday and Phyllis would join him, no longer needing to be afraid of being home alone.

The living room was as I remembered it. I got some newspaper from the kindling box beside the fireplace hearth, spread it on the floor and dug out a piece of the cardboard I'd previously seen in the ashes. I put the cardboard on my newspaper and dug some more until I came up with more bits of cardboard. Phyllis no doubt had her virtues, but building a decent fire was not among them. I looked at the scraps of cardboard. They were charred and black, but there was no doubt that they looked a great deal like they had once been part of the cover of a photograph album.

I put the screen across the top of my bucket and, using Vince's little fireplace shovel, began to shovel ashes bit by bit onto the screen. When I stirred them with my fingers, the ashes fell through and bits too big to pass through stayed on top. If there was nothing interesting on top, I would tip the screen and let the stuff fall into the bucket. A little cloud of soot was soon floating in the air, but I kept at it. When the bucket was full, I took it outside and emptied it in the woods behind the house. But not everything got thrown out. First I found metal rings such as held pages inside photograph albums, and finally, in a far corner of the fireplace, I found what I was hoping and not hoping to find: a bit of negative and part of a photograph, both partially burned but still identifiable.

The photo was of a nude woman and a partially clothed man engaged in what looked like, for her, a very uncomfortable sort of sex. The fire had taken away the woman's face, but had left the rest of her. It had taken away most of Chug Lovell's legs, but had left his face. He looked intent. It was an amateur shot, and I wondered if the woman even knew it was being taken and where the camera had been.

I turned on a floor lamp and examined the negative. A woman on her knees, looking up, her hands cuffed behind her, a nude man before her, looking down. A photo apparently taken from the camera in the ceiling. His face was not shown; I recognized hers.

I went back to the fireplace and screened the rest of the ashes. I found two more bits of negative with contents similar to that of the first one. There was too little left of the negatives to identify the participants. I put the cardboard, the photo and the negatives in a large envelope, and emptied the last bucket of ashes.

Then I found Phyllis's vacuum cleaner and cleaned up the fireplace and the living room rug. No need for Vince to know how careless Phyllis had been with her fire.

Then while I thought things over, I laid a new fire. Paper, kindling, larger pieces of wood, a birch log. Very cozy-looking. A Yule log for the senator-to-be and his wife. Even Phyllis could make this one burn. All she needed to do was light it.

I went to the phone and called Mimi Bettencourt's house. Mimi answered and I told her to tell Phyllis that I was up at her place, and that I knew Vince was coming down in a couple of days, so I was going to clean the house up a bit.

"Oh, how nice of you," said Mimi. "I'm sure she'll be very appreciative."

I doubted that. "It won't take long," I said. "There's not much to do."

"Well, it's very good of you. Drop by on your way home and have some tea. Wait, here she is now. You can talk to her yourself." I heard her call, "Phyllis! It's J.W. For you."

Phyllis's voice was less strained than it had been when last I'd seen her. She asked how I was and I told her that I was fine and then I told her what I'd told Mimi.

"Oh," she said. Then, quickly, "Well, don't bother, please. I'll take care of it. I'll come right up. Thank you very much, but . . . Yes, I'm coming up myself. Right away. I do thank you so much! Come down and visit Mimi instead. She'd love to see you. Goodbye."

The phone clicked and buzzed in my ear, and I sat back to wait, feeling the room slowly grow warmer as the furnace did its work.

I heard the car when it came into the yard, and had but a moment to wait for the sound of the back door of the house opening. I got up as Phyllis came into the living room. She was wearing an unbuttoned winter coat over slacks and a sweater, and there were short boots on her feet. Her hair, as always, looked newly permed. Her eyes flicked from me to the fireplace and back. She put a hand to her mouth and leaned against the deep chair that formed a part of the set of furniture that curled around the front of the fireplace. Her face was pale. She sank into the chair and put her other hand up to that pale face.

I gestured toward the envelope, which lay on the low table in front of the couch. "You didn't do a very good job with your fire," I said. "There are pieces of the albums and pictures here. Some negatives, too. Heather is in one. I imagine that's why you did it."

There was a pause while she looked at the floor. When she spoke, her voice was strange. "I meant to come back, but I just couldn't." She shuddered. "It was all so hateful. Besides, I thought I had time to clean things up. Mimi never told me she'd given you her key. I never knew until just now." She waved a well-groomed hand in a vague gesture. "Mimi just told me. She said she didn't want to worry me. Worry me." She raised her head and looked at me. "I knew then that I'd be too late, but I had to try, I had to hope that you hadn't looked at the fire too carefully. Oh dear, what will happen now . . .?" She put her hands between her knees and shook her head slowly back and forth.

"Do you want to tell me about it?"

She shook her head. "I don't think I should say anything more."

"Did Chug try to blackmail you?"

"I think I should call my husband . . . my lawyer . . ." She seemed uncertain.

"I think you did it because he showed you pictures

of Heather and asked for money. I think you were protecting your daughter."

She looked up at me, her teeth over her lower lip.

I went on. "I think he asked you to come to his house because he had something important to show you. I think that when you got there, he showed you his albums and told you that if you didn't pay him money, he'd sell them to a magazine and tell the island men all about Heather. Is that about it?"

"No!" Then, "How did you know that . . .?"

"I should have known it was you when you spilled your tea at Mimi's house and called someone a wicked man. We were talking about Chug's murder, and you spilled your tea. Do you know anything about archery? About how to shoot a bow and arrow?"

"No. Certainly not. Sport doesn't interest me."

"I understand why you want to lie. You've killed someone and you're afraid . . ."

"I'm not lying! I'm not afraid! I haven't killed anyone!"

"You and Mimi went to school together, and you practiced archery together. Mimi has an album with a picture of the two of you as students on the archery range. I haven't seen it, but Manny Fonseca has, and I doubt if Mimi will deny anything if the police ask her about it." I watched her close her eyes and sink into herself.

"Mimi told me once that you were tougher than you seemed to be," I said. "What I think happened is this. When Chug threatened to ruin Heather, you went sort of crazy. You grabbed his own bow and arrows, and you shot him. You weren't strong enough to pull that compound bow of his all the way back, but you were strong enough to pull it partway, and it was enough to put the arrow into him. Then you took the

albums and the negatives and you went home and
tried to burn them. But you were a wreck and you did
a bad job with the fire, then you fell apart and had to
go to Mimi's place so you wouldn't have to be alone
up here."

As I spoke, she opened her eyes and they grew larger and larger until they seemed to fill her white face.
She wiped at them with her hands. "I need a hankie,"
she said. "I'm not going to say anything. You're not
the police. I know I don't have to say anything."

"That's right. You don't have to say anything, and
I'm not the police. They don't know about you yet,
but if they see the stuff in this envelope, and talk to
the people I've talked too, you'll be in more trouble
than you are now."

She thought about that. "I need a hankie," she said
again, finally. "There's a box in the bedroom. Do you
mind if I get it?"

"This is your house. You can do whatever you
want."

She got up and went into the bedroom. After a
while I heard water running in the attached bathroom. When she came out again, her face had been
scrubbed clean of makeup. She sat down again, and
looked at me. "What do you mean 'if' they see the
things in the envelope? What do you mean by that?
And what do you mean when you say I'll be in a lot
more trouble than I am now? I'm already in trouble."

I looked at her. "Not with me," I said. "Not yet. I'm
not the conscience of my race." I told her how Chug
had tried to blackmail other women. "He was not a really nice guy," I said. "He got some money from
Heather and he's gotten it from other women too, for
years. But I guess it wasn't enough, so he came to you,
because you have a very rich husband. One woman I

talked to hoped that if one of Chug's victims had killed him, she'd get away with it. If I was a cop, it would be my job to make sure she didn't. But I'm not a cop anymore." I paused. "But I've got to know what happened."

She gestured toward the envelope. "It's a crime to withhold evidence. You have to give them that."

I held her eyes. "I haven't decided what to do with that, yet. I want to hear you first."

"Do you have a cigarette? Oh, never mind. I haven't smoked in ten years." She took a deep breath. "All right. First, he threatened to destroy Vince's career. You can imagine what that could have led to, if I'd fallen for that line. I would have had to lie and cheat and pay out a fortune for the rest of my life to keep Chug Lovell quiet. But I'll tell you frankly, Mr. Jackson, although my husband is a man who likes power, I don't care for politics, and I'm not sure that he should be in the senate. To tell you the truth, if that wicked little man had only threatened to show those pictures to Vince, I might have told him to get on with it, because Vince will forgive his children anything, and he would have given up his campaign. And then he would have absolutely destroyed Chug Lovell! Does that astonish you?"

"No," I lied, surprised by yet another woman.

"Vince is a hard man, and I think it best if he remain in the business world, where there are others like him to keep him in check. Did you know that he's actually talking with gangsters in Providence? People who own companies and have influence in the labor unions? But Heather's personal life is another matter. When Chug Lovell threatened to publish those pictures and show them to other men, I ... I ... Something snapped inside of me. I could see that bow of his in the next room. I ran there. I think he tried to stop me, but I got away. There was a quiver of arrows. I snatched up the bow and an arrow. I remember that the other arrows spilled on the floor all around me. We struggled, but I pushed him away. Then he came at me again, and I shot him. I could hardly pull the bow, but it was enough."

She paused and thought. "And you're right. I got the albums and I knew there must be cameras and negatives, so I got them, too. It was very strange. I felt very cool and deliberate, and I took my time and made sure I had everything. I found a camera in the closet and another one up above that mirror on the ceiling. I knew there had to be one there because of some of the pictures in the albums. I had a hard time finding my way up there, and I ruined my panty hose. I put everything in a box and went out. I didn't have to try to wipe away my fingerprints because I was wearing winter gloves." She brushed at something imaginary on her blouse. "I think that's all. I came home and emptied the cameras and burned everything I could. Then I took the cameras and threw them into the ocean down at South Beach." She looked at me. "Then I seemed to fall all apart. Or maybe I was falling apart before that. I couldn't sleep all night. In the morning I drove to Vineyard Haven and called the police from a phone at the ferry parking lot. I put a handkerchief over my mouth like I've seen them do in the movies. I told them about Chug. Then I went to Mimi's . . . What shall I do? What are you going to do?"

I looked at her. Phyllis Manwaring, murderess.

"I don't know what's going to happen to you," I said. "The police are on the case, and they're good at their work, so maybe someday they'll come knocking at your door. If they do, I suggest you get a good lawyer." I took the envelope from the table and handed it to her. "I imagine that if your husband got this stuff in a plain brown wrapper along with a blackmail note made out of letters cut from a newspaper, or some such thing, he might decide to quit the campaign. But whether that happens or not, this stuff is yours."

She stared at me for what seemed a long time, but probably wasn't. "You're not going to the police?"

"No."

Her face had a strange look to it, half hope, half doubt. "I don't know . . ."

"As you said, it's a crime to withhold evidence," I said. "By giving this envelope to you, I'm giving you a hammer to hold over my head. If I turn you in, you can turn me in. Even steven."

She hesitated. "Those pictures are disgusting. I don't really know what Vince would do if he saw them."

I shook my head. "I don't know if they're disgusting or not, because I think that what happens between grownups who agree about what they do to each other is their business. I also don't know what kind of a senator your husband might make, although the way you describe him doesn't make him sound too desirable. I don't live in Connecticut, so I don't have to deal with him. A good thing, too, because we've got enough problems with our own pols here in Massachusetts. I've got to go."

I didn't really have to go, but I didn't want to stay.

She stood up, holding the envelope in both hands. "I . . . I really don't know what to say . . ., what to do . . ."

"Why don't you just say nothing. Your husband will be down in a couple of days. Between now and then you can decide what to do. Maybe the two of you should go away together. A long trip. Around the world on an ocean liner, or something." I went out of the room, then went back in. She was still standing there. "It's Christmas," I said. "The Christians say that God sent his son so that we could be freed from our sins and be born again. They celebrate his arrival on earth about now. You might keep that in mind."

I went out into the winter air.

— 24 —

I drove to Oak Bluffs, parked and went in to see Heather Manwaring. Harriet, her receptionist, recognized me, and said to have a seat, since Heather had a client with her. She lifted a phone and told her boss that I was in the waiting room. I read a copy of *National Geographic* while I sat there. One of the nice things about *National Geographic* is that you can read a copy that's two years old, as this one was, and it will still be interesting. In this edition I read about a city being excavated in Jordan. A place given passing mention in the Bible, but now of considerable interest to archaeologists. Just as I was getting interested myself, the door to Heather's office opened, and her client came out. He nodded to the receptionist, and left. I went in.

"Well?" Heather looked very professional in her woolen suit.

I got right to it. "I think I know who killed Chug Lovell, but I've decided not to tell you who did it."

She stared at me with surprise. "That's a very

strange thing to say. I paid you to find out and tell me."

"Actually, you just paid me to find out. I've done that, I think. But I still have the money you gave me, so you can have it back if you want it. You may need it for your lawyer."

"My lawyer? Why? I didn't kill Chug!"

"We've been over this before. It's not what we do, but what people think we do. You were Chug's girl-friend for several months. Your fingerprints must be all over the place up there. Sooner or later, the police may trace you through them and come to see you."

"But I didn't do it!"

"I know that, but they won't. On the other hand, I doubt if they'll be able to pin the hit on you. They may suspect you, but that's all they'll manage. Insufficient evidence."

"I don't want to spend the rest of my life being a suspect for a murder I didn't commit! You've got to tell me—and the police—who did it!"

"I'm not going to do that."

"Then when they come to see me, I'll tell them ex-actly what you've just told me! Then you'll have to tell them the truth! I'm not going to take blame for some-thing I didn't do!"

"You won't like what I tell them. You'll wish I never told them a thing. I think that if you just keep your mouth shut, you'll be better off. Did you ever touch Chug's bow?"

"His bow? No. I don't know anything about bows and arrows."

"In that case, I doubt if you'll even be much of a suspect. The bow was never wiped clean after the killing, and if your prints aren't on it, they can't stick you with the job. They'll look somewhere else."

"But they'll never stop looking at me! I insist that you tell me what you know!"

"You'll remember that I warned you that I might find out something you would wish I hadn't found out. I think I've done that. I really don't think you want to know."

"You have a lot of gall to think that you know what I want to know!" She sat back and gathered herself together. After a while, she said, "All right. Tell me why I don't want to know."

"Because the person who killed Chug is someone you love very much, who killed him because he had pictures of you that he said he was going to sell to magazines and then spread around on the island, so all of the local men could see them. I've seen a couple of those pictures, myself, and I assure you that you wouldn't have wanted that done."

"You've seen the pictures?"

"Some of them. But now most of the pictures have been destroyed. The negatives, too. The person who killed Chug burned them."

She put a hand to her mouth and stared at her desk. I leaned forward. "The person who burned those photographs did a brave and dangerous thing. And did it for you. That person is the one who is in real danger if I tell the police what I know. You're a pretty tough woman, I think. I hope you're tough enough to keep your mouth shut about this if the cops come."

She stared at me with hard, watery eyes. "You ask a lot! You ask a damned lot! You tell me this and ask me to trust you! Why should I believe you? Tell me that!"

"Because I have told you this. It would have been a lot easier to have told you that I didn't know anything.

Maybe that's what I should have done. Maybe I was wrong to tell you the truth. Maybe you should pick up that phone and call the cops right now."

She glared at me.

I stepped away from the desk. "I'll return your money," I said. "That way we'll be shed of each other." I started toward the door.

"Wait." I turned. She was standing behind her desk. "Keep the money. I don't want us to be shed of each other. We're in this together. I got you into it, so both of us are in it." She leaned on the desk. "Someday will you tell me who?"

I went out of the office without answering.

At 7 A.M. the next day my phone rang. It was Zee.

"Hi," she said. "Come for supper. It's time we planned the Christmas feast."

"It usually takes me all night to plan the Christmas feast," I said, panting heavily into the phone.

"I know! See you at my place when I get home. I've got to run! Bye."

It was beginning to snow again when I drove through West Tisbury, past Alley's store, and past the field where the statues were dancing cheerfully in spite of the midwinter dusk, until I found Zee's driveway. The snowflakes falling slowly out of the dark sky gave renewed promise of a white Christmas after all.

I got a fire going in Zee's fireplace, and put some mulled cider to warm on her stove. I'd add the rum I'd brought when she had her shoes off and was sitting in front of the fire.

She had enough odds and ends of veggies and meats to make up a good refrigerator soup, so I did that. Later, I'd mix up some cornbread to go with it. A meal fit for a queen.

By the time Zee got home from the hospital, it was

dark, and the snow was falling faster. She came right into my arms and stayed there awhile. Then she looked at the fire, and said, "There's only one way to make this better. Wait right here."

She went into her bedroom and soon reappeared wearing her woolly robe and her slippers. She came back into my arms. "There," she said. "Now it's perfect."

I could not but agree, for under the robe was nothing else but Zee herself. After appreciating this for a time, I sent her to the couch in front of the fireplace while I got her a rummy mulled cider, and mixed up the cornbread and put it in the oven. Then I got my own cider and joined her.

She leaned against me and we looked into the fire, as our ancestors had surely done ten thousand years before, when the winter winds blew beyond the opening of their cave and they wondered if the moon goddess would answer their prayers before they perished from the cold, and would make the sun shine longer each day until it was summer once again.

"What's new in the emergency ward?"

"No mopeds, so no moped accidents. A man with chest pains. Indigestion, we think. The usual. What's new in the sleuthing biz?"

I had been thinking about how to answer that question, for she was sure to ask it. We would be getting married in a few months, and I had theorized that once she was my wife it would be a good idea to always tell her everything. It seemed as if that was a good idea, but I didn't know if I would ever actually do it, because there would always probably be things—such as, maybe, a chance meeting with Angie Bettencourt—that would only annoy her. Maybe it was better for husbands and wives to keep a few things to themselves. Had I been more successful as a husband when I'd been one before, I would have had more confidence in my thoughts.

Meanwhile, Zee wasn't my wife, yet, and I wasn't sure what to tell her. Not because I couldn't trust her with secrets, but because being trusted with them might make her life more difficult. She and I didn't walk quite the same moral paths, and what might be ethically acceptable for me could be unacceptable to her.

On the other hand, I thought that thought seemed pretty condescending.

So I told her about finding the pictures and negatives, and about my talk with Phyllis Manwaring, and when I was through, Zee didn't say anything. She just looked into the fire.

My nose told me that the cornbread was ready, so I left Zee and went into the kitchen, and got two trays ready: soup, cornbread and mulled cider. A little salt and pepper and some butter on the side. I brought Zee's tray to her and then got my own. We put them on the coffee table and began to eat. Nobody said anything for a while.

"You never know, do you?" said Zee, finally. "You just never know about people. What they'll do. It never fails to mystify me. So you're not going to tell the police?"

"No. What good would it do?"

"It would give them a killer."

"I don't think that Phyllis Manwaring is a killer. I think she's just a woman who killed somebody who was lucky nobody ever did it to him sooner. What do you think?"

She was a healer by both profession and temperament. "I don't think anybody deserves to get killed."

"I didn't say he deserved it, I just said he was lucky nobody did it to him sooner. Do you think Phyllis should be turned in?"

"No. I don't know. I guess I don't."

"Are you sorry I told you about all this?"

This time she was sure. "No. No, I want you to tell me things. I always want you to tell me."

I pushed my tray off to one side and put my feet on the coffee table. "In that case," I said, "I have another confession."

She flicked her great, dark eyes at me, and stuffed a last bit of cornbread into her mouth. "What?"

"I already planned the Christmas feast. I came here under false pretenses."

She pushed her tray to one side, and put her feet up beside mine. "Oh, dear, what could they be?"

"Allow me to help you out of that robe, and I'll try to explain myself as I go along."

"Gracious me, what can you possibly mean?" Her eyes floated to the clock on the mantel. "Oh, oh! Sorry, Jefferson! The explanation will have to wait. It's time for the Grinch!"

Unlike me, Zee has a television set. So first we watched the Grinch steal Christmas yet again, and then I illustrated my true intentions.

In the morning I made cranberry pancakes for us before Zee went off to work. As I washed up the dishes and made the bed, the idea of being married to Zee, always a good one, was seeming better and better. I was happy.

Later, back in Edgartown, I met the chief on South Water Street. I had just come over from Collins Beach, after rowing in from having a look at the *Mattie* and the *Shirley J*. There was an inch of new snow on the ground, the sky was pale blue and it was cold, but so far there was no ice on the harbor. A few bold, freezing scallopers were still out dragging in Cape Pogue Pond and Katama Bay, and I was glad that I wasn't going to be one of them for a few more days. I was headed for the Wharf pub for a little something to warm my innards.

The chief was hunched against the sunny side of the bank, out of the wind that was blowing down Main Street, getting his pipe stoked up. There weren't any perpetrators in sight, so he had only Christmas shoppers to worry about. No problem.

"Well," he said, "how's private eyeing? Solved the crime yet?"

"Naturally," I said. "The butler did it. I knew it all the time."

"You'd better tell Dom Agganis. He still thinks it was somebody else."

"You tell him," I said. "He probably wouldn't believe me. I'm a mere civilian."

"And I'm a mere small-town cop who can't be trusted to understand anything as complicated as a murder investigation. You haven't come around asking me questions for a while. Why not?"

"It's Christmas. My mind is on peace and good will and cats, not crime."

The chief puffed his pipe. "Maybe you'd better get it back on crime. I called you earlier this morning, but nobody was home."

"I was having breakfast with my bride-to-be up in West Tisbury. What was the message?"

"Got a call from Vineyard Haven. Somebody thinks they saw Joey Percell come off the early boat. I phoned Nash Cortez and gave him the news. Now I'm giving it to you. People are on the lookout for him, but so far nobody's confirmed that he's really on the island. Still, I'd keep my eyes open, if I were you.

Joey's got a thin skin but a long memory, they say, and if he's down here, it's for no good reason."

"If he gets too mean, we can make him go scalloping for a week in January. That should take some of the steam out of him."

"You just watch yourself. We don't have anything on him, so we couldn't pull him in even if we found him."

I looked at the Christmas shoppers on Main Street leaning against the wind that was trying to blow them down into the parking lot in front of the yacht club. They clutched their cheery wool hats with mittened hands while they gazed into windows bright with red and green decorations. They seemed happy and impervious to the cold. There were no Joey Percells in their thoughts.

"If my snitches are right," I said, "Joey's boss is interested in Vince Manwaring's campaign. Something about having pull with some unions Vince would like to have on his side come next November. Vince gets the union votes, Joey's boss gets some pull with Vince. Maybe Joey's down here on that business. Maybe he's going to see Vince. Vince is coming down this weekend, I'm told."

"You're told a lot more than I am. What bird has been singing to you?"

"Phyllis Manwaring has been staying with Mimi Bettencourt. She's the one that says Vince will be down. And you're the one who said Joey's boss was interested in Vince."

"I never said anything about any unions."

"Maybe I just made that up. Anyway, maybe Joey's down here on business."

"I don't think he's here to celebrate the holidays. Question is, whose business is he on? His boss's or his own?" A cruiser came slowly down the street. It stopped, and the chief got in the passenger side. He pointed his pipe at me. "You take care, now." The cruiser took a left and went up North Water Street. Maybe a Christmas crime wave had broken out on Starbuck Neck.

I went down to the Wharf pub and had a bottle of Beck's dark while I did some thinking. It tasted so good, that I had another one. I also had a sandwich. Man does not live on beer alone.

I drove to Nash Cortez's house. He met me at the door. I noticed that his shotgun was leaning against the wall. He followed my glance.

"Got her loaded with rock salt. Won't kill anybody, but it'll sure put the hurt on 'em. Salt in the wounds, you know."

"The zero hour is approaching," I said, as Velcro and Oliver Underfoot came galloping noisily out of the kitchen to see what was going on. "Tomorrow night Mimi gets the kittens that are up at my house, and the next morning Zee gets these two little characters."

Nash looked worried. "Hey, J.W., you sure you won't go out to Mimi's before I show up, and sort of, you know, let her know what's happening? I mean, blast it all, what if she . . .?"

"All right, all right," I said. "I'll go out there ahead of you, and I'll be there when you get there."

He beamed and seemed to grow taller. "Gosh, that's damn fine news, J.W., damn fine!"

Oliver Underfoot was wrapped around my ankle, purring. He seemed to have grown a couple of inches since last I'd seen him. Velcro, too, seemed bigger. She made a jump and attached herself to Nash's pant leg.

"Here, you little rascal, quit that!" Nash peeled Velcro off his leg and held her in his big, red hands. "Gonna miss these little fellers."

"You play your cards right, and Mimi will let you hang around and play with her two."

Nash petted Velcro and I sure hoped I was right.

"Trust me," I said, wondering if I was.

Out in the street I heard a car slow and stop.

"No nibbling," admonished Nash, as Velcro took a tentative nip of his thumb. Velcro nibbled some more. They were gentle little nibbles. Nash said, "No nibbling," again, but he didn't pull his thumb away.

I moved over and looked out the window. A dark car was parked behind my Land Cruiser. I couldn't see its license plate. I heard footsteps on the porch, then there was a knock on the door.

Nash and I looked at each other. Nash put down the cat and walked over to his shotgun. I wished that he had one of those doors that has a window in it so you can see who's standing outside, but such was not the case. I opened the door.

A man I didn't know was standing there, his hands in the pockets of a long, dark winter coat. His face was a very ordinary one. It did not belong to Joey Percell, but maybe Joey had a friend. His hand lifted swiftly out of his pocket. It held a piece of paper.

"Excuse me," he said, "I'm trying to find Pine Street, and this map hasn't helped me a bit. Can you point me in the right direction? It's my first time on the island, and I'm a lost soul."

I looked over his shoulder at his car. Now I saw that the back seat was piled with brightly wrapped Christmas presents.

I told him how to find Pine Street.

He smiled. "Thanks. And merry Christmas!"

"Merry Christmas to you, too."

I watched him get into his car and drive off.

I shut the door and looked at Nash.

"I don't want to live like this," he said. "Do you?"

"No," I said, "but I don't think you have to."

"What do you mean?"

"I mean I don't think that Joey Percell has any reason to come after you. He already gave you his message."

"Damned lot of good it did him!" huffed Nash. "Takes more than a punch on the jaw to shut me up if I feel like talking!"

"Yeah, but now that you've decided to be sweet to Mimi Bettencourt, you've shut up on your own account. You've done Joey's work for him."

"Well, hell . . ." Nash's voice trailed off. "Hmmmmm . . . Damn, J.W., you may be right. Now if that doesn't beat all."

"Let's talk about the kittens," I said. So we did that, and worked out the details of the Christmas deliveries. Then, after assuring nervous Nash once again that I would prepare Mimi for his arrival, I went home and phoned her.

"Mimi, after I left that message from Shrink Williams, did Phyllis ever phone him?"

"Why yes, I believe she did."

"Did she go see him?"

"If she did, she didn't tell me about it."

"Did she go out?"

"Yes, she went out, but she said she was going to do some shopping. What's this all about, J.W.?"

"Is she his patient?"

"Not that I know of. You're awfully interested in Phyllis all of a sudden. What's going on?"

"Are they lovers?"

"Lovers!" Mimi cried, "What an idea . . ." But then her voice faded off. "My goodness," she said, thoughtfully. "Phyllis and Cotton Williams. Well, well . . . Where did you come up with this one, J.W.?"

"Vince isn't around much, and according to Zee, Shrink has a new woman. I found Shrink up at the

Manwaring place looking for Phyllis. He'd heard about the murder in New York and had rushed to the island to offer her aid and comfort. I got the impression that he knew Vince was still on the mainland."

"Ah. And when Phyllis heard he was back on the island, she made a phone call and went out shopping. You may have a case, J.W. Well, well, isn't this interesting? Do you want to tell me what this is all about? Have you joined the moralists or something?"

"I've always been a moral paragon, Meem. You know that. No, it's just that if I got this figured out, somebody else probably has, too."

I rang off and looked up Shrink Williams's office number. His receptionist answered. Yes, Dr. Williams was in, but he was with a patient and couldn't be disturbed. I asked her when his business day ended, and she said that since it was Saturday and the night before Christmas Eve, he would be leaving at four. I told her it was important for me to talk to him and left my name and number.

I noted that Shrink's home and office addresses were the same. He lived and worked on West Chop, not far from where Hazel Fine and Mary Coffin lived. I wondered if they knew each other.

I got my old police .38 out of the drawer at the bottom of the gun case where I kept my shotguns and my father's deer rifle, loaded it and put it in my pocket. I didn't know if I'd have time to pull this off, because the Christmas concert started at seven-thirty, and I'd have to be back home before that to get myself spruced up so Zee would not have to hide her face in shame when the two of us went into the church.

I gave Shrink five minutes to phone me, and when he didn't, I drove to Oak Bluffs.

— **25** —

I went into the hospital emergency room. Zee was there, looking terrific in her white uniform. One of the great things about Zee was that she looked just as good dressed or undressed. It was a virtue shared by few other women I knew. Most of the rest of them looked better either one way or the other.

"Hi," I said.

She had a little Christmas angel pinned on her dress. "Hi," she said. "Are you an emergency?"

"No. I'm looking for Joey Percell. Is he here? If he is, it will save me a lot of time. Do you know him?"

"No. He's that guy that slugged Ignacio Cortez, isn't he? Why would I know him? And why would he be here?"

"Actually," I said, truthfully, "I just came by to see if you're coming by my house before the concert, or if I'm going to pick you up."

"You're going to pick me up, of course. About a quarter till seven. Why are you looking for Joey Percell?"

"He's on the island, they say. I think I know why."

"Why?"

A man and a woman came in through the door. The man could barely walk. The woman wasn't helping him a whole lot, although she had an arm around his shoulder.

"Putting the star on the tree," said the woman in a loud voice. "Fell off the ladder. Some Christmas. Well, isn't anybody gonna help us? Well?" She didn't seem to have too much holiday spirit.

"Excuse me," said Zee, and went to meet the man and woman.

I went out and drove to Vineyard Haven. Dr. Cotton Williams's office was attached to his house. I parked up the street and looked things over. It was cold, and I wished that the heater in the old Toyota worked better. I found the country and western station that I can get from Rhode Island, and listened to the C and W folks mix sentimental songs about the holidays with more traditional ones about people doing or being done wrong. Reba sang the good old one about her man having a lady up in Boston, then Kenny sang "Silent Night," while I hummed along. I was sorry I hadn't asked the chief if Joey had arrived in a car or on foot.

A middle-aged man walked out of a back door behind Shrink's office, circled back to the street, got into a car parked not far from mine and drove away. I thought the back door was not a bad idea. A patient could leave the office and enjoy the illusion that nobody out front would know who had been in there with Shrink. I wondered if that was a normal office design for psychiatrists and psychologists. I guessed it probably was.

There were several cars parked on the street, but they seemed empty. I got out of the Land Cruiser and walked down to the end of the street and back. I had been right. No one was in any of the cars.

I opened the glove compartment and extracted, not gloves, for I have never seen a glove in anyone's glove compartment, but my emergency flask of cognac, which I keep there in case the St. Bernard never comes. I poured an ounce into the stainless steel cup that threaded onto the flask, and sipped it. Not bad.

Emmy Lou was singing a rock and roll song. I don't normally like rock and roll songs, but when Emmy Lou sings one I listen. Emmy Lou and I go back a long way.

The sun was very low when I saw Joey Percell come walking up the sidewalk. He was wearing a winter cap and a down jacket and Bean boots. I imagined that when he finished his work here, he planned to walk back downtown, get on the ferry and go home. I wondered where he'd spent his day after he'd located Shrink's office and home and learned, as I had, when Shrink got off work.

I looked at my watch. Four o'clock. A woman walked out of the back door of Shrink's office, circled to the street and walked past me up the street. Last customer of the day.

Joey paused and pretended to be opening the door of a car. He was very good at blending into a background. He wasn't really doing anything, but he looked like he belonged there. No one would have looked at him twice or remembered him if they had.

After a few minutes, a woman—Shrink's receptionist, I guessed—came out the front door of the office, looked back and called, "Merry Christmas, Doctor!", and walked away down the street.

Joey waited five minutes, then crossed the street to the house. I got out of the Land Cruiser and walked across, too. I watched him press the bell at the front door of Shrink's house, and got to him just as Shrink opened the door.

Joey looked at me. His hands were in his pockets.

"Hi, Joey," I said.

"What is it?" asked Shrink, looking at us. "Hello. Jackson, isn't it? I got your message. In fact, I just phoned you. I'm afraid my office hours are over, gentlemen . . ."

Joey Percell looked at me. "This is none of your business. Get lost or I'll lose you."

"We outnumber you, Joey, so don't get snotty."

"What's going on here?" asked Shrink, uneasily.

Joey kept his eyes on me. "This clown with the glasses don't count. There's just you and me, bucko, and there's more of me than you. So fuck off." He took his hands from his pockets. He was wearing more of his favorite leaded gloves.

"You can give Shrink your message, Joey. We won't try to stop you. But keep your hands to yourself or we will."

Joey flicked his hard eyes up the street. He wanted to look behind him, but he didn't dare turn his back to me.

"All right, what's going on here?" asked Shrink in a semi-firm voice. "What do you men want?"

"We? We who? We where?" Joey's voice was like a rusty knife.

"We," I said. "Me and Smith and Wesson. Right here." I wiggled the pistol in my jacket pocket. "It's three to one, Joey. Not good odds. Why don't you give Dr. Williams your message and then we'll go down to the boat and you can go back to your wife and kiddies so you can all be together when you open your presents Christmas morning." I glanced at Shrink. "This is the guy I wanted to tell you about when I called. His name is Joey Percell, and he works for some big-time hoods over in Providence. He's a messenger. Give him the message, Joey, but put your hands in your pockets first."

Joey stared at me, then put his hands in his pockets. His eyes were thin and flat. He looked at Shrink.

"Break off from Phyllis Manwaring. You gotta have some ass, get it somewhere else. You don't break it off, we cut off your balls and shove them down your fucking throat. And you keep your mouth shut about her and you. You don't, and we take out your fucking tongue."

"What . . .? What . . .?" Shrink was stunned.

"He means it, Shrink," I said. "I don't know if it's good advice, but it comes from his boss's heart."

"Now, see here . . ." said Shrink.

"Think about it," I said. "No tongue, your balls down your throat. Not a good way to live. All right, Joey, I think that's all you have to say. Let's walk downtown. Goodnight, Doctor."

"Now, wait just a moment . . ." said Shrink.

The sun had gone down. Joey Percell was exhaling little puffs of steam in the cold, midwinter air. He looked like some sort of demon. "I'll get you for this," he said to me. "This is twice you've fucked with me. Nobody fucks with me twice."

"If you don't start walking," I said, "I'm going to put six into you right here."

"I'll kill you for this," he said.

"Walk."

He turned and walked down the street. I walked behind him. At the foot of the street we took a right and walked past the library. We walked until we got downtown, then turned left and walked down to the ferry dock. The five o'clock ferry was loading.

"Stop, Joey," I said. He stopped and turned to face me. His eyes were hooded and cold.

"You got your ticket, Joey?" I asked.

"Yeah."

"You have a hard time doing things right on this island, Joey. I don't think it's your kind of place. I think you'll be better off if you never come back."

"You're going to wish you'd never been born."

"You're going to miss your boat."

He turned and walked up the gangway. I waited till the boat pulled out, then walked back to the Land Cruiser and drove home.

I have two showers at my house, one indoors and one outdoors. The outdoor one is the shower of

choice, but not at this time of year. I showered and
shaved, taking my time and wondering if maybe this
year I should grow some hair on my face. A handle-
bar moustache, maybe, or maybe a Vandyke. I put
my comb under my nose. The Charlie Chaplin look.
Nah.

I got into a green turtleneck, matching green thrift
shop pants and my red thrift shop sport coat. Some
guy my size had decided to live a less colorful life just
as I had decided to live a more colorful one. Another
example of God's mysterious master plan.

I drove to West Tisbury and picked up Zee, who,
naturally, was looking splendid. She was wearing a
pale wool dress which contrasted nicely with her long,
black hair. She wore a red, green and silver pin over
her left breast, and looked like one of Santa's favorite
fantasies.

We kissed and went off to church. I don't go to
church too often, so I was interested, as usual, in the
architecture of the place. I thought that it might be
nice to convert a church into a house. You'd have to
use a little imagination, but it could really be neat. I
suggested this to Zee.

"A church is supposed to be a spiritual place," said
Zee. "You're not the spiritual type most of the time."

"I'm more spiritual than most people think," I
said. "Why, I bet that I'm at least as spiritual as . . .
let's see . . ."

Just then, the singers and musicians entered and
took their places. I recognized Mary Coffin and Hazel
Fine. They were wearing long gowns and looked
quite splendid, as, in fact, did their fellow singers and
musicians.

The program was called *Christmas Through the Ages*.
It began with Gregorian chants, continued with
Christmas music from the early, baroque, and classical

periods, and concluded with traditional popular carols sung by both the singers and the audience. I have my complaints about Christianity, but I have to give it credit for having inspired some of the loveliest music I've ever heard.

When it was over, we walked out into the cold winter night, arm in arm. All around us people leaving the church seemed happy and gentle.

"I love Christmas," said Zee, "and I love you too."

"It's because Christmas is a spiritual season and I'm a spiritual person," I said. "Why, I bet I'm at least as spiritual as . . ."

"Good evening," said Mary Coffin. "Did you enjoy the performance?"

"I like the way you asked them that, dear," said Hazel Fine. "Now, of course, they must say that they did, or else run the risk of offending us."

"We loved it," said Zee.

I introduced her to them and them to her.

"Have you time to join us for some Christmas punch?" asked Mary.

"Yes."

So we went to their house and found ourselves mixing with the rest of the singers and musicians and other members of the audience.

Someone had taped the performance, and it was playing as background music. The punch was laced with at least two kinds of rum, and hit the spot.

Zee, being the most beautiful woman there, as usual, had attracted the attentions of several men, and was talking to two or three of them when Hazel floated up to me.

"Have you solved your crime, Mr. Jackson?"

"It's not exactly my crime."

"But have you solved it?"

"Let's say I'm no longer trying to solve it."

"You're an evasive fellow. Has justice been served?"

"I think so. I really did like your performance tonight."

"And I think your fiancée is stunning."

We smiled at each other. "I'm giving her two kittens for Christmas," I said.

"Perfect," said Hazel. She lifted her cup and touched it to mine. "Happy holidays."

— **26** —

It was the day before Christmas, and Ignacio Cortez was a nervous wreck. His two kittens, on the other hand, were feeling good, as they tore after each other through my house.

"Do you think I should wear a jacket and tie? Or maybe even my suit? Or should I just look normal? I mean, you know, wear an ordinary shirt and pants like I usually wear? What time are you going over to Mimi's place? When do you think I should show up?"

It was midmorning, and I was fixing us some pre-Christmas cheer: rum in warm cider. It would warm me up and quiet him down. I gave him his cup.

"It won't hurt you to wear a tie. That way Mimi will know you come in peace. The important thing is for you to keep from making wisecracks."

"What do you mean? What wisecracks?"

"I mean, no remarks about how come she's got reindeer decorations when you'd think that anybody who's an animal rights person must know that Santa is ruthlessly exploiting his little deer by making them pull his sleigh. And no remarks about Rudolph's nose and him being another case of animal forced labor. That sort of thing."

"Say," said Nash, his eyes lighting up. "That's pretty good. I never thought about that."

"Well, don't think about it now, either. And no comments about her food. It'll all be vegetarian stuff. No talk about turkey, or Tiny Tim and his Christmas goose, or about roast beef. You watch your tongue, you might get invited to stay awhile."

"Okay, okay." Nash drank his cider. "You really think this will work? I tell you, J.W., I'm nervous as a cat in a dog pound."

"Relax. It's going to be fine," I said, wondering if it was. "Let's go over it again. Are you sure you have room for the cat boxes in your pickup?"

"Sure. Plenty of room."

"Make sure you warm up the cab before you put them in."

"No problem."

"And don't forget you have to bring their litter box and litter and dishes and kitten food. I'll have it all ready here for you to pick up."

It was a gray day, but not cold. There was still a bit of snow on the ground and some hope of more tomorrow. I like to have some symbolic snow falling on Christmas morning. It makes me feel as I did when I was a little kid, when my father and my sister and I opened our few presents and were happy together.

"You show up at Mimi's at five-thirty," I said. "I'll already be there."

"Make sure you are," said Nash. "Maybe I ought to bring some candy, too."

"Candy can't hurt a bit."

"Flowers, too?"

"It's a good idea, but this is Sunday, so I don't know where you'd find them. I think the kittens will do the job all by themselves."

"Oh, yeah." Nash nodded, then quickly pulled back his cuff and looked at his watch. "Say, I'd better go to Mass! I'm going to be late!" He tossed down his cider and headed out the door. "See you later!"

I put on a tape of the Harry Simeone Chorale singing carols, including the one about the little drummer boy, and let the music fill the house.

I took my Christmas dinner goose out of the freezer so it could thaw, put some scallops in a marinade made out of yogurt and tikka paste, then started four loaves of Betty Crocker's white bread and set them to rise. In the afternoon I made a steamed pudding in the old metal form my mother's mother had once owned, and made up a ball of Aunt Elsie's never fail piecrust to be used tomorrow when I made the apple and pecan pies. I put the ball of potential crust in the fridge, then I baked the bread and, except for the half a loaf I immediately ate, and the bit I fed to the kittens, set the loaves to cool. While all this was happening, I had a few more cups of spiked cider.

Fat city!

I captured the kittens and put them in their boxes, then stacked the litter, litter box, dishes and food beside them.

Time for Zee to arrive. Time, too, to go to Mimi's. I phoned ahead to see if it was okay. Angie answered the phone. There was a lot of noise in the background.

"Everybody's here," said Angie. "Ted and me, and my sister and her husband and their kids are down from the mainland. Mom is happy as a cloud in a blue sky. Come on by."

I hung up as Zee arrived. I told her I was going to

Mimi's and that I'd be back at six, about the marinading scallops I planned to have for supper and that Nash Cortez would be coming by in a little while to pick up the kittens and kitten gear.

"Is Angie over there?"

I'd hoped that she wouldn't ask. My voice sounded abrupt. "Yes. And Just Ted, too. And her sister and her family. And Mimi. And maybe somebody else I don't know about. Do you want to come with me?"

"No. Why should I?" She took off her coat.

"So you can keep an eye on us." I was irked.

She tossed the coat onto the couch. "No. You go on."

My jaws felt tight. I got the bottle of wine I was giving Mimi for Christmas and went out. I was glad to feel the chill air against my face. I wondered if Angie's name was always going to do this to Zee and me.

I drove through the darkness to Mimi's house. It was ablaze with light, and there were two extra cars in the yard. I recognized Just Ted's.

I knocked on the door and was welcomed with kisses from Angie and Mimi. Someone took my wine bottle and put it under the tree. I shook hands with Just Ted and the visitors from the mainland, and met Mimi's three grandchildren. The house had that filled, happy feeling that comes when a family that likes itself has gathered. There were cookies and a punch bowl on the table, and wine and liquor bottles on a chest that had become a bar. The punch bowl held a mixture of fruit juices and soda water, and was popular with both the children and their parents. Just Ted and Angie had opted for stronger stuff. I joined them, then followed Mimi into the kitchen. She was busy stirring this and that and peeking into the oven. The room smelled wonderful.

I told her that Nash Cortez would be dropping by. She hesitated, then began stirring again.

"He comes bearing gifts," I said. "He wants to mend rifts."

"Does he?"

"He does. Now I know that you two have had your differences, but . . ."

"Our differences!"

". . . But he really wants to make peace."

Her spoon clattered against the bowl. "Is that a fact?"

"Yes. Come on, Meem, it's Christmas. Nash wants to be your friend . . ."

"Some friend he'd be!"

"Meem, he really means it. He's been making all this fuss because he likes you."

"Likes me? Likes me? Well, if he acts like he does because he likes me, I'm certainly glad he doesn't dislike me!"

"Meem, he doesn't own any rabbits."

The spoon clattered, then slowed. "What?"

"You remember. He came over here that day I was working here, and told you he only wanted your greens so he could fatten up his rabbits. Well, Nash doesn't have any rabbits."

"No rabbits?"

"No. He was being foolish that day, but all he wanted was to catch your eye. He wants you to see that he's there."

"Oh, I see that he's there! I can see that!"

"He likes you, Meem. He probably more than likes you. He wants you to like him."

"He has a damned funny way of showing it."

"He knows he's been foolish. Now he wants to make up for it. He's coming by and he's bringing you some presents. A peace offering."

The spoon started again. "Well . . ."

"If you don't want him to come in, say so, and I'll go out and head him off before he gets to the door."

"Well . . ."

"He's a pretty nice guy, Meem, and he's been alone ever since Joan died. He just needs the civilizing influence of a good woman."

"The civilizing . . . Don't give me that drivel, J. W. Jackson! My land, where'd you steal that line?"

"In his case, it probably applies," I said. "Well, shall I go outside and intercept him?"

"No, no. Don't do that . . ."

"He really does want to be your friend. He says you and Gus and he and Joan used to be together all the time."

The spoon stopped again. "Yes. We were. All right, J.W., you've done your matchmaking bit. Now get out of my kitchen so I can get my work done."

"He's due in about five minutes, and he'll be wearing a jacket and tie for the occasion."

"Well, he'll just have to take me the way he finds me, apron and all. Oh, my." She tried to catch her reflection in the windowpanes. "How do I look?"

"Just fine. You could be wearing a Santa Claus suit and Nash would think you look terrific. I think he's in love."

"Get out of my kitchen!"

I did that, but she herself was also in the living room when Nash knocked on the door.

"I'll get it," said Angie.

"No you won't," said Mimi, wiping her hands on her apron, and striding forward. "I'll get it."

Angie arched a brow and flashed me a look of inquiry. Mimi opened the door, and there stood Nash Cortez, a badly wrapped box of candy under one arm, each hand holding a larger box. He had a look of worried innocence on his face.

"Well, well," said Mimi. "Merry Christmas, Ignacio. Won't you come in?"

"Oh," said Nash, as though the invitation was more than he had hoped for. "Oh, yes. Thanks, Mimi." He stepped in, and she closed the door behind him. "Here," he said, "these are for you."

He put the two big boxes on the floor and stepped back. The boxes mewed and thumped.

Mimi knelt and opened a box and a kitten jumped out. She opened the other, and the other kitten jumped out. The three grandchildren moved in. The kittens scampered under a table.

"Merry Christmas," said Nash. "This is yours, too." He thrust the candy at Mimi.

"Oh, they are cute!" said Mimi, as the grandchildren tried in vain to catch the kittens. Nash beamed.

A kitten was captured by a child.

"Now, be careful, dear," said the child's mother.

The kitten purred, then, with a twitch, escaped. The child pursued. Mimi laughed. Nash beamed even more.

"Cute," smiled Angie. She lifted her eyes to mine. "I got a present today, too. Have a look." She lifted her left hand and let the diamond on her finger flicker at me. "Ted popped the question and I said yes."

"Congratulations," I said. "Or is it best wishes that you offer the bride-to-be? I forget."

"I'll take both," said Angie. "Please give Zee Madieras the news. It may make her feel better."

I thought she might be right. In a sudden hurry to get home, I congratulated Just Ted on his excellent choice in women, and Mimi on her good fortune in getting her last daughter engaged, wished one and all good night and merry Christmas, and left. As I shut the door, I could hear Mimi asking Nash if he'd like to stay for supper.

It was dark as the pit. There were no stars. Santa was going to need Rudolph tonight. I drove home and turned down my snowy driveway. The lights in my house looked warm, and the candles in the windows seemed to offer comfort to seekers after bed and board. Beyond them I could see the lights of the Christmas tree.

I parked and went in. Zee met me just inside the door and put her arms around me before I could even get my coat off.

"I'm sorry," she said. "I told myself that I was never going to be jealous again, and I was anyway before I could stop myself. I'm really sorry. I promise I won't ever . . ."

I stopped her words with a kiss that lasted a long time before it ended.

She wiped at her eyes. "I have drinks for us. In the freezer. Give me your coat."

"You get the drinks, I'll take care of the coat."

We sat in front of the fireplace and I told her what had happened at Mimi's house.

Zee snugged against me. "So Angie is going to get married. I'm glad." She smiled up at me. "It'll make it a lot easier for me to really not be jealous anymore. I know I promised, but this will make it easier."

"The men and women we knew before we met don't count," I said.

"No. We didn't know we'd be meeting each other, so we can't be held accountable for the people we knew."

"That's it."

After a while, I got up and cooked the scallops. We ate them with rice and green beans flavored with honey, and washed everything down with white wine. Delish. Then we went back to the fireplace again.

"I miss the kittens," said Zee sleepily. She pointed at a window. "Look! It's snowing."

"Perfect," I said. "Now Santa will have a smooth landing."

In the morning, Santa, in the form of a very happy-looking Ignacio Cortez, arrived with Oliver Underfoot and Velcro. A light snow was still falling. Zee, who had been wondering where her present was, was ecstatic. She kissed Nash and me and each kitten.

It was the best Christmas I could remember.

— 27 —

The new year brought some news. I got it from the chief as we leaned against his cruiser in the parking lot at the foot of Main Street. It was a sunny day, and we were drinking coffee.

"Guess what," he said.

"What?"

"Chug Lovell really was a tobacco heir. They found a safe-deposit box over in his mainland bank. Seems like kin of his live down in South Carolina, too, so somebody will inherit his house."

"Such as it is. I thought tobacco heirs lived in mansions."

"Not when there are a lot of heirs and not a lot of tobacco. Chug got a few thou a year, but not enough to live on. He must have had some other income we don't know about yet."

"Maybe he was a police chief in some little town. He'd have made a good living on graft and he wouldn't ever actually have had to do any work."

The chief nodded. "I've made so much money under the table that I could have retired years ago, but greed drives me on. Besides, I like the glory of the job."

In mid-January we had a spell of warm weather that made scalloping almost a summer experience for the few of us who were still out on the ponds dragging for the last of the bay scallops that most people had given up on catching months before. For days on end, Dave Mello and I chugged over the Edgartown waters, our seven drags hauling up rocks, shellfish, seaweeds of various kinds, empty beer bottles and all of the other odds and ends of coastal waters.

Scallop prices were down, for reasons not apparent to us; but like the members of the light brigade, Vineyard scallopers do or die, nor reason why, and charge on into the guns. What other income was there for island fishermen with boats too small to go beyond the waters of the great ponds? Long ago, when the white men first came to these lands, there had been whales for the harpooning just offshore. But those times had long since gone, and now even the scallops sometimes seemed to be disappearing.

Dave and I were dragging Cape Pogue Pond, our oilskins open, enjoying the January sun, feeling almost as if it was late March.

"I tell you," said Dave, "on a day like this, I figure that I won't ever give up this game. I've been doing this for fifty years, but it feels like the first year I went out."

"You're probably right," I said. "Besides, what would you do if you ever gave this up?"

"Hell, I'm seventy-five years old. I never thought

I'd last this long, so I never gave any thought to what I'd do when I retired. Nobody in my family ever retired. They all worked as long as they could move. What do you think I should do?"

"Stay at home with Millie?"

"Haw! You try staying home with Millie. Drive her crazy to have me lying around underfoot while she tried to get her work done."

"Maybe you need a hobby."

"Hobby, hell! This is what I do for a hobby. I scallop all winter and fish all summer. Keeps me out of Millie's hair."

"Go to Disney World?"

"Been there."

"Take a cruise? See the world?"

"I seen as much of the world as I want to. Back in the war. Iwo Jima and them places. Pretty enough, I suppose, if there wasn't any shooting going on, but nothing as good as the Vineyard. Why should I go someplace else when there's no place else as good as where I'm at?"

Spoken like a true islander.

"Beats the hell out of me," I said.

We worked a long time to get our limit, then took the boat to North Neck, unloaded the baskets and put the boat on its hook. While Dave made things fast, I toted the bushel baskets of scallops up the stairway from the beach to the parking lot on top of the cliff. As I brought the last of the baskets up, Dave had the first of them in the truck. He's a rugged guy, seventy-five years old or not.

By boat, it's a long haul back to Edgartown, and if the wind is strong from the north, it can be a wet and dangerous trip between the Cape Pogue gut and the Edgartown light, so when we scallop in Pogue, we bring Dave's pickup over to Chappy and load it up there. All it costs is the effort it takes to haul the baskets up from the beach. That effort is considerable, but I was up to it. Barely.

We got into the pickup. "Ought to build some kind of hoist out here," said Dave, not for the first time. "Someday somebody's gonna bust a gut hauling scallops up them stairs."

"It could be me," I said, glad to be sitting down. We bounced slowly toward the paved road. Dave never drove fast, being an authentic Hat Man, one of those guys wearing a hat who is always at the front of any line of traffic on a narrow road.

The On Time Ferry (always on time because it has no schedule) carried us from Chappy to Edgartown and we drove on to Dave's house. The snows of December had long since melted, and it felt as though flowers should be blooming. Edgartown was quiet, with only a few wanderers on its streets.

"Fire up on West Tisbury road," said Millie, as we unloaded. Like a lot of islanders, Millie and Dave had a scanner which let them keep track of fire and police activities. "Nobody hurt."

"What else is going on?" I asked Millie, as we unloaded and started to open.

"Well, that Manwaring fellow that's got the summer place out by the airport has dropped out of politics, according to the radio. He was running in Connecticut, I think. You know him, J.W.?"

"I know who he is. That's about all."

I wondered if Shrink Williams and Phyllis were still together, and if Vince had quit politics because Phyllis had sent him the picture of Heather, and if Vince and Phyllis would now take a world cruise. I doubted if I'd ever know any of those things.

"Never mind the Connecticut news," said Dave. "We've been out on the pond all morning. What's going on here in town?" Dave, like the *Vineyard Gazette*, took little notice of anything not directly connected to the island.

"Mimi Bettencourt's got another letter to the editor in the paper. Says they should at least stop shooting geese in January and February. Says the Commission should ban all hunting on that Norton land they're thinking of buying. Same stuff as usual."

It seemed that Nash Cortez had not managed to change Mimi's mind about shooters or shooting. I doubted whether she had managed to change his, either.

"So what else is going on?" asked Dave.

"Somebody thought they saw a guy hanging around outside their house. Prowler. Police didn't find anything. Didn't have many prowlers while the weather was bad, but now that it's warmed up, I imagine they'll be out again."

The island had its share of crackpots, but as I stood in the slanting sunlight opening scallops, the word "prowler" made me think of Joey Percell. I wondered if Joey would ever come prowling after me.

"Them guys like warm weather," agreed Dave, opening across the table from me. "Not many crooks abroad when it's below zero."

Consistent with this wisdom, Joey Percell waited until the cold weather was gone.

He came in late April, when I was through scalloping and had relaxed my guard and was getting my gear in shape for the first bluefish of the season, which usually make their appearance about the middle of May, as they come north from the Carolinas. I planned to be ready for them.

I had been mulling over the news that the Commission had finally bought the Norton land and was going to allow all of its traditional uses to be continued. This was a setback for the animal rights people, but not one that would defeat them, for they were a passionate bunch who would never lay down their flag.

I had also been thinking about the rumor that Nash Cortez was seriously courting Mimi Bettencourt. Well, why not? Vegetarian Mimi had lived with an omnivorous man before, so why not again? She and Nash could take turns using the typewriter to write letters to the editor contradicting each other's arguments about guns and gunners.

Joey was a pretty patient guy. As someone said of Italians, vengeance was a meal he preferred to eat cold. Four months had passed since last we'd met, and I was not thinking of Joey. Actually, I was thinking of Oliver Underfoot and Velcro. Following one of their periods of mad pursuit, with first one, then the other in the lead as they tore from room to room, they were now either sleeping or up to no good somewhere else in Zee's house. There was a lot of silence, which could mean either nap time or bad kittens at work. Both Oliver Underfoot and Velcro had grown immensely since I had given them to Zee. Oliver in particular promised to be a large cat, indeed, but his brain had not caught up with his body. Both of them were still all kitten.

I had spent the night in West Tisbury, and Zee had gone off to work at the hospital. I was washing up the breakfast dishes in her sunny kitchen, and listening for the sound of something being knocked off a bureau or rolled across the floor.

Instead, I heard the front door open. Unlike Zee, who locks things up, I leave them unlatched. I looked up as Joey Percell walked in and pushed the door shut behind him. He had a pistol in his hand.

I was flabbergasted and must have shown it.

"Surprise," said Joey. His smile, below a large black moustache that I'd not seen on him before, was not a pleasant one.

My hands were in the rinse water. I left them there. I think my mouth was hanging open.

Joey flicked his hard eyes here and there as he crossed the living room and dining room and came to the door of the kitchen.

I finally got my brain and my tongue slightly in sync.

I said, "Before you start shooting up the joint, maybe you should know that there's a platoon of marines in the master bedroom. How did you manage to find me here? I figured that if you showed up, it would be at my place."

"I figured you'd figure that. That's why I'm here instead of there. I been down here on this fucking island for almost a week following you and your girl-friend around till I got your routines straight. I was careless about you before, but not this time."

I hadn't seen a thing, and told him so.

"You weren't supposed to see a thing. What do you think? I'm so bad at my work that you'd see me? And don't give me any of that marines in the bedroom kind of shit. You're here all by your lonesome." He lifted the pistol. "And you're gonna die all by your lonesome."

I thought he was probably right. I felt very cold and fatalistic. I was conscious of my hands in the warm rinse water. I closed one around the handle of Zee's nice big cast-iron frying pan.

My mouth said, "You don't want to shoot me, Joey. You'd never get off the island."

"I got on it, I'll get off it. Hell, I been staying in the

motel in Vineyard Haven, and I got reservations on the noon boat. Mr. Antonelli, that's me. This moustache makes me look like a real wop, don't you think? Nobody knows who I really am or that I'm here. And nobody will find you till I'm long gone. Your little sugar baby is gonna have quite a shock when she gets home. I wish I could see it."

"I'm not alone here," my dry mouth said. "You've made a mistake."

"No mistake, wise guy. You never should have fucked with me that second time. Nobody does that to me. I can't afford it. I got a reputation to uphold, you know?" He pointed the pistol at me. "Say goodbye, asshole."

I barely got it out: "Goodbye, asshole."

"Smart mouth to the end. You never learn, do you?" The muzzle of the pistol looked as big as Mammoth Cave. I could see his trigger finger tighten.

In the living room behind him something hit the floor with a thud, and there was a rush of sound toward Joey's back. He spun around and fired a shot that would have hit a human dead center, but instead passed well over the heads of Oliver Underfoot and Velcro as they tore into the kitchen, away from their latest mischief. Velcro, terrified by the sound of the pistol, leaped and clamped all four feet onto Joey's leg, further distracting him just enough for me to take two long strides and lay the frying pan onto his ear.

Joey went down like Humpty Dumpty and didn't move.

Zee was impressed when I told her the story. She hugged Velcro and Oliver Underfoot and then hugged me again, and then went to her living room door and put her finger on the bullet hole that was above the knob. Then she cried and said, "Is this how it's going to be when we get married? You having people coming to kill you?"

"Of course not," I said. "They've got Joey on attempted murder charges this time. And I figure they'll make them stick."

But Zee wasn't listening. She had Velcro and Oliver Underfoot in her arms again and was kissing them and thanking them and calling them brave kittens.

Later, she allowed me to fix us each a double vodka on the rocks, and we sat in front of her fireplace. She leaned against me. "I don't want anything to happen to you," she said. "You know, the weird thing is, I was in the emergency room when they brought him in. I helped work on him before they flew him off to the mainland. And after he tried to shoot you! Maybe it's a good thing I didn't know about that until later. You must have really whacked him. He has a fractured skull."

"I whacked him as well as I could."

"Can they keep him in jail?"

"He'll be in the hospital for a while, I imagine. After that somebody will try to post bail for him. But I don't think Joey's going to slip out of this noose. I think my testimony will put him away for quite a while. Unless, of course, he decides to talk about his work with the mob. If he does that, maybe he can make a deal with the D.A. and the Feds."

"Yes, he'll be in bed for quite a while. And my frying pan did it! Oh, I'm glad you're all right!"

"Me too."

"He won't come back here again, will he?"

"He hasn't had very good luck on the Vineyard. No, I think he'll stay far away from here."

Oliver Underfoot climbed into Zee's lap and began

to buzz. Soon Velcro also appeared and attached herself to the front of my shirt.

"Dueling buzzers," said Zee.

In late May, Dom Agganis told me that Joey Percell
had made a deal to talk about his boss in Providence
and was going to enter the witness protection program. Two weeks later, they found Joey hog-tied in
the trunk of his burning car in a junkyard north of
New Bedford. Whoever had put him there had shot
him several times too, just to make sure.

"I guess somebody else besides me found out about
Joey's plans," said Dom. "Saves the cost of his trial,
anyway."

It was a beautiful sunny day and Dom was off duty.
The bluefish had been in for three weeks, and it was
two hours before the last of the east tide.

"Say," I said. "You want to go fishing?"

"Does a wolf howl at the moon?"

So we headed for Wasque.